OUR LAST DAYS IN BARCELONA

BERKLEY TITLES BY CHANEL CLEETON

Next Year in Havana

When We Left Cuba

The Last Train to Key West

The Most Beautiful Girl in Cuba

Our Last Days in Barcelona

OUR LAST DAYS IN

Barcelona

CHANEL CLEETON

BERKLEY
NEW YORK

BERKLEY
An imprint of Penguin Random House LLC
penguinrandomhouse.com

Copyright © 2022 by Chanel Cleeton
Penguin Random House supports copyright. Copyright fuels creativity, encourages
diverse voices, promotes free speech, and creates a vibrant culture. Thank you for
buying an authorized edition of this book and for complying with copyright laws by not
reproducing, scanning, or distributing any part of it in any form without permission.
You are supporting writers and allowing Penguin Random House to continue to
publish books for every reader.

BERKLEY is a registered trademark and the B colophon is a trademark of
Penguin Random House LLC.

Library of Congress Cataloging-in-Publication Data

Names: Cleeton, Chanel, author.
Title: Our last days in Barcelona / Chanel Cleeton.
Description: New York: Berkley, [2022]
Identifiers: LCCN 2021059408 (print) | LCCN 2021059409 (ebook) |
ISBN 9780593098899 (hardcover) | ISBN 9780593197820 (trade paperback) |
ISBN 9780593098905 (ebook)
Subjects: LCGFT: Novels.
Classification: LCC PS3603.L455445 O97 2022 (print) | LCC PS3603.L455445
(ebook) | DDC 813/.6—dc23/eng/20211209
LC record available at https://lccn.loc.gov/2021059408
LC ebook record available at https://lccn.loc.gov/2021059409

Printed in the United States of America
1st Printing

Title page art: Floral border © IndiPixi / Shutterstock.com
Book design by Kristin del Rosario

This book is dedicated to every reader who asked for the other Perez sisters to have their stories told. Thank you!

OUR LAST DAYS IN BARCELONA

prologue

Isabel

1961

PALM BEACH

The night before my wedding, while my youngest sister Maria slept in the bedroom next to me, Elisa in her new home with her husband and child, Beatriz off somewhere saving the world, I painted.

At first, the image was a sea of blues, my brush flying over the canvas, the scene pouring from the secretive place inside me where it lived when I was not yet brave enough to let it wave proudly for the world to see. I added some pinks, orange, a hint of gold streaking across a dawning sky. I painted for hours, the Palm Beach morning rising to greet me. I painted until my mother's heels clacking against the stairs signaled it was time to return to my real life, as the household readied itself for a momentous day, a new chapter for the Perez family. I painted until I took a step back and studied the canvas and realized I hadn't just painted a random assortment of colors, that the tears raining down my cheeks had mixed with the colors staining my fingers red.

I painted Cuba.

I painted home.

M y knees tremble beneath my white lace gown. My fingers clamp down on my father's arm.

The "Bridal Chorus" begins.

The guests rise.

My groom smiles.

I tear my gaze away from him, searching instead for my sisters in their matching pale blue dresses—Maria at sixteen barely old enough to assume the role of bridesmaid; Elisa, despite being younger than me by several years, already a wife and mother.

Elisa and Maria stand side by side, but the space between them is unmistakable and loud, one sister missing. If she had been here, Beatriz would have nicked a bottle of champagne from our parents hours ago and had us all tipsy before this march down the aisle.

You don't have to marry him, she'd whisper in my ear. *You don't love him. How could you? He'll never understand you—where you come from, what you've lost. He can't make you happy.*

My father takes his first step, and my legs move as if of their own volition, following his direction as I've been taught to do, holding on to him to keep me steady, my manicured nails digging into his elegant tuxedo jacket.

You could run away, Beatriz would tell me.

For a moment, I consider it. For a moment, I imagine her standing there at the end of the altar beside our sisters, Beatriz in all her breathtaking glory.

A lump forms in my throat.

Of all the times I daydreamed about my wedding day, it was nothing like this.

Instead of this church in Palm Beach, I envisioned myself walking down the aisle of the Cathedral of Havana, the boy I loved and left back in Cuba awaiting me at the end. I envisioned the church brimming with family and friends, this joyous occasion marked by those I cared for most, Beatriz beside me as my maid of honor. Our brother, Alejandro, should be here, too, smiling that mischievous smile of his. And our nanny Magda—

How quickly life can change.

How much is lost in the blink of an eye.

I thought when I knelt before God, the mantilla that was draped over the shoulders of centuries of Perez brides would be placed over mine, but instead, like all the sentimental family pieces that should have accompanied me on this day, the delicate lace is buried in a box in a backyard in Havana, waiting for us to return.

I try to remember who I was before the revolution, before my brother Alejandro was murdered, before we fled our home in fear for our lives with little more than the clothes on our backs. I try to remember that girl, but she's as lost to me as Cuba.

My side of the church is mostly empty. So many of our loved ones are still in Cuba, waiting to see what changes this revolution will bring.

The groom's side casts suspicious glances my way. I am *not from here*, which is a thing they say in whispered voices just loud enough to not really be whispers at all. It is a second marriage for Thomas, whose first wife died years ago, and the decades between us as well as his business successes have convinced them that I am only looking for a wealthy man to care for me. In truth, Thomas wooed my mother with the extravagant bouquets he sent to our house, but he wooed me with the life he offered: quiet, safe, secure.

You see, I learned something about myself when the world as I knew it ended.

I am not brave. I am not particularly strong. I have no need for daring and adventures. I've had enough turmoil, experienced enough loss in twenty-five years to last me a lifetime. If I had one wish for this life, it would be for peace.

But what of passion? Beatriz's voice whispers in my ear.

I take another step down the aisle, and another, and another.

I had passion—once. I had a fiancé I loved, who loved me.

It's been over two years since we said good-bye in Rancho Boyeros Airport as my family fled Havana for the United States after the revolution, two years since we last saw each other. I heard from friends who came over recently that he has decided to stay in Cuba. That there's a woman in his life. That he's done well for himself under the new regime.

Time moves on without us, even as the past pulls us back.

My gaze settles on my mother standing in her place of honor in the pew at the front of the church.

She is beautiful, always, standing tall and proud, and I know that in this marriage I have achieved something desperately important to her: I have taken us one step closer to respectability. My marriage is giving the family a foothold in this country that so often seems like it doesn't want us here. Thomas is accepted in ways we never will be, has connections we will never have. Perhaps this marriage will open doors for Maria when it is her time to decide her future.

I pass my mother, and out of the corner of my eye, I swear I see her let out a nearly imperceptible sigh of relief, exposing a rare crack in her normally impenetrable armor.

My father stops directly in front of the spot where Thomas waits at the altar, and I follow suit. They are nearly the same age, Thomas and my father, and a friendship of sorts has sprung up between them these past few months.

I search Thomas's eyes for a bit of reassurance, for something that will push Beatriz's voice out of my head for good.

Beatriz is in Europe now, and we've barely spoken since our fight, but I think of her constantly; after all, with only two years between us, it is difficult for me to remember a time in my life when she wasn't with me. There are so many moments I wish to tell her something, when I forget we aren't speaking, that our lives have moved on without each other. I keep hoping that one day she will come back to us in Palm Beach, and I will have a chance to apologize in person. That we will somehow make things right between us once and for all.

My father presses a light kiss on my cheek, and he turns away, joining my mother in the church pew, and I am alone at the altar with my husband-to-be as I embark on this new chapter of my life.

I let Thomas take my hand, and we turn toward the priest as he begins the ceremony.

I feel as though I have left my body, and am watching all of this from a distance, as though I am a guest at my own wedding. I can only imagine the thoughts running through the minds of so many of the others.

I almost snatch my hand back, pick up my skirts, and run from the church, my family, the weight of everything pulling me down. I envision getting in the car and driving somewhere, anywhere. I fantasize about escaping and never looking back.

And still—the familiar fear winds its way inside me. What would I do? Where would I go? How could I start over yet again, in a foreign country where I have little prospects to recommend me? I have never worked, have no real talents, never had the opportunity to go to school past the basics when I was younger. I was raised from birth to follow the path my mother set before me until the world changed and the path was set aflame.

No, let Beatriz travel the world, and rail against her causes. I am sick of war, of revolution, of fighting, of the destruction it causes.

But what about love? Beatriz whispers in my ear as clearly as though she were standing here, even though she is an ocean away in Europe.

Thomas slides the simple platinum band onto my paint-stained finger.

I meet his gaze, and I know with a great certainty that I never, ever want to fall in love again.

chapter one

Isabel

1964

PALM BEACH

It's a crowded party, a veritable who's who of Palm Beach society ready to close out the social season, but I don't care about any of that. I cut through the crowd with a single purpose:

To find Senator Nicholas Preston.

He's standing on the fringe alone, a drink of something dark and heavy in his hands. I was prepared to finagle some privacy between us, to separate him from his coterie of friends and political mates, but to find him alone like this is a blessed opportunity I can't miss. I walk toward him, and as I do, our gazes connect across the room. His eyes widen, and he takes a step forward, and he freezes, his expression changing, as though he saw an apparition only to realize it wasn't real after all.

It isn't the first time I've been told I resemble my sister Beatriz.

I close the distance between us on slightly shaky legs, filled with the unmistakable sensation that I'm inserting myself in a drama that's already started. I stop right in front of him, offering a silent prayer that we haven't just become an object of fascination for the entire room.

"I'm sorry, I know we've seen each other around, but I realize we've never been formally introduced. My sister Beatriz—"

"—I know who you are." He interjects, none of the legendary Preston charm I've heard about on visible display. He looks a bit terrified, and he clears his throat, his gaze drifting down to the glass in his hand as though he'd like to take a swig for courage.

I've never cared for him. What little I knew of him was that he was engaged to another woman and somehow Beatriz became his mistress. I never liked his position on Cuba much, either—his rumored closeness to the late President Kennedy who seemingly abandoned us after the Bay of Pigs. But looking at him now, it's impossible to miss how he's changed since I last saw him. His tuxedo isn't as impeccably tailored as I remember, his body leaner than it used to be, his skin paler than it was, his eyes devoid of that twinkle that used to appear when he'd cast his gaze on Beatriz.

He looks like a man who's lost a great deal, and being no stranger to loss myself, it's almost enough to make me feel sorry for him.

Almost.

"Perhaps if we could go somewhere in private," I reply, more out of consideration for his reputation than mine. As a married woman who rarely engages with society these days, I hardly attract the sort of attention others do. But at present, Nicholas Preston is a single, wealthy United States senator with political aspirations for more, and everyone's eyes are perpetually on him.

He nods, and I follow him from the room, down a hallway, and into a small library just off the main wing of the house. He closes the door behind us and walks over to an elegant desk, leaning against the edge of the wood.

"Is Beatriz all right?" he asks without preamble.

"I don't know. She's in Spain. Our sister Elisa used to speak with her nearly daily, but we haven't heard anything from her in weeks."

He says nothing, but there's the barest flinch at the news that Beatriz is gone, and he looks like a man bracing himself for another blow.

"Did you know she was in Spain?" I ask. "Have you heard from her? Did she leave you? Elisa thinks she has, but Beatriz refuses to talk about it. Are you—?"

"Wait." He holds up a hand. "Stop for a moment. Please."

"I'm *worried*. We're all worried. It's not like Beatriz to just disappear like this."

I've been worried about Beatriz for a long time now, even as she's made it clear that she wants to make her own way in the world, even as she's thrown herself into Cuban politics in exile, her determination to see Fidel Castro removed from power and vengeance won for our brother Alejandro all-consuming.

"Doesn't your family have a cousin in Spain?" he asks. "Has she checked on Beatriz?"

Sometimes it's easy to forget that he and Beatriz shared a life together once, that he was one of the most important people in my sister's world, if not *the* most important person. As much as I dislike him on principle for the tears my sister shed over him, the fact that Beatriz loved him coupled with the evidence before me that he loved her as well is enough to make me rethink my ire.

"She does, but I think Rosa and her husband are traveling out of the country on diplomatic business. They're unreachable. I hoped you might have heard from Beatriz considering how close the two of you are."

"I haven't."

"Are the rumors true—have you really ended things?"

"Yes, they're true. Beatriz left me."

"Did something happen?"

"Isn't that a bit of a personal question?"

"Not when it concerns my sister. All I care about it is Beatriz's safety and well-being."

"And you think I don't? I love Beatriz. I always will. She knows that. I asked her to marry me before she left."

The last part comes out with an air of frustration, the sound of a man who has been turning something around and around in his mind, unable to reconcile himself with the unavoidable conclusion he reaches each time.

Shock fills me.

Our stature in America is nothing like it was in Cuba, and for someone with Nicholas Preston's political ambitions and position in society to throw all of that away on a wife who would never be more than a massive political liability, a wife who had engaged in espionage—

I'd always assumed he viewed Beatriz as a dalliance, worried as only an older sister is wont to do that he was taking advantage of her, but now—

"I would have given up my career, everything to be with her. I told her that."

"And she still left?" I ask.

What of love, Beatriz?

"She did."

"Beatriz—" I struggle to find the right words to describe my brilliant, passionate, complicated sister.

"Beatriz is unlike anyone else. The qualities that made it hard for us to be together were also the things that made me fall in love with her," he interjects. "I'm not sure what that says about me. Maybe I'm a masochist."

"Or you both found each other in difficult circumstances. What happened in Cuba, the losses our family suffered, the death of our brother, it left a mark on all of us. Beatriz perhaps most of all considering how close she and Alejandro were. But that's why I worry about her so much. She's chasing ghosts and fighting old battles that cannot be won, and I've already lost one sibling to this madness. I can't lose another."

"You think she went to Spain because she's still working with the CIA."

"That's what I'm afraid of."

An oath falls from Nicholas Preston's lips.

"I'm sorry, but I don't know why she went to Spain. I haven't heard from her since I asked her to marry me and she ended our relationship. But given the way we left things, and her determination to keep working with the CIA, the current situation with Franco—" He frowns. "Well, I wouldn't be surprised if she's in Spain for political reasons."

I knew it was a long shot coming here, but with Beatriz an ocean away, Nicholas Preston was my best hope for a lead on my sister.

"What will you do now?" he asks me.

"I don't know. We've written to her." Well, *Elisa* wrote to her. I haven't quite summoned the courage to do so. "I suppose we'll keep writing to her in the hope that she will respond."

"I can place some inquiries if you like, reach out to connections

I have at the Agency. I don't know how involved I should be, how involved she would want me to be, but if she's in danger, please let me know. There's nothing I wouldn't do for her, nothing I wouldn't give to make sure she's safe."

"Thank you. I'm just not sure what to do. Beatriz is a grown woman. She's entitled to her life and privacy. I don't think she'd care very much for us inserting ourselves in her affairs. Beatriz doesn't need someone to rescue her; she's always been perfectly capable of rescuing herself. But she's my sister and I love her, and I'm worried about her."

"Just because someone is strong doesn't mean they don't need help, Isabel."

"I know that. But she has made it perfectly clear that she has no room in her life for me—"

"You had a fight. And no one holds a grudge like Beatriz. However, even if Beatriz is still angry with you, she misses you," Nick says, surprising me.

"Beatriz talked about me? About the disagreement we had?"

"She didn't tell me all the details—I imagine there are some secrets that will always be between sisters—but it was clear she was hurting, that she missed you terribly. That maybe she had regrets, too. Beatriz can be proud, and she can be stubborn, but she's loyal, and when she loves, she does so deeply, without reservation." He hesitates. "Trust me, the worst thing is loving someone and having regrets about how you left things between you, the things that were unsaid, the opportunities that were missed."

He says it almost casually, but knowing the keen politician Nicholas Preston is, I can't imagine this wasn't his endgame all along:

"You know, if you're worried, you could always go to Spain to make sure she's safe."

chapter two

As I sit on the flight from Palm Beach to Barcelona, wondering what possessed me to embark on this misguided adventure, it's the look in Nicholas Preston's eyes from our conversation a few days earlier that I remember most. There was no doubt that this was what he wanted, that he was worried about Beatriz as I was, but given their breakup and his desire to respect the boundaries they'd set, he was reluctant to involve himself, choosing instead to appeal to my romantic and sympathetic nature so I would do his bidding for him.

It's a move Beatriz would make in a heartbeat, and it's crystal clear how two people could be both utterly perfect for each other and impossibly doomed.

It's been my experience that relationships are often about balance: one person tends to be the star, and the other is there to support them, to play those all-important background roles of advice and support. And sometimes, maybe, the roles shift a bit, although in my reality it has been almost entirely the man who is held in such a place of honor and esteem. Knowing my sister as I do, and her inevitable draw to the limelight whether intentional or otherwise, I can't see her playing the role of the-woman-behind-the-man while Nicholas Preston ascends to political greatness. And I can't imagine a man with such political ambitions and connections being happy throwing it all away for a life of relative obscurity.

If Beatriz is in Barcelona nursing a broken heart, the big sister in me wants to be there for her.

The flight is uneventful, the last hours passed staring out the window, questioning the decision to send me rather than Elisa as the family envoy, weighing the odds of Beatriz being happy to see me against the far more likely possibility that she'll be less than enthused.

"I have a four-year-old," Elisa pointed out when I suggested she would be more successful and welcomed by Beatriz. "How am I supposed to leave for Spain? Do you suggest I take Miguel with me?" She laughed at that, and given how energetic my nephew is, I can't quite blame her for not wanting to bring him on an international flight to Europe by herself.

In the end, after much prevarication, and a fair dose of pleading with Thomas, who thought it both unseemly for his wife to travel by herself and has always harbored a strong dislike for Beatriz and her reputation, he reluctantly acquiesced, giving me a week away.

Armed with the return address on Beatriz's letters to Elisa, a bit of money, my suitcase, and little else, I step off the plane when it lands at the airport in Barcelona and hire a taxi to take me to Beatriz's home.

After a few initial minutes of conversation in Spanish, the driver leaves me to my own devices, and I stare out the window of the cab as he makes the twenty-minute journey, my gaze on the city.

I thought of dialing Beatriz's number from the airport, warning her of my arrival before I showed up on her doorstep, but any attempts to call her before this trip have been met with silence, and I must admit I worried a bit that if Beatriz did answer the phone *this time*, she might tell me to turn back around and return to Palm Beach.

The farther we get from the airport, the more congested the city becomes, and I realize we're near the center of Barcelona now.

Beatriz's return address from her letter is a smart building on Las Ramblas with a beige stone facade and little balconies with red wrought iron railings. The taxi lets me off right before it.

It's the sort of place I can imagine Beatriz living—elegant with a dash of whimsy. I can envision my sister leaning over the balcony railing, her dark hair billowing around her as she calls out good-naturedly to pedestrians, her laughter ringing down Las Ramblas. It is quintessentially Beatriz, both the privilege seeped in living in one of the city's most desirable locales and the slight bohemian bent a city like Barcelona thrives on: art, music, and culture seemingly on every street corner.

It is a far cry from my life and the one our mother wanted for us in Palm Beach; no doubt, much of the allure for Beatriz was escaping to a place where there is anonymity in the crowded streets and bustling pace, where the need to see and be seen does not reign paramount.

But still, it raises the ever-important question that has been on my mind since Elisa first told me Beatriz had left:

Why?

Why Barcelona?

And given the environs where she's chosen to live, who is funding this adventure?

A list of names of apartment residents is affixed near the building entry. I scan the directory until I settle on a "B. Perez."

I set my suitcase down on the ground and lift my gloved hand, my heart pounding as I press the buzzer next to Beatriz's name.

Why did I let Elisa talk me into this? I should have pushed harder for her to come, should have found another way around me standing here to see my estranged sister. Why did I think we could just sweep past the fight we had, the words I hurled at her?

Could all of the danger Beatriz constantly finds herself in, the recklessness, have been avoided had I been a better sister to her, more concerned with her well-being than the damage that her affair with an engaged man had on our reputation? I've always prided myself on the importance of family and loyalty, but in this I was disloyal to the sister I love, and that has been the hardest pill for me to swallow.

No one answers.

I momentarily consider the idea of just staying here, sitting down on the front step with my suitcase beside me until Beatriz returns, but I barely ate on the flight, too nervous to even think about food. Now, I'm hungry and tired, my clothes rumpled, makeup mussed, and more than anything I want to eat a good meal, take a shower, and fall asleep.

I'll find a hotel nearby, call Elisa, and formulate a plan to find Beatriz.

I've never traveled alone, much less to another country, and while I know it's foolish for a twenty-eight-year-old woman to be this intimidated, I can't help but be daunted by the city and the unexpected adventure I have embarked on. Once, when I was younger and single, I might have viewed this whole exercise as exciting and daring, but I've become so used to being married, to belonging to someone, that striking out on my own like this terrifies me.

I scan the street, yearning for a place to sit down and rest, to gather my thoughts, my suitcase beside me.

There's a little restaurant nearby and I choose to sit outside, eager for the fresh air after so many hours on the plane. A waiter shows me to a table near a man eating alone with a bouquet of red roses beside him. I order a drink and a sandwich, my gaze trained on the people walking down the street.

When the food comes, I dig into the sandwich with gusto, the crusty bread and savory meat and cheese doing the trick to replenish my flagging energy.

Ten minutes pass after I finish my meal, then twenty, thirty, but there's no sign of Beatriz.

I pay my bill with some of the money I exchanged at the airport, carefully counting the remaining amount. I ask the waiter for a suggestion for a local hotel, and he gives me one that's close to Beatriz's place and sounds reasonably priced. Thomas has never been one for extravagance, and the budget he allotted me will only go so far.

I pick up the suitcase and head over to the main entrance building of Beatriz's apartment.

My sister wouldn't give up, and I won't, either.

I ring the buzzer once more to no avail.

I scroll through the list of names in the directory, trying two more before someone answers and I explain who I am and why I am here. The woman knows who Beatriz is and agrees to tell her I'm looking for her next time she sees her, no doubt taking an extra bit of pity for me and the way my voice wobbles over the story when she agrees to buzz me up so I can leave a note for Beatriz under her front door.

Beatriz lives on the fifth floor, and I drag my suitcase up the flights of stairs. When I arrive at her apartment, I reach into my handbag, pulling out the little notepad and pen set Thomas bought me for Christmas last year.

I scribble a note for Beatriz letting her know I am in town, that I'm desperate to see her, and I leave the name of the hotel where the waiter suggested I stay. I rip the paper from the notepad and fold it over once, twice, until it is a neat square.

As I nudge the folded piece of paper under the door, I push against the wood, and where I expect to meet resistance, there is a give as the door opens, exposing a sliver of Beatriz's apartment.

Could she have been here the whole time?

"Beatriz," I call out through the crack in the doorway, peering through the opening. A pair of shoes is discarded near what looks to be a dark green velvet couch, a sequined dress draped over the arm. "Are you home? It's Isabel."

Beatriz's bright and cluttered apartment comes into full view as I nudge the door open the rest of the way. The room is eerily quiet when I cross the threshold, only the faintest scent of Beatriz's favorite perfume lingering in the air.

I shut the door behind me gently and lock it.

Clothes are strewn about the room, books discarded on table-tops, a cabinet ajar. The familiarity of Beatriz in all her chaos transports me to our teenage years when she used to tease me over the fact that I color coordinated my closet and I—

I haven't seen them in years, but those are definitely my sandals.

There's a noise behind me, a rustling, a creak, and—

"Beatriz?"

I whirl around.

When I entered the apartment I turned the lock, but now the door is open again, and a tall, lean, dark-haired man in a trench coat stands in the doorway.

There's a gun in his hand.

"You're not Beatriz," he says.

He steps back, closing the front door behind him with his free hand.

There's a statue sitting on top of Beatriz's end table, and I wrap my hands around the little marble figure, its weight somewhat of a comfort. It's not the best weapon, but it's better than nothing, and I'm not going down without a fight.

His eyes widen, his gaze drifting to the statue clutched in my hand and back to my face.

His lips curve.

He lowers the gun.

"You're Isabel."

"How do you know who I am?"

"Beatriz told me about you. The resemblance is clear, as is, well—" He gestures vaguely in my direction, at the statue in my hand. "You're brave like your sister. I'm not going to hurt you. I promise. I didn't come here looking for you, and I didn't break in, either. I have a key."

He holds his hands out in the air, the key glinting in the light, before slipping the gun in his coat pocket.

I don't lower my weapon.

"You came here looking for Beatriz, and you came here armed. Where is my sister? And who are you?"

"Hell if I know where Beatriz is. I'm looking for her myself. She was supposed to meet me last night, and she never showed."

"Who are you?"

He hesitates. "Diego."

"Who are you to my sister?"

"A friend."

The sorts of friends my sister likely has, given her work with the CIA, aren't exactly reassuring.

"Prove it."

"Prove what?"

"If you're Beatriz's friend, prove it to me."

"And if I don't?"

"If you know my sister, surely she has told you something about her life. If Beatriz trusts you, I'll trust you."

"Fine. You're Isabel. You're the eldest of the Perez sisters, who, according to Beatriz, at least, are known for leaving scandal and a trail of broken hearts in their wake that spans from Cuba to Palm Beach. I'll confess when Beatriz told me about you, I had a hard time picturing it, but now I'm thinking she underplayed it if anything." He smiles. "Four Perez women. I can only imagine."

"You could have gathered that information through gossip. That hardly proves anything."

"True. What else can I tell you?" He pauses. "You and Beatriz are constantly arguing. She said it was because the two of you are so different, but from where I'm standing, I bet you're more similar than you realize. She told me about the last big fight you had, how you exposed her relationship to your mother and the fallout it caused. She didn't tell me who the man was—after all, Beatriz is fiercely protective of the people she loves—but she told me enough to know that she regrets how things turned out between the two of you, even if she can't admit it."

It's as apt a description of Beatriz as I can imagine, and those details of our fight are as intimate as it gets. It's also remarkably like what Nicholas Preston said about my sister.

I still don't lower the statue.

His eyebrow raises.

"Beatriz is more trusting than me."

His smile deepens. "Hell of a thing," he says more to himself than to me. "Well, Isabel, last I heard from Beatriz, you were safely ensconced in some mansion in Palm Beach. So, what are you doing here in Barcelona?"

I don't trust him, not really, but Beatriz clearly did confide in him to tell him those things, and if he was going to harm me, he's already had ample opportunity. If he has information on Beatriz's whereabouts, perhaps if I give him a bit of information, he'll share what he knows.

"I came to Barcelona because I'm worried about my sister."

"You came all the way to Barcelona because you're worried about Beatriz?" He sounds faintly incredulous.

"Yes. When was the last time you saw her?"

"It's been almost two weeks. It's unlike her to be out of touch for this long. Like I said, we were supposed to meet last night, and she never showed."

"Beatriz missed our sister Maria's birthday a few weeks ago in March, which she would *never* do. Knowing what she was involved in before—" I'm unsure of how much I should share with him, how much he knows. "We're concerned she's in trouble," I finish. "Perhaps because she's mixed up in something she shouldn't be. Speaking of trouble, what are your intentions toward my sister?"

He laughs, the sound full and rich. "I see you're still helping Beatriz navigate her love life."

I can't deny it, even as I promised Beatriz I wouldn't interfere again. I don't know how to explain what it's like to love someone so fiercely that you want to protect them from harm, even when you know it isn't your place, even when you know you can't possibly keep them safe in a world like this.

"I apologize," Diego says. "It wasn't meant as a criticism. Beatriz spoke of her big sister Isabel as though you would do anything to protect the people you loved. Said you were fierce in your devotion. She's lucky to have someone like you in her life. Lucky to have someone who cares so much.

"Beatriz is an intelligent, fascinating woman. A beautiful one, too. But our arrangement is not a romantic one. I told you—we're friends. We've spent some time together since she came to Spain, and she's one of the few people I'd trust with my life. I think she'd say the same about me."

"Maybe. But if you're so close, where is she? She didn't mention anything to you?"

"I'm sure you know your sister has her secrets, and that they're necessary ones for her protection and for the protection of those she cares for."

She has her fair share of enemies, too, which is what worries me.

"That doesn't give me much reassurance considering who she's chosen to align herself with. You're a spy for the CIA, aren't you?"

His eyes widen, but he doesn't answer me.

Suddenly, I'm exhausted, the weight of the trip and my worry over Beatriz crashing over me. I sit down on the edge of the couch, the statue still clutched in my hand.

Diego doesn't move from his perch by the door.

"I don't understand why she came to Spain. Her involvement in Cuba, her anger toward Fidel, I could understand even if I didn't like the choices she made, even if I would have made different ones. But this isn't Cuba. Why would she keep doing this? Why risk everything? Why put herself in danger?"

It's the same argument I had with Alejandro first, and then Beatriz. How many siblings am I going to lose?

"I can't speak for Beatriz," Diego replies. "But I have gotten an opportunity to know her better in the months since she arrived in

Barcelona. We spoke of the situation in Cuba, of what's going on in Spain. Franco is a brutal, ruthless dictator, something your sister understands. He has a stranglehold over Spain, and despite their political differences, he's building a relationship with Fidel. Beatriz speaks Spanish fluently. She's an asset."

"I would have thought Franco objected to Fidel's communist leanings," I counter.

Just because I have little interest in politics doesn't mean I haven't grown up surrounded by it.

"Perhaps if he was truly driven by ideology, but there are also practical considerations at play. Times are tough. Franco needs allies. Fidel publicly decries Franco, but they both value a strong trade relationship, particularly considering the historic ties between the two countries."

"My sister is risking her life because Cuba and Spain have developed a stronger trade relationship?"

"Beatriz wants to undermine Fidel however she can. And after her experiences in Cuba, she understands the threat Franco poses."

"Sometimes I wish I could save Beatriz from herself," I mutter half under my breath.

"If you came all the way here to save Beatriz, you'll have your hands full. How long do you plan on being in Spain? Have you found a place to stay?"

"A waiter at the café across the street recommended a hotel. And I'm going to be here as long as it takes."

"As long as it takes for what?"

"To find Beatriz, of course."

"Have you ever been to Barcelona before?"

"No."

He looks like he wants to say something, but he's silent.

"Do you think she's in danger?" I ask.

Do you think she's alive?

"I don't know. I don't understand what happened. She's been working at the consulate here, socializing with Spanish government officials. She's good at that sort of thing; she's the life of the party, flirting, drawing attention to herself while gathering information. She has a knack for pretending to be someone people are constantly underestimating until it's too late for them to realize what fools they've been."

"Who else is she close to? Who might have information about where she could have gone?"

"Beatriz doesn't trust many people," he replies, confirming for me once more that he does indeed know my sister well. "Have you tried searching her apartment to see if she left anything behind that could help shed light on her whereabouts?"

"No, I was about to before you came in."

His gaze sweeps across the apartment. "It's difficult to tell if anything is out of place when it's like this."

"Tell me about it. Beatriz was always messy, even when we were younger."

"I guess we should start looking."

"I'm not sure we're a 'we' now," I counter.

"Reluctant allies, then."

Diego begins his search of Beatriz's apartment in the living room, but having the benefit of almost twenty-seven years of life together, I've learned my sister's habits better than anyone. Throughout the years, Beatriz has hidden love letters from boyfriends, political pamphlets, daring dresses our mother would never let her wear. Even when she was younger, she'd pilfer cosmetics and lipsticks from our mother's vanity, and late at night she'd sneak into my room and do my makeup, Elisa occasionally joining us.

I open the top drawer of the nightstand next to her bed and spot it immediately—the little datebook Beatriz keeps. We all have matching ones, Christmas gifts from Elisa a few years ago. Mine is a pale blue with my initials on the exterior, Beatriz's a vibrant red with hers embossed in gold.

There's little visible method to Beatriz's organization— sometimes she uses initials next to appointment times; other times she writes out the person's name. A few entries are written neatly on the lined pages; others are scrawled upside down or at an angle, Beatriz's handwriting boldly taking up the entire page.

Diego's name appears a few times, seemingly confirming the story he has told me, that he is someone in my sister's life, someone important to her. There's no evidence of the nature of their relationship—no obvious hearts surrounding his name—but Beatriz has never been the overly romantic type.

My heart pounds as I flip through the pages.

Her last appointment is only five days old.

12 A.M. Camila's.

I take the datebook and close the nightstand drawer behind me, heading for Beatriz's closet and her favorite hiding spot—the top shelf, right-hand corner behind a pair of shoes.

It's too high for me to see what's up there, but I run my fingers along the wood, my hand brushing against a thin sheen of dust.

There's nothing there.

Maybe if it was related to her work, she would have to get more creative, more inventive. I have no idea what sort of tricks spies have; Beatriz's skills have likely evolved since our childhood.

If she did have some sort of secret information—

As I turn away from the closet, I spy a piece of paper discarded on the floor, wedged between a pair of lilac pumps. I pick it up, confusion filling me.

"Did you find anything?" Diego calls from the living room.

It's an innocuous thing—a black-and-white photograph of a man and woman sitting at a café with a young child. Without anyone telling me, I know that the photograph must be from 1936 or 1937, but certainly not later than the spring of 1937.

When we left Cuba, we didn't take any old photographs with us, but throughout the years some have been smuggled out by family members and friends, so it's easy enough to identify myself as the young girl in the photo. I must be one or two years old. My mother is recognizable in the image as well; in her youth, she looked a lot like Beatriz. This is a version of my mother I'm less familiar with, though. She's looking at the man sitting across from her, the child—me—between them, and the expression in her gaze—

There are two things that jump out at me in the photograph.

One, the man my mother is across from is most certainly not my father. I've never seen him before in my life.

And second, even though I've never been to Barcelona before, I'm staring at an image of me as a young girl sitting at the exact same café where I ate less than an hour ago.

chapter three

W hat did you find?" Diego asks, and I jump at the sound of his voice. I was so engrossed in the strange photograph that I didn't even realize he had approached me.

"Nothing you're looking for, but for some reason, Beatriz had this." I hand him the photograph.

"Do you recognize the people in the photo?" he asks after studying it for a second. "The woman looks like Beatriz."

"That's our mother. And that's me when I was younger."

"I thought you said you hadn't been to Barcelona before."

"I didn't think I had been."

"There's no date on the back of the photo," he muses, turning it over. "You must be what, one or two in the picture? Maybe three?"

"I couldn't have been older than two. Beatriz and Alejandro were born in December of 1937, and my mother doesn't look pregnant in the picture, plus her dress and mine are rather lightweight for colder weather, and if my childhood experience is anything to go on, if there had been a chill in the air, she would have dressed me in a sweater or coat. The picture would have been taken either spring or summer of 1936 or spring or summer of 1937."

He frowns. "Those weren't exactly the best times to come to Barcelona."

"What do you mean?"

"Well, the civil war started in the summer of 1936. You were born in Cuba like Beatriz, right?"

I nod.

"It's strange that she'd leave Cuba and come to Spain with a young child in such an uncertain and dangerous time."

It is, and supremely unlike my mother, who was terrified during the revolution in Cuba, who has always valued safety and security above all else. Did my father accompany her to Barcelona? I can't imagine my mother traveling by herself with me from Cuba to Spain. It's just so at odds with every impression I have ever had of her. She would have been nineteen or twenty years old at the time, nearly a decade younger than I am now.

"It's so strange. I've seen the few remaining family photos we have left from Cuba, and I've never seen this one."

Our parents were never particularly close to us growing up. So much of our rearing was left to our nanny, Magda, and when they were involved in our upbringing, it was more my father trying to prepare Alejandro to take over the family business or our mother drilling etiquette and comportment into us. There wasn't much in the way of nostalgia or shared family history beyond the importance of our responsibility in always upholding the Perez name in our choices and our actions.

"Did you find anything else?" Diego asks.

"Beatriz's datebook, but that's it. Part of the problem is it's difficult to tell what is a normal mess for Beatriz, and what might be something more. The unlocked door makes me nervous. And the fact that it was open."

"Beatriz isn't always cautious."

"No, she isn't, although I have to imagine her line of work has taught her to be more prudent than she would normally be. I hope so, at least."

"Did she keep a diary?" Diego asks.

"No. When we were younger, our mother had the staff snoop in our rooms. We all had to be creative with preserving any secrets we wanted to keep. I think Beatriz just held everything inside rather than risk someone uncovering hers."

"I looked for her purse and didn't find one."

"That's a good sign, right?" I ask. "Maybe she went somewhere and took her things with her."

"Perhaps."

"Well, what's next? You're the spy; how do we find Beatriz?"

"I told you—I'm not a spy."

"And yet, somehow I don't quite believe you, and at the moment, you know more about her movements and whereabouts than most."

"She has a job at the consulate. Someone there might know something. Worst case, we can at least find out how long it has been since she showed up for work. Beyond that, there's not much we can do."

"No."

"'No'?" he echoes.

"No. That's not good enough. If my sister is in danger, I'm not going to just sit around waiting to see if her body turns up somewhere."

"If Beatriz is in danger, do you think looking for her is a good idea?"

"She's my sister. My family is all I have."

"And for that, you're willing to risk your safety?" Diego asks.

"If not for my family, then why else?" I scan the apartment once more, searching for any obvious clues we might have overlooked. "Did you find anything in the living room?"

"Just this," Diego answers. "It was in her wastebasket."

It's a matchbook with a black backdrop. The name of the place is scrawled across in an elegant white font.

Camila's.

"Are you familiar with this place? According to her datebook, her last appointment from a few days ago was at Camila's. If she brought the matchbook back home with her, at least we know she made the appointment. I thought it might have been a person's home. It doesn't say who she was meeting there, though."

"Camila's is a bar in Marbella."

"Have you been there before? How far is Marbella? Why would Beatriz go there?"

"It's a popular vacation spot. It's beautiful and attracts a social crowd. I've been to this bar and it's a nice place. I'm not sure why Beatriz would go there, though. She never asked me about it. I don't think we've ever even talked about Marbella. It's very far from Barcelona. A full day's drive, at least."

"If it's a popular vacation spot, it must get international tourists. Maybe she's meeting a contact there—someone who she was passing information to or who was passing information to her. They might remember her at the bar. Beatriz doesn't exactly blend in wherever she goes."

"Perhaps."

He's giving me so little to go on, and all I can think is that the longer this takes, the more time we're wasting if Beatriz is in trouble.

"Can we go to Marbella?" I ask him.

"There's that 'we' again."

"If you don't want to help find my sister, I can hire a car and make the trip myself. I just thought you had your own reasons for wanting to find Beatriz. After all, if she's been working with you, carrying your secrets, you wouldn't want those to get in the wrong hands."

"'Carrying my secrets'?"

I get the sense he's trying not to laugh at me.

"I didn't say I wouldn't help," he replies. "We've just come a long way from you threatening me with a statue to now wanting to go to Marbella with me. It's not exactly close. We could take a train, but it would be better to have a car to get around the city especially if there is trouble and we need a quick escape. Still—why wouldn't you just wait here in Barcelona for Beatriz? I thought you were supposed to be the quiet one, the cautious one."

"I am the quiet one, but I told you—I'm going to do whatever it takes to find my sister. The only thing we know is that she was in Marbella a few days ago."

"Isabel." His tone gentles. "It's not much of a lead to go on."

"It's better than nothing. I can't be here forever. I have responsibilities and obligations back home." I'm too embarrassed to admit that there's no chance Thomas will let me stay longer than the week he afforded me. "And if Beatriz is in trouble I can't just sit here in Barcelona waiting around for her to show up. I need to do something. I'm going to Marbella whether you're willing to help or not."

"Your sister will kill me if something happens to you." He sighs. "I'll pick you up tomorrow morning. Early. Very early."

"I'll be ready."

Once I am safely ensconced in my room after Diego drops me off at the hotel the waiter recommended, the first call I place is to a harried Elisa to let her know I have arrived safely and to tell her where I'm staying. I was too scared to remain at Beatriz's apartment considering the danger she may be in and the chance that someone would go there looking for her.

"How is Beatriz? Did you see her?"

I sit up in bed, Elisa's voice loud in my ear through the phone. It's growing dark in my room, the barest sliver of daylight breaking through the heavy drapes as the sun sets over Barcelona.

"Beatriz is gone."

"What do you mean 'Beatriz is gone'?"

"I went to her apartment and she wasn't there. It's a mess. You know how she is. But there was a man there, a friend of Beatriz's, I suppose, and he was looking for her as well."

Elisa is silent for a beat. "What sort of man? A lover?"

"Possibly, although he denies it. They certainly seem to share common interests. He was handsome enough, too."

"Do you think she's in trouble?"

"I don't know. I'm worried she is."

"Isabel, be careful."

"I will."

"Should we do something?" Elisa asks. "Ask for help? Maybe this is too big for you to take on by yourself. If she is involved with *those people* again, you shouldn't be there."

It's hard to know what's safe to say over the phone, who to trust. We learned the value of discretion in Cuba, the necessity of keeping our heads down and guarding our secrets lest we draw attention from the wrong circles.

"I left a note for her in her apartment with my hotel information and asked her to be in contact with me as soon as possible. We found a matchbook in her apartment for a bar in Marbella."

I wish I had more assurances to offer Elisa. I promise to give her another update tomorrow, and I hang up the phone and call my husband.

My conversation with Thomas is quick, his ire with my trip to Spain clear. He's not the sort of man to raise his voice and shout, and we're hardly a couple who lives in each other's pockets, but I can sense how perturbed he is by this shift in our relationship and the fact that we're in this unusual situation of me being so far away from him and much too independent for his liking.

Marriage is more of a balancing act than I ever realized.

It's difficult blending your lives when you come from such different places, distinct cultures, your experiences too divergent to be easily conveyed or explained away. He tries to be patient, I think, and I try to be less *everything*, and what is marriage if not an exercise in sacrifice and an attempt to make yourself more pleasing to your partner?

The instinct to soothe his worries, to reassure him that I will be home soon, that he will hardly miss me, that I have made sure there is enough food for him until I return, is as innate as breathing. But when the time comes, I am too tired from the jet lag that is creeping in to say much of anything, resenting the fact that I must always comfort him when he never does the same to me.

Despite the fear in Elisa's voice, the annoyance in Thomas's, it's the third call I make that I'm most anxious about.

It takes a few minutes for us to be connected, to hear my mother's voice on the other end of the line.

If I could have avoided telling her I was coming to Barcelona, I would have, but Thomas is hardly as well versed in the art of subterfuge as my siblings, and I doubt he could hold my parents at bay when they began asking to know my whereabouts.

When I told her I was going to Barcelona—omitting our fears that something had happened to Beatriz—her face went pale, and for a moment, I thought she was going to tell me I couldn't go, treat me as though I was still a little girl. Instead she said nothing, moving on with the conversation as if I hadn't spoken at all, changing topics so swiftly I questioned whether I had even voiced the news aloud myself.

"Isabel. What's wrong?"

"Nothing. I'm in Barcelona. I arrived safely."

For all that my mother and Beatriz argue, she worries about my sister, struggles to understand how her daughter has chosen a path so different from the one we were raised to follow. The last thing I wish to do is cause her more angst, so I shift the conversation past mentions of Beatriz, instead focusing on how lovely the city is, babbling on about the charming hotel room I am staying in, while she says nothing at all.

I can't resist asking—

"I saw a picture in Beatriz's apartment. Of us when I was a little girl sitting in a café here in Barcelona. I didn't realize I'd been here before."

"You haven't."

For as long as I can remember, I was taught not to question

things, that my parents were the final authority in my life. My siblings may have been more willing to challenge them, but I have always been the one to keep the peace in the family. Still, with the picture in hand, the café I sat at earlier near Las Ramblas clearly visible, I can't accept what she's saying to be true.

"No, there's a picture of me in a café in Barcelona—"

"You must be mistaken. It's simply not possible; you've never been to Barcelona, Isabel. Neither have I. I have to go now."

"Wait—I—"

She's off the phone before I can finish my question, before I can tell her that the picture contradicts everything she's saying, before I can ask her why she's lying to me.

I wish Beatriz were here so I could ask *her* about the photograph— how she got it and what she thought of it. I wish Beatriz were here so I would know that she is safe.

I turn off the lamp next to the bed, certain sleep will elude me tonight with so many questions and fears rattling around in my mind. But the jet lag is more powerful than my worry, and as my eyes close, one thought runs through my mind:

Who is the man across from my mother in the picture?

chapter four

Alicia

1936

BARCELONA

W e're almost there," I whisper to my daughter, Isabel, her body heavy on my hip after the long distance we've traveled. She is just over a year old, her footsteps still unsure, her preference to be carried everywhere we go.

She doesn't respond, but she burrows into the curve of my body, her arms wrapping around me tightly, her familiar scent filling my nostrils.

The truth is, I have no idea how far we are from my parents' home, the Barcelona streets running together, the unfamiliar city overwhelming me.

When we got off the ship from Havana, I was so grateful to have my feet on firm ground that I told myself the hard parts of this voyage would be over, imagined myself home, safe at last. And now that I am so close, it somehow seems even farther away.

We turn down another street, and Isabel lets out a little cry.

Not now. Please, not now.

I can't blame her for the tears welling in her eyes, the impending onslaught of cries building to a crescendo, my own emotions overwhelming me, but I am simply unprepared for her to have a fit when I am alone.

I should have brought Isabel's nanny, Magda, with us.

I should have thought this out better.

I regret the way I left Havana, that I didn't send a letter of warning to my parents so they would have someone waiting for me at the dock when we arrived, but at the time, all I could think of was getting as far away from Emilio as possible. Even the offer to stay with his cousin, my dearest friend, Rosa, at her marital home in Havana wasn't enough distance between us after what he did.

Does an ocean drown a sea of marital troubles?

I can only hope so.

"Mami—"

"We're almost there," I say again, praying that this time it is true.

I wish I had taken more jewelry to sell. I didn't think of all the costs that would go into this trip, the luxuries I have taken for granted since I married Emilio, how expensive this journey would be.

And then I see it—my parents' street—the place where they have been living since they fled Havana during the revolution in '33. My father liked Machado, backed him initially, believed in his promises for Cuba, but when Machado proved to be another strongman, more concerned with his own interests rather than Cuba's future, my father could not be silent, and his critiques became more pointed until he could no longer stay safely in Cuba. My father had some friends in Spain and thought Barcelona might be a good place to start over, our ancestors having come to Cuba from Spain generations ago.

I jostle Isabel on my hip, my strides quickening as I count down the numbers until I see the familiar address that I have never visited and have only seen previously scrawled across the envelopes of the letters we write each other.

I stop in front of the elegant building and set Isabel down at the base of the steps to the entrance door. She fusses slightly, reaching for me, her mouth open as though she is about to cry.

I straighten the skirt of her dress—one my mother-in-law purchased for her at El Encanto—running my fingers through her dark hair and the loose curls there. There's so much of her father in her, but sometimes I see glimpses of myself, too—in her hair, in her eyes, in the stubborn look that crosses her face when she wants something and it's denied her. She'll learn as she grows older how she will need to bend and shape herself to conform to the world around her, to fit others' expectations of her. She'll find herself changing, until one day she will look in the mirror and be unable to recognize the reflection staring back at her.

I take her hand and we walk up the front steps to my parents' house.

I knock quickly and decisively lest my courage fail me now. Their butler answers the door, and after I explain who we are, he shows me and Isabel into the sitting room while he goes to notify my family of our arrival.

There's a cry from somewhere in the house, and my sister Consuelo rushes in. She's just seventeen, but in the years since we last saw each other, she's grown so much, the photographs she's sent me hardly doing her justice.

"Alicia!"

I rise, my legs trembling as I walk toward her, as we embrace, as we exchange kisses on the cheek.

Her gaze drifts behind me to my daughter seated on the couch.

I hear footsteps in the hallway, and I turn just as my mother enters the room.

She embraces us both, and despite the smile on her face, the clear joy she has at seeing Isabel in person after all the photographs I've mailed to them from Havana, I can see the worry in her eyes, too, for her daughter and granddaughter to have shown up on her doorstep unannounced like this.

"Where is my father?" I ask her.

"He is at the clinic. One of his patients isn't doing well, but I've sent word to his office to let him know that you're here. You both must be exhausted. To have come all the way from Cuba . . ." Her eyes narrow as though she is working it all out in her mind. "Are you hungry?"

I nod.

"Let's get you some dinner. We'll have rooms prepared for you. Isabel can sleep in the guest room next to yours if that's amenable to you."

"That would be wonderful, thank you."

"Did you bring anything with you?"

"Our bags are arriving later. I'm sorry I didn't write to tell you we were coming."

She waves me off with a flick of her hand. "It's no matter. The house is certainly big enough, and I know your father will be happy to see you as well." Her gaze meets mine. "Is it just the two of you here?"

"It is."

She lowers her voice. "What happened? Where is Emilio?"

For the first time since I boarded the boat in Cuba, I say the words out loud—

"I've left my husband."

"Tell me everything," my mother demands once Isabel is asleep and we are alone in my parents' guest room.

"I left Emilio." I've had the whole sea voyage to try to acclimate myself to this decision, but on the ship, I could be anyone I wanted to be, the anonymity making me bold. Now that I am telling my family, it seems real.

Our parents were longtime friends, the sort of relationship that always made us more like family, so it was perhaps natural that there would be talk of Emilio and me being intended for each other even when we were young. If Emilio gave much credence to the talk, I never saw it when we were children—he paid me little attention at all, and I spent more time with his sister Mirta and his cousin Rosa than I did with my "intended." But Machado fell out of favor, and the revolution came, and my father realized it was safer for his family to leave Havana for Barcelona, and suddenly, the opportunity to marry his daughter off to his godson—the son of his oldest friend—before he left for an uncertain exile became salvation for my parents' worries over my future.

Emilio never told me how he felt when his father proposed our marriage, and maybe that was part of the problem—that we were both so concerned with honoring our families' wishes that we never discussed our expectations for our marriage, chose duty over understanding our own desires.

"What did he do?" my mother asks.

"There's someone else."

"Alicia." She pales. "Are you certain?"

"As sure as I can be. I saw them together."

"Maybe you were mistaken. Perhaps you misinterpreted what you saw."

"Some things cannot be misinterpreted."

An uncharacteristic curse falls from her lips. "How could he?"

"I don't know. I've been asking myself that since I found them together in his office. I meant my vows when I said them. And when we had Isabel, I thought we were happy. I thought he loved us. I thought we were a family."

"Do you love him?"

"I was on my way to loving him, I think. Emilio can be charming. He's smart and he's well-mannered, and he was always a polite husband. I never thought he would do this." My voice breaks. "He has humiliated me."

"Oh, Alicia." She wraps her arms around me, and it's like I am a little girl again, safe in her embrace. I didn't realize how badly I needed someone to comfort me, how badly I needed my mother. "I'm so sorry. When your father proposed that the two of you marry, I thought it would be for the best. We didn't know what awaited us in Barcelona, what sort of future we would be able to offer you and your sister, and I believed Emilio to be an honorable man. That he would be able to give you the life you deserved."

"I know you did. I don't blame you for wanting me to marry him."

"Who is she?" she asks. "Does he love her?"

"I don't know. I asked him, and he said he didn't, that I didn't understand, but what is there to not understand about a half-naked woman on his desk?"

"Is he going to give her up?"

"I didn't ask. Regardless, the damage has been done. I thought we were building a family together; I thought we were building a life. He has ruined all of that. I don't know how I can ever look at him the same way. I don't know how I can ever trust him again. I'm a fool for not realizing there was someone else. For thinking he might learn to care for me as I had begun to care for him."

"What will you do now?"

"I don't know. I didn't think about much beyond my need to leave. I told him I wanted to see all of you in Barcelona, that I needed to be with my family. He wasn't in a position to make demands or object."

"Does he realize you've left him? That this isn't just a trip to visit family, but something more?"

"No."

"And what will he do when he realizes you aren't returning to Havana? That's it, right—you plan to make this move a permanent one?"

"I don't know. I haven't thought that far ahead. I just needed you."

"I'm here for whatever you need. We all are. Of course, you and Isabel can stay with us. You will be safe and well cared for." She's silent for a beat. "If I were you, though, I would think about what you want sooner rather than later. She is his daughter. Do you really think he will let you take his child? Despite the losses his family suffered after the revolution in '33, Emilio is still a man who holds some influence, a man to be reckoned with. Be careful, Alicia."

I lengthen my strides as I walk toward my favorite café in the city. It's still early in the morning, not yet dawn, but it's already a hot one this July, sweat trickling down my back and threatening the makeup I so carefully applied earlier.

Isabel and I have been in Spain for a few weeks now, and I have yet to acclimate to the time difference, the sea voyage from Havana taking its toll on me. I sleep little, the combination of travel and my worries over the situation with Emilio keeping me up late and waking me in the night. I try to be strong for Isabel, but sometimes I look at her and I am so filled with fear that Emilio will come take her away that it steals my breath. So, in the mornings, I rise before most of the household is up and come sit at a café near my family's house, and write letters to Rosa in Cuba.

I quicken my steps as I near the café, glancing over my shoulder, once, twice. Maybe it was foolish to come out this morning, dangerous given the whispers spreading through Barcelona of the growing political violence in the city, but I could not resist. There are so few opportunities for me to be alone with my thoughts before I am surrounded by my family, before Isabel needs me, and in these quiet mornings I am just myself, not a mother or estranged wife, merely Alicia.

I sent Emilio a letter to let him know we have arrived safely, a few short lines scribbled on my mother's stationery, but I have received no reply from him.

A group of tourists speaking English comes toward me, and I move out of their path quickly, pressing against the building to let them walk around me. They look as though they have been up all night and are just now trickling back to their hotel rooms to catch a few hours of sleep, considering the early hour.

Barcelona strains at the seams with all manner of people and tensions. Thousands have traveled to Barcelona for the People's Olympiad where athletes from all over the world will compete in the event organized to protest the upcoming Summer Olympics hosted by the Nazis in Berlin.

The current democratically elected Republican government

wishes to modernize Spain, but many oppose their efforts and the government has been weakened by infighting, strikes, and uprisings. There are many factions at conflict, and as an outsider, not privy to the history that led up to this moment despite my family's ancestral ties to Spain, I walk a tightrope as I navigate a country that is not my own.

Whether the tensions will convert themselves into full-fledged war remains to be seen.

I lengthen my strides once more, nearly at the plaza when a loud boom explodes in the distance. I trip, almost falling on the pavement, my ears ringing.

There's another boom, and a quick series of pops, one right after the other, that are unmistakably familiar—the sound of gunfire that we often heard in Cuba, political assassinations, and violence an all too regular occurrence in Havana.

I glance around me, the street nearly empty. The tourists that just passed me by stop as well, their gazes drifting to the sound of the noises as well. And then I see them—

Coming up from an adjacent street, Spanish soldiers march toward the square, their weapons drawn.

A loudspeaker comes on, sirens blaring in the city.

Off in the distance, someone screams, the sound piercing the square.

I turn back, ready to run toward my parents' house, when I spy a group of soldiers heading toward me, their presence blocking my safe exit.

A man runs up to me and grabs my hand, and I reflexively try to yank it away from him, but he keeps a tight hold on me.

"Come on," he yells. "We need to find somewhere safe."

I hesitate for a split second, but my fear of the soldiers wielding guns in their hands is greater than my concern over what may befall me with a stranger.

We run down a side street, away from the square, away from the soldiers, surrounded by people doing the same. It's a melee in the streets, some joining the fighting, others running away from it. Bodies push me, arms brushing against me, and I tighten my grip on the stranger, grateful to not be alone in this.

We're still far from my parents' house, and I look around this new street, trying to get my bearings when the rapid sound of gunfire erupts again.

More screams. More people pushing.

Isabel.

I cannot leave my daughter like this, cannot leave her alone, forced to make her own way in the world. She needs her mother. She needs me to survive.

The straps of my sandals bite into my feet, and I almost consider bending down to take them off, but I'm hesitant to slow down, the sight of those soldiers and their guns filling me with terror. My lungs burn from the exertion, my leg muscles shaking.

Ahead of us, a soldier emerges from one of the side streets, and some of the citizens begin picking up rocks, anything they can find on the ground, and hurl them at the soldier as he aims his gun at them.

My arm is wrenched free of the stranger, and I turn, trying to see where he went, attempting to get a better sense of my bearings, but when I look back, he's gone, chaos surrounding me.

It's undeniable now—

War has come to Spain.

chapter five

Rosa

1936

HAVANA

I practice the speech I've rehearsed once more in my mind. It won't do for me to be accusatory, to appear as if I am complaining about our circumstances. Better to make him think this is a natural conclusion to a conversation we have already been having, smarter for him to arrive at the decision on his own with some gentle guidance from me than to maneuver him into it.

I descend the elaborate staircase, my fingers trailing against the banister, the simple gold band on my ring finger gleaming under the chandelier. After only two months of marriage, I still have not grown accustomed to living among such wealth and privilege, and I doubt I ever will.

My foot hits the bottom step of the staircase, and I turn right, careful to keep from making too much noise and disturbing the others this morning. Privacy is difficult to find when your in-laws reside under the same roof, and as enthusiastically as Gonzalo has taken to us living with his parents, I still feel as though I am surrounded by strangers who would be happier if I wasn't around.

I find my husband sitting in the dining room, blessedly alone.

"Rosa," Gonzalo says in greeting, looking up from his breakfast with a smile, a newspaper folded next to his formal place setting. "Have you heard?" he asks, gesturing to the newspaper beside him, his voice filled with excitement.

There's something about Gonzalo when he's like this. He is handsomest when he is passionate, when he is consumed by his interests, and as the recipient of such intense focus you are often left with the sensation that you are about to have your life changed by the force of his excitement and enthusiasm.

It was like that when we met—a friend of mine at the University of Havana invited me to a political meeting held in a little bar around the corner from the university. As soon as we walked in, we were engulfed in a cloud of smoke, a group of students crowded over a table littered with discarded cigarette butts and empty glasses, their voices just loud enough to be heard over the din of the room as they quoted political philosophers back at one another, some a little drunker than others.

I asked Gonzalo once what he thought when he saw me that day, and he just shook his head and smiled as though it was his secret to keep, but that day he motioned me over, and somehow there was an empty chair next to him, and I sat down, our bodies pressed indecorously close together at the small table, and he went right back to speaking politics, his gaze occasionally cutting back to me, his leg warm against mine under the table.

He courted me vigorously for weeks until one day, I had a ring on my finger, and I was no longer alone, but a wife, part of a new, complicated, intimidating, terrifying family.

"What has happened?" I ask Gonzalo, sliding into the chair beside him.

"They're fighting in Spain. There was a military coup organized by some generals."

Alicia.

My cousin by marriage and closest friend has been in Barcelona for weeks now. We promised to write regularly when she left Havana with her daughter, Isabel, but I've yet to receive word from her.

"How bad was it?"

"The coup was defeated in Barcelona and the Republicans still control the major cities, but the Nationalists seized territory in the countryside. Some of the athletes who traveled to the People's Olympiad remained in Spain to fight with the Republicans. Men from all over the world will volunteer for the Republican cause. I'm going to join them."

For a moment, I think I misheard him. I'm too filled with worry for Alicia and Isabel.

"What are you talking about?"

"I'm going to Spain. To fight with the Republicans. If we're going to defeat fascism once and for all, it's going to take more support than the Spanish have now."

"You could die in Spain."

The look in his eyes absolutely terrifies me because it's clear that there's no discussion to be had. He's already made up his mind. I open my mouth to say something, but before I can find the words I'm searching for, Gonzalo turns his attention back to the newspaper.

Not for the first time, a gulf has appeared between us, and I have no idea how it came or how to erase it.

Marriage is much harder than I ever imagined it would be.

I want to argue with him, want to convince him to stay, but if I've learned anything in our short marriage, it's that when Gonzalo's mind is made up, there's no changing it.

"If you're going to Spain, I want to move out of your parents' home and into a place of our own while you're gone."

The words come out as of their own volition, borne out of my frustration and hurt, and the sense that I am the voice most easily ignored in this household, my feelings and opinions often pushed to the margins.

It was the point I wished to discuss with him when I came down here in the first place, before I knew about the fighting in Barcelona and his desire to leave, but now that I am to be alone in this house, the need for freedom is all-consuming.

Gonzalo looks up from his newspaper. "Are you joking? Why would we ever leave?"

"Because we are married. One day we might have a family of our own. Your brother will return to Cuba and marry, and as the eldest he will inherit the house. Are we to live under the same roof as Felipe and his wife, as their children? Are we to raise our families in this house together?"

"I imagine Felipe is quite far off finding a wife of his own or even wishing for one, so I don't think you need to worry there," he replies. "And my parents like having me here."

"They haven't adjusted to having me here." I take a deep breath, attempting to steady myself. "I appreciate that they have given us a place to live, but what about the life we talked about before we got married? Finding a little apartment close to the university. Working while we finish our studies. I want to build a family of our own, just the two of us."

"And who do you think will pay for that apartment?" Gonzalo asks, frustration in his voice. "Would you have us huddled together in some tiny room with threadbare furnishings, a mattress on the floor, wondering how we're going to make ends meet?"

It's on the tip of my tongue to remind him that my own upbringing wasn't far from that, and still we were happy—my parents loved each other, and they filled my life with laughter and joy. There's so little of either of those things in this mausoleum of a house.

"At least it would be ours."

"I am an Aguilera. My family would never countenance me living in such a manner."

"So, what am I supposed to do? Stay here while you go to Spain?"

"You're my wife. Your place is here while I am gone."

"And what if something happens to you? What if you don't come back? Please don't do this. Please don't go to Spain."

"Nothing is going to happen to me. You'll see. I'll return to Havana with a hero's welcome."

chapter six

Isabel

1964

BARCELONA

I must have been more tired than I realized because I sleep soundly, waking just before I agreed to meet Diego to drive to Marbella.

The matchbook and datebook I found in Beatriz's apartment are as flimsy a lead as they come, but when I asked the front desk if there were any messages for me, they told me there weren't, so Beatriz must still be gone. No matter how angry she might be with me, the estrangement between us, the sister I know would never ignore the note I left for her.

I dress quickly, repacking my suitcase. Diego said we'd be driving all day and would need to stay the night in Marbella after visiting Camila's before returning to Barcelona. He gave me the name of a hotel he recommended, which I leave with the clerk at the front desk in case Beatriz returns to her apartment while I'm gone.

The sun is barely rising when I walk out the hotel entrance, my suitcase gripped in my hands, Diego's red convertible idling at the curb.

"Good morning," he says as he steps out of the car, his eyes shielded by dark sunglasses. He takes my suitcase from me and loads it into the trunk of his car. "Did you sleep well?"

"Better than expected," I admit, nerves filling me. As badly as I want to find my sister, it's difficult for me to countenance getting into the car with a strange man, trusting someone I barely know. Last night, he seemed to be who he says he is—a man in my sister's life, a man Beatriz trusts—but my sister is also involved in things I struggle to comprehend, a world of secrets and lies I want no part of.

Is Diego really a friend or is he caught up in the web of espionage I fear has ensnared Beatriz?

He must see the indecision in my eyes because he says, "You can trust me, Isabel. I promise."

I wish it were that easy, that people could just say things and you could take them at their word, but my experience in life has proven otherwise. I've learned that often it is not what people say, but what they do, that shows you who they are, and in this there is little for me to do but see where this journey takes me.

There's also the pair of beauty scissors in my handbag.

Not big enough to do serious damage, but hopefully sufficient to give me a chance to wound him and escape should I need them.

I grip my purse a little more tightly as he holds the passenger door open for me.

I consider telling Diego that I've changed my mind, that there's no possibility of me traveling to Marbella with him, but instead I slide into the convertible, sitting there quietly while he shuts my car door and gets into the driver's seat.

We don't speak as we begin the journey, the early hour and strangeness of the whole situation keeping me quiet. I look out the window as we drive through the city, curiosity filling me. Based on my age in the photograph, I would have been too young to remember my trip here, but I can't help but wonder why we traveled from Havana and why my mother would bother to deny it.

"What are you thinking?" Diego asks, breaking the silence between us. "Contemplating making a run for it?"

"I was earlier. Once I sat in the car, I figured I was somewhat committed. No, I was thinking of the photograph I saw yesterday."

"Were you able to talk to your mother? Did you learn the story behind it?"

"No. I called home to let my family know I arrived safely. I told my sister Elisa I was going to Marbella with you," I say pointedly lest he think there aren't people who know who I'm with and where I'm headed. "But my mother insisted that I've never been to Barcelona."

"That picture is unmistakably Barcelona."

"I know."

"Why would she lie?"

"I don't know. My mother isn't the sort of person who invites questions."

"Is she as formidable as her daughters?"

"Oh, more so, undoubtedly. After all, we learned from her. Unfortunately, it makes it difficult to get the truth from her at times. It just seems like a strange thing to lie about."

I've learned people lie about all sorts of things, their motives often difficult to comprehend. That Diego has agreed to help me, going so far as to drive me all the way to Marbella, makes me wonder about *his* motives.

"Are you one of Beatriz's coworkers at the consulate?" I ask him. "You told me you and Beatriz share common interests, that she trusts you, but you never said how you met."

"No, I don't work at the consulate, but I did meet your sister while she was working there. My family does business with the American government, and since I'm an American citizen it helps to have me involved."

That he's American *and* Spanish makes me wonder if my earlier suspicions were true, if Beatriz met him through her involvement with the CIA.

"What sort of business?"

"Manufacturing. It's been around for generations. One of my uncles is preparing to turn the reins over to me."

"I know a thing or two about family businesses," I murmur.

"Beatriz mentioned that. Does your husband work in the family business?"

"No, Thomas has his own interests."

"And what do you do in America? Palm Beach, right? Beatriz mentioned that, too. Do you have children?"

"No."

Silence falls, and I surprise myself completely.

"I paint."

"So, you're an artist."

"Not professionally or anything like that. It's more something I like to do in my spare time. I—I have a hard time sleeping sometimes and painting relaxes me." I flush, realizing I'm talking too much and likely saying utter nonsense to a stranger. What does he care if I paint or not?

"What do you paint?"

I hesitate. This conversation is becoming more personal than I'd like, my art something I don't even share with my family or Thomas.

"I paint my memories, I suppose. Things I loved."

Things I lost.

Home.

I paint home.

"What a wonderful gift that must be, to be able to preserve the pieces of your life, to bring them alive on the canvas and know that wherever you are, you are always able to carry your home with you. I think I envy you that ability. You must miss Cuba a great deal."

I can't quite formulate a response to his comment, the urge to cry embarrassing me. I have never been comfortable with my emotions. Beatriz is content to wear her passions proudly on her sleeve, Elisa's kindness and openness drawing people to her, and Maria speaks of Cuba as though it is her past, her life in Palm Beach her present and future now. But I can't move past it, can't reconcile my grief. It's easier to never speak of it at all. I know how it makes people see me, that the rest of my family thinks I don't care, that I left a fiancé and a life back in Cuba as though it was nothing. The truth is the things I don't speak of are often the ones that hurt the most. There aren't words that ever seem adequate to describe what this exile has meant to me, so I merely respond with,

"Yes."

"When did you leave? Beatriz speaks so little of her life in Cuba."

"Right after the revolution in 1959. We stayed a few months, hoping it would all blow over, but—it didn't, of course. It all seems so hard to believe now, the fact that we thought we would only be gone a few weeks, months at most, and it's now been over five years."

"It's difficult when you love your country, and you watch it struggle, know that you deserve better, that it could be better, but the people in power seem determined to not make it so," he responds.

"Have you lived your whole life in Barcelona?" I ask him.

"No, I was actually born in New York. I grew up there. I didn't come to Spain until later. My mother was Spanish, but she was forced to leave during the civil war. My father was American, a soldier in the International Brigades, so they fled to New York when things became too dangerous. She was pregnant with me, and the war was growing more violent."

I open my mouth to respond when suddenly he says—

"There's a car following us."

"What do you mean, 'there's a car following us'?"

"There's a black sedan. It's been two cars back since I left my house this morning."

He says it almost casually, but his hands tighten on the steering wheel.

Instinctively, I turn my head—

"Don't look."

I can't not look, and out of the corner of my eye I see that there is indeed a dark sedan a few cars behind us. I can't make out the passengers without obviously craning my neck and perhaps drawing their notice.

"Why would they be following us?" I ask. "Did you tell anyone you were taking me to Marbella?"

"I told my secretary I would be out of town and to cancel my appointments, but I didn't mention where I was going or who I was going with."

"Do you think this is about Beatriz? Could someone have been watching her apartment and decided to follow us in the hopes of finding her?"

"I don't know. I worry about Beatriz sometimes," he confesses, surprising me. "She thinks she's invincible, but she should be careful. Especially now."

"Do you think I haven't been telling her that from the time we were children? She throws herself into dangerous political situations, ramifications be damned."

"Well, if you're worried your sister disappeared, maybe there's some reassurance in the fact that if men are following us to get to Beatriz, they don't have her."

"Or we're leading them to her," I counter. "What are you going to do about them?"

"About the men following us? Nothing. Let them drive all over Spain if they wish. If they don't get too close, we should be fine."

"What do you mean 'get too close'? Are we in danger?"

I struggle to keep my voice calm, to push past the fear clawing at me. Sometimes, it can take the littlest things to catapult me back to those terrifying days before we left Havana: the sound of a car backfiring so similar to a gunshot, the sight of Fidel's face in news reports, the noise from an airplane like that one that carried us from Havana. There are all sorts of moments that sneak up on me and leave me breathless, panic gripping me. It is impossible to not always worry the worst will happen to you when the worst *has* already happened to you.

"You're a tourist so there's that, but that doesn't mean you don't have to be careful. You're wearing a wedding ring. A married woman in the company of a single man can be perilous. Spain is opening to travelers who enjoy our beautiful sights and beaches, but it's still dangerous. People are being executed for so-called war crimes; there's a morality police ready to root out any subversion they find. We're all walking a fine line. Franco controls everything, and it is not good to draw attention to yourself."

I slip my wedding ring off my finger and plop it into my bag.

His eyebrow raises. "Just like that?"

"We can say we're brother and sister."

He grins. "Or you could have left your wedding ring on, and we could have said we're husband and wife."

"We'll say we're cousins," I decide, ignoring the obvious flirtation in his voice.

He laughs. "Cousins, then."

I look down at my naked ring finger, surprised to see that the skin where the band used to be is a little paler than the rest of my hand, the thick gold band I've worn for the past nearly three years blocking me from the sun. Now that the ring is off, it's as though a remnant of my past, of who I was before I married Thomas, lingers.

"How would your husband feel about you traveling around Spain with another man?"

"I doubt he'd care very much. He knows I'm not swayed by a handsome man however charming he might think he is."

Diego laughs. "Should I be flattered that you think I'm handsome or insulted that you don't find me charming?"

"Neither considering I'm married."

"Happily married?"

"Decidedly married."

"As someone who is decidedly *unmarried*, you'll have to tell me what's so wonderful about the state of holy matrimony. What was it about your husband that first drew your notice?"

On its face, it isn't an objectionable question, and yet, I'm loath to answer it, to share such intimacies with a stranger.

The night I met Thomas we were at a party hosted by some business associate of my father's in Palm Beach. When we were first introduced, I hardly thought much of it. He was more my parents' contemporary than mine, and I wasn't over my broken engagement back in Cuba. That I even drew his notice that night hardly registered in the face of the other worries that plagued me: the pinch of my too-small secondhand high-heeled pumps, the thin smile my mother plastered on her face as guests looked over us as though we were simply invisible, the way my father's voice boomed a little louder than it normally would, as though he were trying to carve a place for himself in this world that clearly had no interest in him. It wasn't until later when I was back in my bedroom removing my earrings, slipping off my shoes and stockings, when my mother came in and mentioned to me that Thomas hadn't been able to take his eyes off me, that his presence even really registered beyond that of just another man at the party.

"He is kind," I say, even as I realize that isn't really the word I'm looking for. Perhaps "uncomplicated" is a better one, and I suppose in my view "uncomplicated" is a kindness in and of itself in that it tends to protect the recipient from the sort of strings that come alongside passionate personalities. It would be strange to say that he is peaceful, but that is part of my husband's allure—that it is easy to know where you stand with him, that for better or worse there are no unpleasant surprises.

Perhaps "predictable" is a better one.

Safe.

"How long have you been married?"

"Nearly three years."

"Beatriz didn't approve."

"Did Beatriz tell you that herself or are you guessing?"

"She told me once over too many drinks. You can't be surprised that she wouldn't approve."

"What's that supposed to mean?"

"Just that she loves you and was worried about you. She thought your marriage was something you did for your family."

"We don't all have the luxury of living as Beatriz does. I admire my sister's ability to follow her passions. Maybe I even envy it. But what we went through in Cuba—I did what I thought was best for myself and my family. I could not live as Beatriz does even if I wanted to. I have responsibilities the others don't have."

"That sounds like a lot of pressure, though, to carry the weight of so many. Is that why you paint, because it's the one time you're able to do what you want without worrying what everyone else thinks?"

"I think I understand why you and Beatriz are friends," I say, sidestepping his question and the emotions it evokes. "You push just like Beatriz does. You're very similar."

"Maybe I do. I'm not sure if you mean that as a compliment or not, but I'm going to take it as one. I can think of worse things than to be compared to Beatriz."

"You care about her, don't you?"

"I do."

"Be careful with her. She's had enough heartbreak in her life. She doesn't need to be caught up in more troubles. She needs some stability in her life. Peace."

"Is that what you were looking for?"

"What do you mean?"

"When you married your husband? Were you also looking for stability and peace?"

"That is a terribly personal question."

"And yet, when we first met you had no problem asking me questions about my relationship with your sister—who I might add seems more than capable of taking care of herself. Some might even say that if I was involved with Beatriz romantically, and one of us was to carefully guard our heart, it should be me not her."

"People make that mistake with Beatriz. Just because she's strong, independent, fearless doesn't mean she doesn't hurt like the rest of us, that she isn't vulnerable."

"Are you vulnerable, too?"

He says it so softly that I'm almost disarmed by the tone of his voice, the look in his eyes.

"We're not talking about me. I'm asking you to be careful with Beatriz."

"I told you my interests don't lie with Beatriz. Perhaps they lie elsewhere."

He says it casually, as though it is a perfectly normal conversation to have with a married woman, and while I know there are so many in the society set who conduct affairs publicly with little concern for the consequences, I've never been that sophisticated.

"Don't look so surprised," he teases.

"I'm—" I can't find the right words to respond to such a statement. "I'm not looking for a liaison. Not even a little one."

His lips quirk. "Now you have me wondering what exactly a 'little liaison' entails."

"You're mocking me."

"I'm not. Not really. I apologize if I was too forward. I promise for the rest of our trip I will say nothing of the sort. I wasn't sure if—"

"If I was going to engage in a torrid affair with you in Marbella?" I laugh at the absurdity of such an idea. "Hardly."

"Not a 'torrid affair,' perhaps just a 'little liaison.'"

I can't help but smile at that. He's surprisingly fun company, and it's then that I realize somewhere along the way he distracted me from the fact that we were being followed at all.

But when I look out of the corner of my eye, the sedan is still there.

"They're going to follow us all the way to Marbella," Diego predicts.

"How do you live like this? How are you so unbothered by it?"

"My experience since I came to Spain four years ago has been defined by fear. The fear that if you speak your mind and the wrong person hears you, you will be punished; the fear that you trust someone and they turn you in to the government; the fear that if you do not support the regime enough you will be punished; the fear that one day you will be driving down the road with a black sedan following you several cars back."

"Are things very difficult . . ."

My question trails off because I know a thing or two about not being able to speak your mind in a country where speech is not free.

"Yes."

There's an understanding that passes between us, an awareness and caution that comes from living in a country run by dictators.

"My mother died a few years ago. My father passed away a year before my mother."

For as difficult as my own relationship with my mother can be, I cannot imagine how alone I would feel if I lost her, considering for better or worse what a dominant force she has been in my life.

"I'm so sorry for your loss," I reply.

"I came to Spain four years ago because my parents are gone, and I grew up on my mother's memories of Spain, her love for her homeland she was forced to flee during the civil war. She spoke of her childhood in Spain daily, told me of all the places she wanted to take me when she felt safe to return, when Franco was no longer in power. I lived Spain through her memories, and after she passed away and I no longer had her stories to connect me to my heritage, I wanted a chance to experience it myself.

"I wanted to know where I come from, where my family comes from. I wanted to know my relatives, to stand on Spanish soil and feel as though I belonged somewhere rather than having parts of me scattered and torn. But Spain wasn't what I thought it would be, and living here made me aware of dangers I never faced in America. At some point, though, I just stopped being afraid. It cost me too much. If I can't speak, if I can't trust others, if I can't live my life freely what's the point? You must preserve parts of yourself they can't touch. You have to fight back."

I can't speak past the lump in my throat, the urge to cry overwhelming me. There is a change your soul undergoes when you experience loss, in exile, and you recognize that essence in the people you meet who have undergone such a transformation themselves, who know what it's like to not belong anywhere. It is as though you say to each other:

I see you. I understand you. I recognize your pain.

chapter seven

Alicia

1937

BARCELONA

It's been eight months since the attempted coup in Barcelona last summer, since violence erupted, civil war breaking out all over Spain, its reverberations felt around the world.

Thousands have traveled from other countries to join the International Brigades on the Republican side including many from Cuba, support for the Republicans widespread among my countrymen and abroad. On the other side of the conflict, Italy and Germany sent weapons and manpower to help the Nationalists overthrow the Republican government.

It was a bloody and terrifying autumn that had me questioning the wisdom of staying here, but the violence has since tapered off in Republican-held territories like Barcelona.

I contemplated returning to Cuba, my fear for Isabel's safety and the worried letters I received from Emilio pulling me back toward Havana. It seems imprudent to remain in a country fighting a war that isn't mine, but at the same time, I can't leave my family here, either, and they can't return to Cuba, considering my father is out of favor with the government once more.

When my time isn't spent with Isabel and Consuelo, I come down to this café with a book and watch the people walking by. At first, I was afraid to return to the square, as though being back here would conjure up bad memories, my time in the city spent avoiding this part of Barcelona, but little by little, I realized that the more I avoided it, the harder it became for me to envision ever enjoying something that once brought me such pleasure.

I often write letters to Rosa in Havana, filling her in on the details of my life in Barcelona. Even though we are only cousins by marriage, she holds my secrets, and I trust she won't tell Emilio anything I'm not ready to share with him. Today, though, brought me to the café for a far more somber task. There's a stack of correspondence sitting next to me, and I stare down at the blank piece of paper in front of me, willing the words to appear on the page.

It is a difficult thing to pen a note that accompanies a dead body. I have sat at this café for hours now, my pen hovering over the crisp, blank page, the words eluding me.

I'm so sorry for your loss hardly seems sufficient for a beloved cousin an ocean away who has now become a widow entirely too soon—is there ever a time when it is appropriate or expected, even, for a woman to become a widow? This war has certainly made too many already and it has just begun.

I stare down at the blank page, trying to find the right words to offer Rosa in this difficult time, the letter that will accompany her husband's dead body back to Cuba.

Gonzalo was a fine man. He died a hero, I add.

I'm not being entirely truthful in my assessment of Rosa's husband, but I cannot say what I really thought of Gonzalo, that I never liked them together, never felt he was sincere in his character or worthy of her affection.

I scribble a few more lines about how much I miss Rosa, how I wish we were together, the words flowing more easily now. When I've finished writing the letter to the best of my satisfaction, I get up from the table, accidentally bumping the edge. The breeze catches the papers, and they flutter to the ground.

I lean down to pick them up, just as a man walking by bends over, rescuing one of the pages from my letter to Rosa.

"Excuse me, miss, you dropped this."

I look up, and farther still, at the man standing over me, my letter to Rosa in hand.

Just as I move to rise, he crouches down so we are nearly eye level, the sun glinting off his dark hair.

I recognize him instantly, the sight of him transporting me back to Cuba and my youth—

"Nestor."

He doesn't speak for a beat, the paper fluttering in his hands. "Alicia."

I rise to my feet unsteadily. "What are you doing here?"

He was one of my father's students when he taught medicine at the University of Havana, and later they worked together before my father left Cuba, but it's been years since we last saw each other.

"At the café? Or in Spain?" he asks, a smile playing at his lips.

"Both."

"I came to offer my medical services. My cousins left Havana to join the International Brigades, and, well, I'm not a fighter, but the stories coming out of Spain—it seems like there's great need in a conflict like this. I thought I could offer medical help to some of the refugees."

Refugees have fled to Barcelona from the countryside and other cities when the Nationalists took control. Many have lost everything, caught in the middle of this conflict, their lives destroyed.

"I stopped by your parents' house—your father and I still exchange letters—and I saw Consuelo. She mentioned that you were here having coffee and that I should come see you and say hello."

"I'm glad you did. I'm sorry, I think I'm just a little shocked to see you. How long has it been? Years?"

"Since you were engaged. I'm sorry I couldn't attend the wedding, but I heard it was a lovely affair. Marriage agrees with you. You look as beautiful as always. Is your husband here with you?"

"No. He's still in Havana. His business keeps him busy, and I wanted to visit my family, for my daughter Isabel to meet her aunt and grandparents."

"I'd heard you had a baby. Congratulations."

"Thank you." I gesture toward the table beside us, flustered. "Would you like to sit? Have some coffee? I'm sorry—I'm just caught off guard. I never imagined I would see you here."

"I felt the same way when your sister mentioned that you were here in Spain. I never expected that our paths would cross again. I've thought of you often since your marriage, wondered how you were. I've missed you."

"I've missed you, too," I reply.

"I thought about stopping by to see you after you married."

"Why didn't you? I wish you had."

"I wasn't sure if it would be appropriate. I didn't want to overstep."

The fact that Emilio could take a lover but a family friend visiting me would have been frowned upon isn't lost on me.

"I wish you had. I would have liked to see you very much. I'm glad you're here now, even if we're meeting under difficult circumstances. Would you like some coffee?"

"I would. I can sit for a moment perhaps, and then I must return to the clinic. We're understaffed; in fact, your father offered to help out when he can, although I gather he's busy with his own practice."

"How long have you been in Barcelona?"

"Just a week. Will you stay in Barcelona much longer?" Nestor asks me.

"I think so. My plans aren't set."

"You should come by the clinic." He takes a piece of paper and jots down the address for me. "We can always use some help. You were so good with the patients at your father's practice."

I take the note from Nestor wordlessly, still reconciling the fact that he is sitting here before me. I've thought of him often in the years since we last saw each other, wondered how he was doing. We were friends once despite the seven-year age difference between us. He never seemed to mind how I would follow him around, hanging on his every word. I used to spend my days as his "assistant" at the clinic in Havana.

"I'd like to see you again while I'm still in the city," he says. "Maybe we can meet for coffee another time."

"I'd like that. I'm often here in the mornings on Tuesdays and Thursdays. Isabel and Consuelo go to music lessons nearby, and I wait for them here."

"Then I hope our paths cross again."

We stand near the table, staring at each other, not speaking.

Seeing him transports me to another time, before I was Alicia

Perez, before I was a mother, when I was simply a young girl whose biggest concern was the terrible—and unreciprocated—crush I had on my father's most promising student.

If Nestor ever noticed my crush, he was too kind to show it. I used to imagine that one day when I was older, he would see me in a new light, that the friendship I cherished so deeply would evolve into something different, that he would feel the same way I did.

At fifteen, I thought for sure that one day I would be Nestor's wife.

I outgrew the dream, of course, when he never showed any interest in me that way, when my parents decided I should marry Emilio. But now, seeing him again, all those old memories come rushing back.

Nestor extends his hand to me, and I take it, shaking it gently, before he releases me and walks away.

I stare after his retreating back for longer than I care to admit, before I'm ready to return to the correspondence I brought with me, the one I saved for last.

A letter sits waiting for me, unopened, my husband's familiar handwriting on the envelope.

Emilio has written twice since the war broke out eight months ago. The first letter was perfunctory at best, his words directing me to come home with Isabel.

I sent him back a few lines letting him know that we were safe with my parents, but the second letter was more insistent, and now this third letter—

I scan the words scrawled there, fear filling me.

Emilio is threatening to come to Barcelona if I don't return to Havana with Isabel.

chapter eight

Rosa
1937
HAVANA

My knees tremble beneath my black linen dress, the sun beating down on my back as I stare at the coffin being lowered in the ground of the cemetery in Havana.

"He was a good man," someone murmurs around me, but I don't bother looking up to see who speaks, my gaze trained instead on my husband Gonzalo's interred body.

My cousin Mirta stands beside me, her strength a balm in these difficult times.

I am left with a letter from one of his fellow soldiers, recounting to me the events of my husband's last days, his time spent fighting in the International Brigades with so many of our countrymen who traveled from Cuba to Spain.

Gonzalo died alongside other brave Cubans in the Battle of Jarama, one of thousands of men on both sides of the conflict who lost their lives that day. It's impossible to think that while my husband's body lay bleeding in a valley in Spain, I passed a normal day an ocean away in Havana, unaware that my life had just come crashing down around me, the man I married lost to me forever.

I keep my gaze trained on the coffin as it rests in the hollowed-out ground.

Men shuffle forward, carrying shovels, each one taking dirt and scooping it onto the gleaming coffin.

With each mound of dirt that hits the rich wood, something tightens in my chest, and I want to throw myself on the coffin, want to join my husband in the grave. Now that I am alone, I cannot bear the idea of a life without him, of navigating this future on my own. It seems unfair that I was promised forever, only to get a few months with him and now a never-ending widowhood.

A pair of shoes enters my line of sight.

I close my eyes, praying they will walk on, that I will be left alone in my grief. I have used Mirta as a barrier to keep everyone away from me; she can be fierce when she wants to be, the Perez haughtiness useful when employed for good, and I have no desire to speak to anyone.

When I open my eyes, though, the shoes are still there, attached to a dark pant leg.

They don't move away.

"Rosa."

Dread fills me, the voice belonging to the immaculate leather shoes, the elegant trousers, unmistakably familiar.

Mirta squeezes my hand as though she could infuse some of her strength to me.

I look up from the ground, drawing the moment out for as long as I can to avoid the encounter. Six feet or so later, my gaze locks with Gonzalo's older brother's scowling face.

He's been in New York for so long, since before Gonzalo and I married, that I'd wondered if he'd even make it back to Havana for his brother's funeral, but he showed up last night just when I thought there would be a reprieve.

Despite being siblings, there's little similarity between them. Gonzalo was slenderer and a few inches shorter, his manner easy and carefree. Gonzalo was the sort of man who everyone wanted to be around, a man who could inspire others to follow him in whatever scheme he'd hatched along the way. Gonzalo was charm personified.

His brother is none of those things.

I swallow. "Hello, Felipe."

Felipe has always been serious, rarely prone to smiles, his head for business and little else. Only four years separated them, but I often got the sense that Felipe carried the weight of the world on his shoulders, whereas Gonzalo did as he pleased, consequences be damned.

I don't hear his response to my greeting over the white noise rushing in my ears, over the rapid beating of my heart, the sun's rays suddenly making it unbearably hot in my heavy black dress.

When was the last time I ate? Yesterday? The day before? I can't remember.

I sway unsteadily, Mirta reaching out and taking hold of my elbow while Felipe steps forward, and all I see is black.

I s she pregnant?"

"She must be pregnant."

I wake slowly, the sun intruding in between the open curtains in my bedroom, the one Gonzalo and I shared for just a brief time before he left for Spain, the sound of voices in the hallway carrying through the door that's been left slightly ajar.

Memories flood back at me—Felipe's perfectly polished shoes, his outstretched hand, the faint look of disapproval etched on his patrician face. My in-laws have never failed to make their disdain clear, and I fear that this last embarrassment—me fainting in front of Havana's high society—has proven in their eyes what they've always suspected: that I am unworthy of their son's hand in marriage.

It's hardly the first time they've wondered if I'm pregnant, that same sentiment levied at us when Gonzalo brought me home the first time and announced we'd married. The only thing that saved the entire affair was that I'd married the younger son, and not the heir apparent.

I rise from the bed, belatedly wondering how I made it from the graveside to our—my—bedroom, and how many people saw my embarrassing faint.

The door opens and Mirta walks into the bedroom.

"Oh good, you're awake. I was so worried about you." She closes the door behind her, turning the lock before facing me. "You cannot stay in this house."

"Was it that bad? I heard what they were just saying right now, but I imagine it was much worse."

"They're horrible, Rosa. They seemed more concerned with you fainting and their fears that it had caused a scene than they were with their son's funeral."

"I heard the pregnancy speculation. You would think it would have occurred to them that since Gonzalo has been gone for six months now and I've yet to show, that possibility is unlikely. I was silly. I should have eaten something at breakfast, I was—"

"You're in mourning. You've experienced a terrible loss. It's understandable. But you should be surrounded by people who care for you. By your family. You shouldn't force yourself to live in this place." Her gaze drifts around the bedroom, a distasteful expression on her face. "It's like you're in a mausoleum or something."

I once said the same thing to Gonzalo. I had vaguely entertained the idea of trying to get my own apartment when he went to Spain despite the disagreement we had when I first broached the subject, but I hadn't the funds to achieve it, and Gonzalo insisted that a wife's place was with her husband and his family, that I should do the proper thing and wait for him here, giving him one less thing to worry about while he fought in Spain.

Speaking of family—

"Who carried me in here?"

"Felipe did."

Horror fills me. "No."

"He didn't look too pleased about it, either."

I can imagine.

"I can help you if you'd like. Anthony and I could—"

"No, I won't be your charity case."

"It's not charity; it's family."

"Still. I can't. Don't worry, I have a plan. I'm almost done with my teaching degree at the University of Havana. If I can just stay in this house a little longer and finish my studies like I promised my mother, I'll be able to get a job to support myself. I can withstand anything for a short enough time if it ultimately gives me freedom."

Mirta reaches out and takes my hand, squeezing it gently. "I know you loved Gonzalo, and I cannot imagine losing Anthony, particularly at such a young age and in such a terrible manner. You aren't alone. You have family who cares for you and who will be there if you need them. You are always welcome to stay with me and Anthony in New York."

"Thank you. I really appreciate your offer and all your kindness. I'm sorry I'm so out of sorts, that I'm irritable, that I—"

"Rosa, you've suffered a terrible loss. There's no need to apologize. Of course you're going to be unsettled and things are going to feel strange. That's perfectly understandable."

I swallow past the tears evoked by her kindness. "Thank you. I can't imagine what this would have been like without you here, if I had been alone. You didn't have to come, but the fact that you did—"

"We're family," Mirta replies. "We Perez women have to stick together."

Mirta returns to New York shortly after the funeral, and days pass, then a week, Gonzalo dead and buried, and I am alone once more. When the house has gone to sleep, I enter the room off our marital bedroom the family had converted into Gonzalo's personal study and sit down at his desk, running my fingers over the divots in the wood. We have now been apart longer than we were married, and I fear that one day in the not-too-distant future, I will forget what he looked like, will miss the feel of his lips against mine, the press of his body.

I cling to the intimacy of sitting at his desk, my fingers caressing the metal typewriter keys, that familiar rush flooding me.

For an hour, I catch up on my schoolwork, on the lessons I've missed in my grief, my professors giving me a few days to sort out my personal affairs. When my studies are finished, I turn my attention to other matters.

By day, I am silent, tiptoeing around this house, struggling to make myself invisible when faced with the reality that so many people don't want me here; at night, all the words that have been bottled up inside of me push to escape.

Far too many women are controlled by their families, by expectations, hemmed in by a lack of opportunities. There are all manners of controlling women in Cuba, from the obvious ones, like the laws that are in place, to the hidden, like the unspoken societal expectations of what makes a good Cuban woman—elegant, demure, respectful, obedient—and I am so tired of feeling as though we exist in this country solely for the ways in which we serve men—in the house, in the bedroom, with our bodies.

While we won the right to vote a few years ago, our journey can't end there. There is more work to be done.

> Women in Cuba deserve better. We have done our part for Cuba, continue to do our part for ourselves and our family. Many of us have mothers, sisters, grandmothers, aunts who fought for Cuba's independence from Spain and were left with nothing for their efforts.
>
> When my grandmother Marina fought for independence from Spain, she believed that women were on the precipice of being treated as equals, but instead their bravery and dedication was forgotten.

My finger hovers over the next key, just as a noise sounds from somewhere in the house—the creak of a floorboard.

I pause.

I very much doubt someone would come into my bedroom in the middle of the night, but the risk of Gonzalo's family finding out about my writing is too great for me to simply ignore. They may have been willing to look the other way when it was their son disrupting the order of things, but I doubt they will be so charitable with me.

I have little illusion over the fact that they're allowing me to live here because throwing their son's widow out on her own would bring attention, scandal, and shame to the family name, but there's nothing they'd like more than to see me gone.

The sound of footsteps fills the hall, and I realize it is Felipe perhaps coming in from a late night. He wasn't at dinner this evening, has been largely absent from all family events since the funeral, and we have yet to see each other since the day I fainted.

When the hallway is quiet once more, I return to typing, trying to keep my fingers as light as possible, wincing each time the key makes a loud noise. I've already decided that if anyone ever asks me why I'm typing so late at night, I will say that I am writing a letter to Alicia in Spain, or perhaps Mirta in New York, but more likely than not the rest of the household is happy to leave me to my own devices.

Sometimes I write about the fighting in Spain, passing the information Alicia sends me in her letters to my countrywomen who have banded together to support the war effort and aid the women and children of Spain. We've raised funds and awareness for the cause at the regular meetings we attend. When Gonzalo was alive and fighting overseas, it felt like my way of supporting his efforts from Havana. Now, it is a purpose to keep me going when my grief overwhelms me.

Tonight, the words come quickly. I write until I cannot write anymore, and I gather the pages, sliding them under the mattress of the bed I once shared with Gonzalo. In this house, it's as if there are eyes and ears everywhere you turn.

I am asleep almost immediately after my head hits the pillow, and when I dream, I am a little girl once more, running around my parents' farm that my family rebuilt after it was razed by the Spanish during the war for independence, helping with the horses, my grandmother Marina telling me stories of her life in Cuba.

chapter nine

I rise early the next morning and dress quickly. I retrieve the typed
pages I wrote last night and tuck them into my purse. I avoid the
dining room altogether, forgoing breakfast for this chance to slip
out of the house and onto the streets undetected.

It would be easier perhaps to ask one of the family's servants to
deliver this for me, but I am certain Gonzalo's mother knows
everything that is going on in the household, and I wouldn't discard
the possibility that she'd read my mail, too. More than that, though,
there's a danger these days to being caught with any material that
could be considered subversive to the government, and I wouldn't
put that risk on anyone but myself.

It's not a far walk from the Aguileras' house in Vedado to the
printer's shop near the University of Havana, but the sensation that
I am doing something illicit follows me each step of the way, and I
can't help but look over my shoulder several times, my purse
clutched tightly in my hands. The words I've written shouldn't be
that controversial, but the anonymity my published pieces provide
me seems prudent given the high tensions in Cuba these days.

It's quiet as I near the printer's shop, the nondescript storefront designed to look as though it sells newspapers and a few essentials, the back of the store where the true business happens. On any given day, a variety of political ideologies come in and out, the printer agnostic in the beliefs he publishes. The topic of women's rights in Cuba is not regarded as controversial as some of the other things I could be writing about, but it's difficult to know what will be tolerated and what will be viewed as a threat.

I'm nearly at the shop when a black sedan pulls up in front of the store. The car doors open, and three men in military uniforms jump out.

A scream rises in my throat, the sound trapped by the fear pushing and shoving inside me.

One of the men looks in my direction before turning his attention to the printer's shop.

The three men stride into the store, the car idling at the curb.

The urge to run consumes me, and still, I stay where I am, unable to look away from the travesty unfolding before me.

A moment later the men emerge, hauling the printer behind them. He's too far away for me to make out his expression, but his head is ducked, his shoulders hunched over, and he has the walk of a man who knows his luck has just run out.

Almost at once, the people around me who were watching the printer be taken just a moment ago return to busying themselves, scurrying back inside the buildings they peeked out of, no one wanting to draw attention to themselves and risk catching the police's wrath.

I can't help it. I stride forward and call out.

"Wait. Where are you taking him?"

As soon as I ask the question, I regret it, as the big man turns on me, his gaze pinning me. I barely can register the movement before his hand connects with my face, the blow knocking me to the ground.

Pain explodes across my cheek, my back, shock filling me.

I look up at the man, already shielding myself in case he hits me again, but he has turned away from me, as he and the others hustle the printer into the black sedan.

The car peels away from the curb.

I stand, and head back in the direction of the Aguileras' house.

We never exchanged more than a few pleasantries, but the printer seemed like a nice enough man. Does he have a family who will be targeted because of his political activities? Will he be let off with some threats, violence, and a warning, or is this it for him? Will he simply disappear?

Undoubtedly, they'll question him about the sorts of people who left pamphlets for him to produce. Most of us likely used aliases, but will he give up what he knows? Will he tell them that on the first Tuesday of every month, a young woman would come in and give him some pages on women's issues in Cuba to print, which she later distributes at political meetings? No doubt, it's just a matter of time before they return to the shop with more men and seize his equipment, the publications he's printed.

If I had been a moment earlier, if I hadn't taken that bit of extra time to stare up at the ceiling when I first woke this morning, I might have been there when they stormed in.

By the time I reach the Aguileras' house, my heart is pounding, a thin trail of sweat dripping down my back beneath my black dress.

What if someone followed me here?

I close the front door behind me, heading toward the grand staircase that leads up to my bedroom when I hear my name—

"Rosa."

I had hoped we could put off another interaction between us, that he would simply go back to the United States, and we could avoid each other completely.

Instead, Felipe is standing outside of his father's study.

"How are you?" he asks. "You look—better . . ."

I don't, really, and we both know it, but at least he's too polite to say anything to the contrary. I resist the powerful urge to run my hands over my wrinkled gown and wipe the sweat from my brow. Gonzalo may have liked to dress like a man of the people when he was outside the house, but Felipe has always dressed elegantly and conservatively, nary a hair out of place, leaving me feeling utterly disheveled in his presence.

"I'm fine. Thank you. Well, as fine as can be expected," I amend, wholly at a loss over the proper etiquette in a situation such as this one.

"Can we talk?" he asks.

It's on the tip of my tongue to beg off, to say anything to avoid an undoubtedly awkward conversation. At the same time, I am not the only one who is grieving, and it seems churlish to not give him this.

I follow him into the study, tilting my head to the side, trying to keep the part of my face the man hit averted from his gaze.

I remember sitting in this very room with Gonzalo, my hand clutched in his as he announced to his parents that we had married.

I sit down in the same chair I occupied that day while Felipe takes the seat opposite me behind the desk.

"My parents think you should remarry."

"No."

The word escapes before the full import of what he has said

sinks in, and I'm half out of my seat, his statement propelling me to move, to fight.

"Their son just died, how dare they suggest that I remarry. I am not a possession to be sold off because they have no use for me, how could you—"

"Rosa. I didn't say I agreed with them—I don't—but I wanted to warn you of their intentions before they spoke to you."

I sink back down to the chair, my legs shaking beneath me.

I knew the family didn't like me, that they—Felipe included—were probably eager to see me gone, but for them to try to fob me off onto someone else—

"Do they have someone in mind for me? Some business associate? Wait, they probably don't consider me good enough for that. After all, I certainly was never good enough for their son. You don't think I—"

I don't realize I'm crying, or that Felipe has moved, until he's crouching in front of me, a handkerchief in hand. He holds it out to me wordlessly, and my fingers shake as I take it from him and dab the tears on my cheeks.

"What happened to your face?"

In my tears, I forgot about the blow.

"I—I fell on the street earlier."

"It doesn't look like you fell. Did someone do that to you?" Felipe asks, his voice laced with fury.

"Really, it was nothing. I fell. I'm fine."

"You're not fine. Your cheek is swelling already. Does it hurt?"

"A little."

"Stay here. Let me get you some ice. That will help with the swelling."

"I'm fine—really—"

"The ice will help."

Felipe leaves me alone in the study, and when he returns, it is with a bundle of ice wrapped in what looks to be one of his mother's dinner napkins.

"Try this." Felipe crouches before me once more and passes the bundle to me.

I lift it to my cheek. "Thank you for the ice," I reply.

Felipe clears his throat, rising swiftly to his full height, his handkerchief still clutched in my free hand. "If you're in trouble, if something happened, you can tell me."

"Really it was nothing. I tripped and fell. I've been so distracted lately, and I haven't been myself. At the funeral—Mirta told me you were the one who carried me upstairs after I fainted. Thank you for that. I'm sorry I was upset earlier, that I reacted so—"

"You shouldn't apologize for speaking up for yourself. I didn't mean to upset you by telling you, but I wanted you to be prepared. My family can be difficult; the last thing you need right now is my parents trying to strong-arm you into something against your will. For the record, I told them I thought it was a terrible idea and that they should allow you to grieve in peace. If you don't wish to marry, you shouldn't be forced into it. It must be very difficult for you to imagine being with someone else after you loved my brother so much."

He turns his back to me, and I stare down at my clenched hands, at the fine linen handkerchief clutched there, Felipe's initials peeking out from one corner of the fabric.

"Perhaps we could start over," he suggests, his back to me. "Be friends. Family. You will need an ally in this house if you intend to remain."

"You mean to stay in Cuba? You won't be going back to New York? I thought your family's business kept you there."

"My plans have changed. I will stay in Havana for the foreseeable future." Felipe turns, facing me, and he extends his hand to me. I'm reluctant to give him mine, but I reach out and our palms connect as we shake on it.

"To being friends," he echoes.

We break apart, and he walks over to the desk and picks up an envelope sitting there.

"I also wanted to give you this. In this house—let's just say private correspondence doesn't always stay private."

"So, it is safe to assume your mother reads all incoming mail."

"Unless you can find someone to intercept it for you."

"Thank you."

I leave him in the study, and walk upstairs to the safety of my bedroom, my head spinning with all that has just transpired.

When I reach the privacy of my bedroom and lock the door behind me, I sit on the edge of the bed and tear open Alicia's letter, eager for news from Barcelona.

chapter ten

Alicia

1937

BARCELONA

*A*s I walk through the house, I pass the framed painting on the wall—the Perez wife who sailed from Europe in an arranged marriage, and reportedly ended up falling in love with her husband in Cuba. I've spent more time than I'd care to admit in this big house, studying her visage, wishing I could talk to her, that she could guide me on how to be a Perez wife.

There are expectations that come with such a last name, with a house such as this, my mother-in-law unafraid to communicate her disapproval with a terse nod of her head or a clipped word.

And Emilio—

I thought we were partners. That even though we weren't the great love match I had dreamed of, that we cared about and respected each other.

I hoped we might have a chance to be happy.

Emilio is in the breakfast room. He glances up when I enter, setting the newspaper down on the table next to his plate, a hint of warmth in his eyes that I used to take as a sign of his affection for me.

"I saw you."

I say it quietly, lest the staff hear us, lest our daughter walk into the room even if Isabel is too young to understand. I say it quietly and firmly, as I practiced in my bedroom in front of the gilded mirror, struggling to keep the tears from filling my eyes, from letting my cheeks redden with embarrassment over the indignity of my husband choosing another.

Emilio has never been one for signs of emotion, and so I do everything to control mine, as though we are little more than a business transaction, as though my heart hasn't broken a bit.

He looks ruffled, and then he blinks as though righting himself.

"What do you mean, you saw me?"

"Yesterday. In your office. With that woman. On your desk. She's very beautiful."

There's an instant when I think he is going to deny it, but instead he looks down at his plate, averting his gaze from mine.

"I'm sorry you saw that."

I'm sorry you saw that? Not I'm sorry I broke our wedding vows, but I'm sorry you saw me break them?

Anger fills me, cutting through me like a knife, sharp and sleek.

"Is she your mistress?"

I want him to be shamed for what he has done, to feel the hurt he has caused me. I want to hurt him, too.

Emilio looks up from his plate, the expression on his face unfathomable.

He doesn't answer me, which is an answer on its own.

"Do you love her?" *I ask him.*

Love has never been part of the agreement between us. We married because our families wished us to, and we are both dutiful children, following the path we were set on. Our marriage has never been one of great passion, but I thought we were learning to care for one another. I thought we'd become friends.

"No, I don't love her."

I'm not sure if that makes it better or worse, only that I am convinced he cannot possibly love me and treat me like this.

"Does she love you?"

"I don't think so."

"Then why?"

For the first time since I've known him, Emilio looks unsure of himself, as he searches for an answer that seems to slip from his grasp.

I knew, of course, what I was going to do before I walked down the staircase. There's no chance I'm going to stay in Havana and allow Emilio Perez to make a mockery of me while everyone speaks of his infidelity, while I share his affections with another woman, no possibility of me playing the fool for this man.

I don't bother waiting for a response, but instead turn and walk out of the dining room. As I step over the threshold, I look over my shoulder and say—

"I need a vacation. I'm going to take Isabel to Barcelona to visit my family."

I wake early, the dream leaving me nervous and unsettled, the memory of that moment between us haunting me, Emilio's recent letter an inescapable tie to my past and a reminder of all the unfinished business between us.

I thought distance would give me the answers I sought, that being with my family again, away from Emilio, I would find peace.

I've physically left Emilio, but his presence lingers in the gold ring on my finger that I can't bring myself to remove, in the knowledge that I am still a married woman, even as I worry that my husband continues to betray our wedding vows, that he is somewhere in Havana with his lover, my absence a mere annoyance to him.

Part of me wonders if I should go back to him, for Isabel alone, if I should accept this state of things as I'm sure so many before me have. And maybe I could, if not for the affection I held for him, and the disappointment his actions have wrought.

I wish I had the vocabulary to discuss my hurt with him, to broker some new arrangement in our marriage, one where we try to make things work. I've sat down and tried to write such a letter so many times, and with each attempt words fail me.

And so, we remain in this stalemate of sorts, an ocean between us.

My days are spent with my daughter and sister, and while it was daunting at first being on my own, I have grown accustomed to it, welcoming the freedom to be myself even as the world around me and the conflict in Spain grows more frightening.

I have taken to assisting at my father's clinic, using the nursing skills I developed in Havana when I used to help my father treat his patients. Nestor has come by a few times, but it's been too busy for us to exchange more than a few words.

He did mention that he would try to visit me at the café where I sit and wait for Isabel and Consuelo when they're at their music lessons.

This morning, I linger over my clothing options longer than I normally would. I'm brushing my hair when the door to my bedroom opens, and Consuelo enters the room.

Now that she's eighteen years old, her birthday celebrated a few months ago, Consuelo keeps to herself more than she used to when she was younger and would follow me everywhere I went.

She doesn't speak as she walks across the room and sits down on the edge of my bed, still dressed in her nightgown and robe.

"You look pretty today," Consuelo says with a knowing smile. "Far too pretty to just be walking me and Isabel to music lessons."

I flush. "I don't know what you're talking about."

"What are you planning on doing when we're at our music lessons?"

"I will sit at the café as I always do."

She grins. "And will you be alone at the café?"

Her tone of voice is so dramatic that I can't help but laugh. She's always been a romantic, sneaking books our parents would never normally let her read, begging me not to tell them. I know they hope for her to marry soon, and while marriages in wealthy families are so often about more than the couple themselves, I pray they will let her follow her heart. There's so much sweetness in her that I worry that a man who is not worthy of her will crush her spirit.

"I *may* be alone at the café," I reply, my tone of voice as teasing as hers.

It's good to see Consuelo so happy. These past few months have taken a toll on her and all of us. She's been unusually quiet lately, sick more often than not, and as this war continues on, everyone is worn down by the weight of it all.

"Well, I hope you aren't," she replies. "You deserve some fun, too."

After I drop Isabel and Consuelo off at their music lessons, I walk toward the café, my steps a little quicker than normal.

If Nestor isn't there, it will be fine—I brought pen and paper to write letters to Mirta and Rosa. Truthfully, I feel frivolous for putting extra attention into getting ready today, more than a little embarrassed over the flutters in my stomach, but I enjoyed our conversation when we saw each other again, and so much of our days are spent worrying and fearful, that pleasure is such a welcome luxury during these difficult times.

When I reach the café, it's already quite crowded despite the early hour and the cold morning, and I scan the tables, disappointment filling me when I don't see Nestor. I'm about to find an empty table to sit by myself when I spy him at one of the tables, a bouquet of red roses wrapped in white paper resting on the tabletop next to him.

I'm already smiling by the time I reach the table, and when he rises, the flowers in hand, I no longer feel so foolish for the extra care I took with my appearance.

"These are for you." Nestor holds out the flowers. "I hoped you'd be here this morning. I saw the flowers earlier when I was at La Boqueria, and they reminded me of you."

"Thank you. They're beautiful."

He smiles. "Like I said, they reminded me of you."

Perhaps it's silly to be moved by such a simple gift when I am a married woman and a mother, but there is something powerfully kind in the notion that he was at the market and saw them and thought they might brighten my day.

Our fingers graze as I take the roses from him.

"I'm sorry I haven't been able to come by your parents' for dinner," Nestor says. "Things have been busy at the clinic."

"Have you been waiting long?" I ask as I sit in the chair opposite his.

"Only about an hour or so." He gestures toward a book lying facedown beside him. "I read while I waited."

A waiter takes our orders, and then we're alone once more, silence descending between us. The last time we saw each other, the conversation flowed easily, but now that we're here, and he brought me roses, I can't help but feel nervous despite the friendship we enjoyed in my younger years.

"I'm sorry if this is a personal question, but I confess, I've thought about it a great deal—have you left Emilio?"

"No."

Even as I ignore Emilio's requests to return to Havana, I can't turn my back on the vows we made when we married in the Cathedral of Havana. For all I know, Emilio is back in Havana with his mistress at this very moment. In his letters, he speaks of Isabel returning to Cuba, but there are no words for me. Does he miss me? Does he want a divorce? Is he angry I've left and stayed away for so long? I wish I could read between the lines he writes; I wish I could understand what he wants and could sift through the parts of our marriage that exist out of duty to see if there's any affection between us that remains.

"I'm sorry," Nestor says. "I didn't mean to shock you, but we always were able to speak candidly together, were friends, and I've been worried about you since I saw you here. If you don't mind me saying it, you don't seem like yourself—not the version I knew in Havana, at least—and I wanted to make sure you were all right."

"It's fine. Things are—complicated, I suppose you could say."

There's something in his gaze that makes me think it isn't just seeing me in Barcelona that precipitated his questions about my marriage—

"You've heard rumors, haven't you?" I don't say the rest of it, can't bear the embarrassment.

"Yes. There were whispers in Havana, but I wasn't sure if they were more than idle gossip until I saw you here in Barcelona and I realized there might be some truth to them. I'm sorry. I can't fathom how he could possibly— He's a fool to have treated you as he has. He doesn't deserve you.

"If you need anything, if you or Isabel ever need anything, I'm here for you," Nestor vows.

"Thank you. Being here in Barcelona—it's nice to have my family close by, but sometimes I feel very alone, cut off from the people I love back in Cuba. It's good to have you in my life again. I've missed our talks. I had a terrible crush on you when I was younger," I confess, a smile playing at my lips as I remember how giddy I used to be when I was around him, and how patient and kind he was with me. There's something so sweet and innocent about the memory, a simpler time when my biggest worries were when I would see Nestor again rather than the concerns I face now. "You must have realized. I'm a little embarrassed now when I think of how I probably followed you around, peppering you with questions."

"I did realize, but you shouldn't be embarrassed. It was very sweet, and I was honored by your admiration, while I had it. I loved being part of your family, to have all of you in my life. Those years in Cuba were difficult—the revolution and the depression challenging— and you always brought so much joy. You would light up a room when you walked into it. That's part of why the patients loved you."

"You make me sound like someone I must admit I hardly recognize."

The waiter brings our food before Nestor can respond. I reach for the silverware, and my hand connects with his resting on the table, our fingers brushing against each other once more.

"Alicia."

I jerk at the sound of my name and whirl around, surprise filling me at the sight of Consuelo and Isabel walking toward us. While Consuelo is certainly old enough to go out in the city on her own, these are dangerous times, and I usually pick her and Isabel up from their lessons.

I glance down at my watch. How could I have missed when I was supposed to pick them up? But no—my watch confirms that there's still twenty minutes left in their lesson. "What's wrong? Why did the lesson end early?"

"I wasn't feeling well," Consuelo replies.

Consuelo does indeed look like she's going to be ill, holding Isabel's hand. Normally, she would be bombarding Nestor with questions, but she's surprisingly quiet.

I rise from the table, turning my attention to Nestor, worry filling me. "I'm sorry, but I should get the girls home."

"Of course. Can I walk you back to the house?"

"Yes. Thank you," I reply, gathering the flowers he gave me.

Nestor tosses some money down on the table for the meal, and I thank him, offering to pay my share, but he waves me off.

No one speaks on the short walk back, and each time I look at Consuelo, her shoulders are hunched over as though she is in pain.

When we reach the house, I turn toward Nestor. "Thank you for accompanying us, and for all of your assistance."

"Of course. I hope you feel better," he says to Consuelo.

"I probably just need to rest," she replies. "Thank you."

"Alicia—what I said earlier—if you ever need anything at all, I'm here for you."

We say our good-byes on the doorstep, and I open the front door, ushering the girls into the house, my worry over Consuelo eclipsing all else. She's been sick lately, but no one thought it was anything serious, and now I fear I have missed something important, that she is seriously unwell.

"Let's get you settled in," I say to Consuelo as she lies down on her bed after I've taken Isabel up to the nursery. "Do you want me to ask our father to come look in on you?"

"No. I need to talk to you."

"What's wrong? Did something happen at music?"

Consuelo is silent for a beat, and she begins crying softly, her shoulders shaking. "I think I'm in trouble."

"What do you mean? What happened?"

Our gazes meet, and my heart breaks at the expression on her face, at the pain she is so obviously in.

She takes a deep breath. "I think I'm pregnant."

chapter eleven

Isabel

1964

BARCELONA

The drive from Barcelona to Marbella is as long as Diego warned it would be, and between the jet lag from my flight and the bright sun shining down through the open convertible, I spend a good bit of it sleeping, waking as we near the city. When we arrive at the hotel, Diego announces that the sedan is no longer behind us, but that hardly gives me much comfort considering we still don't know why they were following us in the first place.

Spain's Costa del Sol is stunning, the streets lined with elegantly dressed tourists and locals sightseeing, shopping, and generally attending to business.

We arrive at our hotel, a white-tiered birthday cake affair on the beach. The staff ushers us to rooms a few doors away from each other, and we agree to meet in the lobby in an hour to go to Camila's.

I shower and dress quickly, using the remaining time to call my hotel in Barcelona and check my messages.

Nothing from Beatriz.

Diego waits for me at the bottom of the steps when I walk downstairs to the hotel lobby. He's changed since we parted ways an hour ago, his casual suit abandoned for a more formal black one, his dark hair slicked back with some sort of pomade, his skin freshly shaven, a hint of his cologne in the air.

He looks handsome, and while there's little resemblance between him and Nicholas Preston, I wouldn't blame Beatriz for a minute if he'd struck her fancy.

"You changed your dress," he says when I reach him.

"I did. I hardly thought it was a good idea for me to wear the same one I'd been traveling in all day."

He's silent for a beat. "You look beautiful," he finally replies, his voice so quiet I can barely hear him over the sound of the music playing in the lobby.

I flush.

"Not that you didn't look beautiful before—wrinkled dress and all."

Earlier in the car, he was flirtatious in his manner, but the sincerity in his voice and in his eyes makes it difficult to laugh his words off.

Camila's is close to our hotel, so we decide to walk rather than drive. Diego is silent beside me, his gaze on our surroundings. Mine is similarly occupied as I keep my eyes peeled for Beatriz, and also, I can't help but notice the people strolling down the street, the beautiful fashions and the energy in the air.

Camila's is the sort of place I can easily imagine Beatriz frequenting, the music good, the drinks flowing abundantly, the women dressed in stunning and daring gowns. It's sinuous and sexy, and reminds me of the places we used to sneak into in Havana, and I envision my sister winding her way through the crowd, her hips sashaying to the beat of the music, glancing over her shoulder at me, laughter in her voice.

Come on, Isabel.

"This looks like Beatriz," I murmur to Diego.

He scans the crowd as though he is attempting to assess all potential threats.

"Did you see the sedan from earlier outside?" I ask.

"No. Let's sit at one of the tables and order a drink and some food. It's been hours since we stopped for lunch, and I'm famished. I brought a picture of Beatriz. We can see if one of the staff members remembers her."

We take a seat in the back and order drinks—a vodka martini for Diego, champagne for me. We show Beatriz's picture to the waitress, but she can't place her and tells us to check with the bartender who was working the night Beatriz was supposed to be here.

"I'm going to go up to the bar and talk to the bartender to see if he remembers Beatriz. Wait here," Diego says.

"No."

"'No'?" he asks.

"No, I'm coming with you. We're a team, remember?"

"So, when Beatriz said you were the quiet one, she was, what—completely wrong? She made it seem like you were the sister who went along with everything, but you've disagreed with me at nearly every turn."

"I—"

"No, don't apologize. I like it; it keeps me on my toes. I'm just having to revise my opinion on some things. The way Beatriz described you and the reality aren't quite aligning. Makes me wonder what other things I have to learn about you."

"I wasn't apologizing," I interject. "And I am the quiet one, although I'm not sure that's saying something with my family and sisters. I'm also the persistent one, so if you keep trying to leave me out of things, we're going to keep doing this dance."

He grins. "By all means then, lead the way, Isabel."

The bartender is busy mixing drinks when I show him the picture of Beatriz that Diego brought with him. It's a good one of my sister—taken recently at a party—and she appears happy, her lips curved in a wide smile.

"We're looking for someone," Diego says, sliding some money across the bar next to the photograph. "Have you seen her here before?"

The bartender glances at the photograph for a moment. He shrugs. "Lots of women come in here. It's a popular place."

"Please," I interject. "It would have been recent. If you saw her, any light you could shed on her whereabouts would help so much. She's disappeared."

The bartender sets the liquor bottle down and picks up the picture, studying the image.

"She looks like you," he says.

"She's my sister."

"She might have been in here last week."

"Was she alone? Did she speak with anyone?"

He pauses. "She sat in the back, near where the two of you are sitting now. She wasn't alone. There were two people with her—I remember because it struck me as a little strange. Most people come here looking for a good time, some romance, but she was here with an older couple. Her parents, I think."

"Her parents? That's not possible."

"I'm just telling you what I saw. The woman—they looked similar. I didn't pay a lot of attention to them—it was a busy night—but they seemed friendly enough. Familiar for sure."

"Did they leave together?" Diego asks, looking just as confused as I am.

"I don't know. Like I said, it was a busy night. Sorry."

"Were they Spanish?" Diego asks.

"I think they were speaking Spanish, but honestly, I'm not sure. They were too far away for me to hear what they were saying. It was loud that night. Same as it is every night." He slides the picture back to us, pocketing the money Diego left him before he turns back to making drinks.

We return to the table, my mind racing with this new information.

Diego sits down next to me, the picture of Beatriz resting on the table between us.

"It definitely wasn't our parents. Last week my mother was in Palm Beach telling me my place settings were tacky. There's no chance she would have been here in Marbella, so clearly he's mistaken."

"Why are your place settings tacky?" Diego asks.

"They're not. Why is that relevant?"

"It's not, but I can't say I'm not curious. The look in your eyes when you said that your mother cast aspersions on your place settings' honor was quite extraordinary."

"How can you joke at a time like this?"

"You'd be surprised what I can do in all manner of situations. You get used to it after a while. All in all, I think we have hope that Beatriz might be safe. You heard the bartender—she sounds like she was fine when she came here."

"Then where is she?" I ask, frustration and exhaustion getting the best of me.

"I don't know. I'm sorry. I know you're scared, and I wish I could give you the answers you seek. I wish I could take the worry away from you."

"Why do you care? Beatriz is my sister, and I know you are friends, but for you to help me this much—it seems like a tremendous amount of risk and effort."

"It isn't just for Beatriz."

I flush. "You hardly know me."

"I know enough to know that I like you and I want to help you."

"Thank you. For everything. I'm sorry I insisted we come here. We're no closer to finding out where Beatriz is or if she's even safe."

"Tomorrow we'll go back to Barcelona. I'll talk to some people and see if they have any leads on Beatriz."

"You don't have to do all of this. I know I pressured you earlier, and I'm sorry for that, but it was kind of you to drive me all the way here. I understand if you want to walk away from this."

"We're partners, remember?" he replies. "I'm not walking away."

chapter twelve

Rosa

1937

HAVANA

It's been a week since I tried to take my article to the printer's office, my days spent attending classes at the university, the papers still resting under my mattress, and I've only had the courage to go by there once since then, my heart pounding as I did my best to look as though I was out on a leisurely stroll lest anyone be watching. There were no signs of life outside the storefront, everything abandoned and seemingly as the printer left it the day he was taken.

The bruise on my face has mostly healed, the makeup I use to cover it saving me from awkward questions.

Today, when I walk past the store, I make a point not to slow down, hurrying past the shop to the private room down the street from the university where my women's club meetings take place. As much as Felipe's warning that his parents hope to see me married off stuck with me, I can't deny that the proximity of their home in

Vedado to both the university and to my meetings is enough for me to keep living in their house for as long as possible. There are so many barriers to a woman receiving an education that anything I can do to make it easier for myself is welcome.

I take a seat in the room, grateful to see that I am not the last to arrive.

"I'm so sorry for your loss," the woman next to me murmurs.

"Thank you," I whisper back as the speaker takes center stage.

There are many calls for a new Cuba, but what that should look like depends on who you talk to, the country divided. Some seek change without putting a name to it, others advocate for communism, and there are those who yearn for a democratic government. Many want another revolution. But what will a revolution usher in?

The thing about revolution is that sometimes the problems it was supposed to defeat remain long after the dust has settled. When Machado was removed from power in 1933, when the revolution was "won," many believed Cuba had a bright future ahead of her, that the problems that plagued us would disappear. The truth is, in the end, Machado is gone, and still, we struggle.

Like my husband and the others who have gone overseas to fight, many of the women's groups and charitable organizations have set their sights on the conflict in Spain. It is easy to feel helpless in one's own country, but maybe we can make a difference somewhere else. As the fighting intensifies, reports of orphaned children and refugees have spread to Cuba, and the island has come together to help the Spanish people.

The speaker begins with the opening business, suggesting that one of the things we can do to help the children of Spain, many of whom have lost their parents and homes, is to sew blankets and coats for them. There is also an effort to raise funds to send to Spain. Many of the women in our group lack independent means, are reliant on allowances from parents or husbands, but we discuss how we can pool our resources and encourage other Cubans to lend their assistance as well.

"It is not just a Spanish fight," the speaker says once the fund-raising discussions have quieted. "These Spanish Nationalists are the past. The same past that condemned our citizens to reconcentration camps. We fight for a new world. Let the women of Cuba do their part for a free Spain."

The meeting ends as it always does, on a powerful note, the company of other women making me feel both uplifted and invigorated, as though anything is possible. When we are united, there is nothing that can stop us.

I exit the building and say my good-byes to a few of the women who sat near me, and I stop in my tracks, surprised to see Felipe standing outside waiting for me.

It's not the part of town where one would normally find him, his university days long past him, the family's business offices farther afield. I'm hardly the only one who has noticed him, his reputation resulting in more than a few curious glances being cast his way. Everyone knows I married into the Aguilera family, but the sight of the eldest son and heir waiting for me outside a political meeting will likely cause its fair share of gossip throughout certain circles in Havana.

"Did you follow me here?" I ask him.

"No, but I was looking for you, and the staff mentioned that you were often gone on Wednesday afternoons after your classes. I remembered that you used to come to meetings here, and I thought I might find you. I wanted to discuss something with you, and it's easier to talk when we aren't in the house where the walls seemingly have ears." He pushes off from the building he was resting against. "Let me walk you home."

"Is this what you meant when you said we would be friends now? You waiting for me outside political meetings?"

"Maybe," Felipe tosses over his shoulder before striding off in the direction of the house, leaving me little option but to trail after him if I want to continue the conversation.

I quicken my steps to keep up with him, and he shoves his hands in his pockets, slowing down a little, matching my stride with his own.

"How was your meeting?" he asks.

"It was fine. We were talking about the conflict in Spain and what we can do to help here in Cuba."

"Just promise me you'll be careful. Those meetings, helping the people of Spain, that's one thing. But the other political activities can be dangerous. You don't want to draw unwelcome attention to yourself within the government."

"I'm aware of the dangers. When I agreed that we could have a truce between us, that we could be friends, I didn't mean that I was looking for a caretaker, someone to monitor my movements and keep me out of trouble. I am perfectly capable of managing my own affairs."

"I know you are. I have no illusions about your ability to take care of yourself. But I'm only concerned about you. We all are."

"*That* is not true. Your family has little tolerance for me. I don't need to be part of some family duty or guilt over the need to take care of your brother's widow."

He swears softly, surprising both of us, I think.

"It's not family duty, Rosa. And I can't speak for my family's sentiments, only for mine. I know they can be difficult, that they have been supremely unfair to you, and for that I am sorry."

"Difficult? Difficult hardly covers it."

"Why do you stay here? You said it yourself—you don't need anyone to take care of you."

"I promised my mother before she died that I would get a degree from the University of Havana, that I would finish my studies. She wanted me to have a career, to be independent. She wanted me to have opportunities.

"The farm I grew up on—my parents wanted me to have choices in my life, and they did everything in their power to educate me at home, to give me books so I could learn about any number of subjects. They taught me to read and write, to do numbers, with the hope that I would be able to be independent, that I would never have to rely on a man to take care of me.

"Education empowers, and that power is what is going to bring about the change Cuba desperately needs. After all, what is the purpose of the vote for women if we don't understand what we're voting for, if our vote doesn't matter and have a chance to effect change in Cuba?"

"I'll never understand," he mutters under his breath.

"Never understand what?"

He stops and turns to face me. "How someone like you ended up with my brother."

That many found me unworthy of Gonzalo has been painfully obvious, but to count Felipe in those ranks—

"How could you not see him for who he was? That he was the sort of man who said one thing and did another, who espoused beliefs he did not practice, who cared little for people and their lives, only for his own ego and personal gain?"

The words fill me with shock; the anger in his voice and in his gaze leaves me reeling.

"Gonzalo gave his life for what he believed in," I argue.

Felipe opens his mouth as though he is going to speak, as if he wishes to belabor the point with me, but he closes it abruptly, turning away from me.

chapter thirteen

That evening, when I come down to dinner earlier than the family's normal time to try to sneak in a quick bite before the Aguileras eat, I am surprised to find Felipe and his parents already seated at the table.

I pause in the entryway to the grand dining room, more than a little ready to flee back to the comfort of my room, hunger be damned.

Just a few more months, I tell myself as my gaze connects with my in-laws' disapproving looks, and finally Felipe's apologetic expression.

Just a few more months, and I will have my degree, and freedom will be mine. I've come so far now that I should be able to withstand anything for a few months—even their scorn.

"Good evening," I say in greeting when I come to the inescapable realization that there is no way around this awkward encounter.

Gonzalo's mother, Elena, flashes me a bitter smile while his father says nothing at all. Despite the tension between us this morning, I take the seat next to Felipe, eager for an ally in this awkward tableau.

Felipe leans over. "I'm sorry," he murmurs. "They insisted on an early dinner. I didn't want you to have to deal with it alone."

I flash him a grateful smile.

"It's impolite to whisper at the table," Elena snaps at us.

For most of the meal, I keep my head down, focusing on the food in front of me, idly paying attention to the conversation going on around me.

A couple times, Felipe tries to engage me out of what I assume must be politeness, but he quickly seems to realize that I have no desire to draw more attention to myself than I already have, and he lets me be, deftly carrying the conversation with his parents on his own.

We're nearly at dessert when Elena says more loudly than normal—

"Felipe, will you be attending the Garcias' dinner tomorrow night? I know they so hoped for you to meet their eldest daughter. It's really time for you to start thinking about settling down, and she would make a wonderful wife."

It's another affair I haven't been invited to, not that I would go if I had. The Aguileras have been in mourning for Gonzalo's death, but they still socialize with a select group of families.

"I wasn't blessed with a daughter; the least I could do is gain one through marriage," she adds.

I shouldn't care what she says; I've seen enough of how she treats the staff and people around her to be able to discount her opinion entirely, and yet, it still stings to hear her write me off in such a caustic manner, to know that I married into a family where I thought I would be accepted, only to find myself alone once more. I can't help but wonder if she knows the scandal that will come her way if she throws me out of the house herself, so instead she's trying to make it as utterly unbearable as possible, to inspire me to make the choice myself.

"Rosa is a wonderful addition to the family. We're all very fortunate to have her in our lives," Felipe replies pointedly.

Her cheeks redden, but she doesn't say anything else, and while part of me is grateful to him for sticking up for me, the discord that thrums through this house causes a sinking sensation in my stomach; the need to always be on guard, to always put up my defenses, is utterly exhausting.

I set my napkin on the table.

"Excuse me." I rise from my seat.

Felipe makes a move to stop me, but I shake him off.

"I know what you think of me," I say to Elena. "You have made it abundantly clear. And I suppose if I had a son who brought home a wife I didn't know, I would be protective of him and his heart. But I loved Gonzalo. I had no idea he came from all of this, and to be honest, had I known, that might have changed my feelings on how compatible we were. I didn't marry him for his money, and all I want is to be able to finish my degree and put this part of my life behind me."

It is little wonder that I cannot sleep that night, hours spent staring up at the ceiling, my mind racing over all the things that were said at dinner. When it's clear sleep eludes me, I rise and try working on a new essay, but there, too, the words do not come. Finally, I turn to the sewing I have agreed to attempt, the coats and blankets for the refugees and orphans in this terrible war. The more stories we hear from Spain, the more letters I receive from Alicia, the more I worry as the conflict intensifies.

I take my sewing and head downstairs to one of the smaller sitting rooms in the Aguileras' home, eager for better lighting while I sew. When I was a girl, we made our own clothes, my grandmother Marina not much of a seamstress despite her best efforts, but my mother, Isabella, always quite skilled with a needle and thread, a talent that seems to have skipped a generation.

The coat I'm working on today is based off a pattern that was shared with us at the meeting, but so far, the shape I've created hardly resembles the image on the page. I set the fabric down, looking over the design once more, as though I am reading something that is in a language unknown to me, the directions growing more confusing each time I review them.

"What are you doing?"

I jump.

Felipe walks into the sitting room, still dressed in the same clothes he was wearing for dinner. He's rolled up the sleeves of his dress shirt, so his forearms are bare, and the first few buttons are undone at the neck.

"What does it look like I'm doing?" I ask, embarrassment filling me as I gesture at the fabric laid out before me.

He grins and takes a seat in a chair near where I'm working on the floor. "I can't quite tell to be honest. I confess, I never envisioned you sewing, and it is a bit difficult to make it out what it is." He leans forward slightly, until we are nearly level in my seated position. "A blanket? Curtains?"

"It's a coat. I haven't started making the sleeves yet."

"Why are you making a coat? Tonight was unbearable, but don't tell me my parents are forcing you to sew your own clothing."

"It's not for me. It's for the children of Spain. It is cold right now, and surely they will need the extra clothes considering how many of them are struggling."

"That's very kind of you to think of their needs."

"Making a coat or raising some funds hardly seems enough, but it's something at least."

He looks like there's more he wants to say, but he doesn't speak, merely shaking his head instead.

"What?"

"Nothing, I just—my brother—you're so different."

I stiffen. "So, we're on this fight again. Why? Because we come from different places? Because he grew up with money and I didn't?"

"No, because you care about helping people. Because you are trying to make a difference in people's lives."

"Gonzalo cared about making a difference."

"No, Gonzalo liked talking about making a difference. Gonzalo enjoyed the admiration of others more than he cared about helping those who need it. It's easy to sit at a table with a rapt audience and share your thoughts about the world with anyone who will listen."

"That's unfair."

"I never had Gonzalo's talent for prettying up the truth."

I'm not wholly surprised by the way he speaks of his brother; I know better than anyone the tension between them, but I still can't resist the urge to defend my husband, or maybe on some level, I can't resist the urge to defend myself and the choices I've made, to try to make Felipe understand how we ended up together. In this family, our marriage has been viewed with suspicion, as though I chose Gonzalo for his wealth rather than love, tonight's spectacle at the dinner table proof of that.

"Gonzalo believed in more than words. After all, he went to Spain to fight. He gave his life to the war. How can you say he wasn't willing to do the right thing when it counts?"

"Maybe because I know my brother. I very much doubt he went

to Spain thinking there was even a possibility that something could happen to him. Gonzalo looked out for himself better than anyone I know. More likely, he enjoyed the idea of going to war, the romanticism of being a hero, without knowing the first thing about sacrifice."

"You could help me, you know," I say, changing the subject. "If you're so concerned with doing something."

He sits down beside me. "All right, I will. Fair warning, I've never sewn anything in my life, but looking at what you've come up with, it can't be that much worse."

I glare at him, and he chuckles, his head bent over the fabric.

We work in silence for several moments, and I can't help but sneak a peek at the progress he's made so far.

"How is it that you've never picked up a needle and thread before, and yet, your design looks like that and mine looks like this?" I ask, holding up the misshapen object.

He grins. "It's a valiant effort, but you're right, your skills clearly lie elsewhere."

"You never know, I may improve with practice."

"I have no doubt you will. I don't think there's anything you couldn't accomplish if you wanted it badly enough."

My cheeks heat at the admiration in his voice.

"I'm sorry about dinner," Felipe adds. "What my mother said to you was abominably rude."

"It was. We've never gotten along, not since Gonzalo first introduced us. I'm sure I'm not the bride she would have chosen for her son."

"And yet, you were far more than he ever deserved."

I freeze mid-motion, the needle hovering in the air.

"Are we ever going to talk about it?" Felipe asks.

My heart pounds. "I don't know what you're talking about."

Felipe moves closer, obliterating the distance between us until he's so near that if I reached out, I could touch him, until I must crane my neck to look up at him, our gazes meeting.

"Coward."

He whispers it like it's another secret we have kept between us, and I stiffen, anger sliding down my spine.

It's a taunt, and a threat, and a condemnation, and for as much as I want to deny it, as much as I want to take some of the grief and rage that has been swirling inside me like a maelstrom and throw it back at him, I can't.

The undeniable truth is that no matter what protestations I may come up with, no matter what excuses I may make, I married Felipe's brother even though I loved Felipe first.

chapter fourteen

Isabel

1964

BARCELONA

We drive back to Barcelona the following morning, the ride less eventful with no black sedan following us. It's late in the evening once we reach the city, stopping only a few times for meals and necessary breaks, and Diego drops me off at my hotel with a promise to check on me the next day once we both have gotten some rest.

I rise the next morning to a knock on the door of my hotel room.

Beatriz.

I climb out of bed, grabbing the robe I discarded the night before from the foot of my bed and slipping it on over my nightgown, belting it quickly.

When I open the door, it isn't my sister standing on the other side of the threshold, but Diego, still wearing the same clothes he left me in the night before.

"She's in Barcelona," he says immediately.

"Did you see her?"

"No, but after I dropped you off at the hotel last night, I went to an underground card game Beatriz sometimes attends."

"I thought you were going back to your apartment to rest."

"You were so disappointed when we said goodnight. I could see the worry on your face. I wanted to do something to help. The card game is a good place to gather intelligence, and I asked around to see if Beatriz had been there recently, and it turns out she was there two nights ago, the same night we were in Marbella."

"Was she by herself? Did they say how she seemed?"

"She was by herself. They said she seemed fine. I don't know why she was there, though. I'm sorry. I had to be careful about the questions I asked. If Beatriz is involved in something she shouldn't be, I didn't want to draw even greater attention to her. But at least it's a lead. We know she's in Barcelona."

"She can't have been back at her apartment or she would have received the note I left for her and called me. I checked in with the front desk before I went to bed last night, and she hadn't left a message. I'm going to go wait by her apartment building to see if she returns," I decide.

"I'll come with you," Diego volunteers.

The café is more crowded than it was the last time I was here, and we snag one of the last available tables outside.

"This underground card game—were you there all night?" I ask Diego as he gulps down the coffee the waiter brings him.

He nods.

"Do you do that often?"

"Stay up all night or go to underground card games or both?"

"Both."

"When the occasion calls for it."

"That must get exhausting."

"It does, at times."

"Is there someone—"

"—waiting for me when I get home?"

I nod.

"Are you asking me about my love life, Isabel?" he teases.

I flush. "Call it curiosity. I can't imagine your life would be an easy one."

"No, it isn't. It can be dangerous, and unpredictable. It's hard to ask someone to accept such circumstances. So, no, there's no one special left to worry if I am home safe. Maybe it's better that way."

"I'm sorry."

He shrugs. "Don't be. It's the life I've chosen, and I haven't regretted it. There are sacrifices, but what doesn't come with difficult choices?"

"How do you do it, though? Do you ever feel as though you are living as two versions of yourself? You presumably go to meetings and work in your family's manufacturing business, and there's this other side of you . . ."

My words dangle between us, and I can tell in his expression that there's a part of him that wants to trust me, that wants to give me the answers I seek, but just like my sister Beatriz, he's caught between two worlds and all the secrets that come with them.

"It's not as dramatic as you probably think it is," he answers carefully. "I am a businessman. I travel internationally a great deal for my family's company. I speak two languages fluently, a poor imitation of French, and a bit of Italian. I am American, and I am also Spanish, and because of my family's experiences during the civil war, because of my mother fleeing her homeland and arriving in the United States, I have certain allegiances. And sometimes, those allegiances might align with others', and sometimes, in my business dealings, in my travels, there are moments when I am able to do some good, to do things I believe my mother would be proud of for the hope of a country she loved so dearly. It's not exploding pens and rocket-firing cars; sometimes it's just connecting people and passing information. But that doesn't mean there isn't a cost sometimes. Or that I always agree with the methods and goals of the people I encounter. Just that I am doing what I can for my country and my family."

The rest of his words fall away.

Beatriz walks down the street, her head tilted to the side, her gaze cast away from us. She looks well, certainly better than I feared when I was filled with worry. She's dressed in a stunning emerald green coat and matching hat, her makeup effortlessly applied, her hair perfectly coiffed.

I move without thinking, rising from the café chair and striding toward her, Diego somewhere behind me calling my name, all my attention focused on Beatriz.

The moment she sees me, she stops in her tracks, and by the look of shock on her face, it's clear she never received my messages, had no idea I was searching for her, that I was in Barcelona as well.

Neither one of us speaks as we stare at each other. Once, I would have thrown my arms around her with relief and joy that she's safe, but now there's an awkwardness between us.

"What on earth are you doing here, Isabel?" Beatriz asks. "And how do the two of you know each other?" she asks, her gaze shifting to Diego, who now stands behind me.

"I've been worried about you. We've been worried about you—

me and Elisa." I don't add the part about going to see Nicholas Preston. Not yet, at least. "We didn't say much to Maria because we didn't want to worry her, too, but I think she knows something is wrong. We've tried writing you, tried calling—"

"I've been away," Beatriz replies.

As much as I love her, as much as I am relieved to see that she is safe and well, it is so like my sister to simply take off and leave the rest of us concerned for her.

"I see that." I know how stiff my voice sounds, but all I can think of is the worry I've felt, the fact that I've flown here to help her, and she's been fine the whole time. "I'm sorry. I didn't realize you were on a vacation. If I had known—"

"I didn't say it was a vacation. Just that I've been away," she retorts. "I'm surprised you would leave Palm Beach just for that. Did you have to get permission from your husband or is he somewhere here, too?"

While I've earned her anger, it hits harder than she likely intended, considering we both know that compared to her, I have settled for a much smaller life. As much as I disapproved of her relationship with Nicholas Preston, she didn't hesitate to let me know how little she thought of the decisions I made, my ability to marry a man I did not love.

Beside me, Diego steps forward so he is standing next to me, his shoulder a hairbreadth away from mine.

Beatriz's eyes widen slightly, a hint of defiance in her gaze as though she has noted that he's standing beside me and doesn't like the implication that I have somehow aligned myself with her friend—or perhaps, more importantly, that her friend has aligned himself with me.

There's always been a rivalry between me and Beatriz. Sisters, and all that, plus as the two eldest girls it was almost natural that we would vie for toys, dolls, parental attention, boys' admiration, and just about everything else. I am the eldest, yet in matters of glamour, sophistication, and dare I say happiness, my younger sister has eclipsed me.

And in truth, none of that matters. I love her so much. I envy her the freedom I've never had. You can't be reckless when you're the one everyone expects to keep the siblings in line, when you're the responsible one, the one your parents count on, the peacemaker. The boring one.

Beatriz must see the hurt in my eyes, because some of the anger and tension seems to seep out of her. That's the thing about Beatriz: for all that she has a temper, she's always had a good heart.

"You really came all the way to Barcelona because you were worried about me?"

Embarrassment fills me, because when you put it that way, I suppose it does sound silly. But the truth is, when you've been through the things we have, when you've lost a sibling as we have, it's not difficult to imagine all the things that could have gone wrong, all the loss that may further await you.

Having lived through a revolution shapes you in so many ways that are difficult to explain. That loss, that fear, stays with you, and even when you think you've outrun it or outgrown it, it sneaks up on you and surprises you in wholly unexpected ways. Fidel didn't just take our home from us; he took a piece of us, too.

"We hadn't heard anything, Beatriz. You were in regular touch with Elisa and you simply disappeared. You missed Maria's birthday, which was so unlike you. Knowing what you were involved in before, well, we were concerned that you were here because you were in trouble." I shoot her a meaningful look. "Perhaps because you were mixed up in something you shouldn't be."

Her eyes widen slightly as though she finally understands my true meaning and the sense of urgency that precipitated my actions. "You shouldn't have worried. I am fine. I *am* surprised to see you here and not Elisa. I would have thought that if you were worried I was mixed up in something you would have decided I deserved it."

So, she isn't going to let me off the hook. Fine. Better to air our grievances now than let them fester. When she came back to Palm Beach over a year ago, we put on a polite face and danced around each other, our interactions barely skimming the surface but for the occasional well-placed barb.

We both grew up in a family where unpleasantness was never addressed, any hint of discord seen as too likely to bring scandal to even be entertained. We never spoke of how we felt about things to our parents, were never given the space to be ourselves, but there was always something about our bond as sisters that operated differently, because we were allies in that house, allies in exile, and so maybe we trusted each other a little more.

Confrontation has never been a natural choice of mine—I'd much rather avoid it than court it—but this situation with Beatriz has gone on for too long, and I have too much to lose.

"Beatriz. Can we talk? Please? I came all the way here because I'd like to change things between us. There's much we have to say to each other. Things I would like to say to you if you would give me a chance."

The expression on her face changes so quickly that, if I'd blinked, I would have missed it, but it's enough for me to know that Beatriz isn't as unmoved as she pretends to be, that there's a crack in the armor that she wears to protect herself from the rest of the world. She's good. She always has been. Sometimes it's easy to think that she is as she portrays herself; sometimes it's easy to forget that I've seen her at her most vulnerable, that for as strong as she is, she has always needed the same support the rest of us do, no matter how much she would wish to pretend otherwise.

Diego breaks the silence between us. "Perhaps I should leave the two of you alone for a few hours. It sounds like you have business to settle between you. Will you be fine, Isabel?" he asks, the last part delivered for my ears alone.

I nod, just as Beatriz's gaze whips to him. "How did you two even become acquainted in the first place?" she asks again.

"We met in your apartment," he answers. "Isabel threatened to bludgeon me with a statue until I convinced her that we're friends, that I didn't mean you any harm. She was quite terrifying."

"I wasn't."

He grins. "You were. You are. I'll come by later. If you need anything, you can call me." He reaches into his pocket and removes his business card, which I take from him wordlessly, and he turns away from us and walks down the street.

"He likes you," Beatriz murmurs, her gaze focused on Diego's back.

I flush. "He's been kind. Helpful. That's all it is."

"Of course that isn't all it is. But if that's how you'd like to leave it, that's your business. I suppose we should go upstairs to my apartment if you'd like to talk." She turns toward her building, leaving me to follow behind her in her wake as she leads me up to her home on the fifth floor.

"Well, you're here," Beatriz says with little fanfare once we're in her living room. "And you said you wanted to talk."

"I owe you an apology. For a long time now. I was too ashamed to say anything to you, and maybe too proud to admit that I did something wrong, but that day that we fought after the Bay of Pigs, when our mother overheard us arguing about your relationship with Nicholas Preston—it was never my intention to betray you like that. I didn't realize she was in the house at the time, and if I had known, I certainly would have been more discreet about it. I was angry with you for causing a scandal when it seemed like there were already so many eyes on us and so much censure cast our way, but it was never my intention to jeopardize your relationship. I thought he was a lark. I thought he was—"

"No." Her voice trembles over the word. "He wasn't a lark. Far from it."

Shame fills me, so much emotion contained in the simplicity of those few words. The truth is, I wonder sometimes if I didn't recognize the love Beatriz had because I've never had it myself. Because even though I've been engaged twice, married once, I've never felt that kind of passion, or felt safe enough to throw caution to the wind with another person.

"I know. I'm sorry. I went to see him." I'm not sure if sharing this will make things worse between us or if honesty is the best course. "Elisa and I were worried about you, and we wondered if Nicholas Preston might have some news of you, if you had been in contact."

"How was he?" she asks.

"He didn't seem himself, at least not as I've seen him before. I think he misses you. A lot. He was concerned when I mentioned that you were in Spain, that no one had been able to get in touch with you."

She turns, her back to me. "Have there been any rumors about him seeing anyone? Do you know if he—"

"Beatriz. I don't understand. It's clear that you still care for him. That you both still love each other. I'm not privy to all the rumors in Palm Beach—we hardly occupy those circles—but I haven't heard anything about him with another woman. If you care about him this much, why don't you come home? Why did you break things off with him?"

Beatriz turns, facing me, the pain in her eyes staggering, the raw emotion there catching me off guard.

"You wouldn't understand."

"Help me. Somewhere along the way we stopped talking to each other, stopped trusting each other, started misunderstanding each other's motives. I'm *trying* to understand. Why would you come here, so far away from your family, from the things you love? What is this hold that the CIA seems to have over you? Of all the things you could do with your life, why spying? I thought you weren't involved in all that anymore. With Cuba. Or with the CIA. Why are you still doing this sort of thing?"

"I'm not involved with Cuba. Not the same way, at least. But that doesn't mean there aren't terrible things happening all over the world. Places where I'm able to do something. Besides, Spain's relationship with Cuba only increases despite the ideological differences between them, so it's not wholly unrelated."

"And Diego? He's CIA, too?"

"I think I should let him explain himself given the way he was looking at you earlier. Diego is a good person. I don't trust many people, but I trust him."

"I'm worried about you, Beatriz. If you're involved in these kinds of intrigues, you're putting yourself in danger again. When it was Cuba and your desire to avenge Alejandro, I could understand, even if I didn't agree, but why do you keep chasing these situations, why do you have to live on the edge—"

"What would you have me do, Isabel? Pretend like nothing is happening in the world? Is that what you do?"

"We are women. Cuban women without a home. We don't have power or influence. I never wanted you to get involved with the CIA to begin with, never understood how you could make an alliance with them given all the horrible things they've done throughout the world. Our father played politics, tried to court influence and power, looked the other way when he aligned himself with the wrong people, and see how that worked out for him? How could you think to do the same? Have you learned nothing from what our family went through in Cuba? From what we lost?"

"What else am I going to do? What is the point of all of this if I'm not fighting with everything I have in me? I'm not you, Isabel. I can't lead the life you lead; can't marry a man I don't love and tell myself I'm living my life."

The blow lands as she likely intended it to, and despite the truth in her words, I can't ignore the urge to defend my life and the choices I made.

"Don't presume to know my marriage. Thomas has given me security, and my marriage has opened some doors for us that otherwise wouldn't be available. We are more accepted in Palm Beach because of my marriage; Maria has better opportunities because of it. I am grateful for that. I'm not you, Beatriz. I'm not looking to be reckless and call it brave."

Beatriz sighs. "Less than an hour together and we're already fighting. Why do we do this to each other?"

"I don't know. Too different, I suppose."

"Maybe. But maybe we have more in common than you think. After all, look where we came from and what we've been through. I don't know that anyone else can understand the same way we can."

"That's true. And if anything, that's even more reason to support each other. I'm sorry for what I said to you when we fought."

"We've both said so much to each other throughout the years." She shrugs in that fabulously "Beatriz" way of hers, as though she can cast off the weight of the world with the arch of one elegant shoulder. "We're sisters. We fight."

"Elisa always seems to manage to stay out of the fray."

"Elisa might be the best of us."

"It's funny you would say that. I suppose I've always wished I could be more like you."

Beatriz's eyes widen. "How so?"

"The way you look at the world like it should step aside for you. How you aren't afraid to be bold. You're unapologetically yourself. I suppose I envy that."

"Some might call that selfishness."

"You're not selfish. At all. If anything, you're one of the most loyal people I know. I'm sorry if I've made you feel otherwise. I suppose there was a part of me that was jealous. It felt like you and Elisa had moved on and built lives for yourself, and while of course I was happy for you, I envied you that ability."

"That's funny you should say that because I felt like you were leaving me behind, getting married and such."

"You make me sound so adult."

"Aren't you, though?"

"Hardly. I thought I would be once I married," I admit. "I thought it would change me somehow, that being Thomas's wife would give me the chance to have order in my life. Peace. Security."

"It didn't?"

"It bought me some things—physical security, at least. But there are things I can't seem to outrun, no matter how hard I try. I wanted to reinvent myself. I wanted to make a home in the States, a life there. I thought that by looking forward, by forgetting all that I left behind, all that *we* left behind, I might have a chance at some semblance of a happy life. But it sneaks up on me at the most unsuspected times. I'll smell a flower, or taste a fruit, and suddenly, I'm not in Palm Beach anymore. I'm in Cuba and everything is different, and as it should be." I take a deep breath, the pressure building in my chest, struggling to get air in my lungs. "I feel like I'm wearing a costume, like I'm draped in someone else's life, and as the years go by, I keep thinking it will become easier, that Palm Beach will feel like home. I *want* it to feel like home, desperately, but no matter how hard I try, how much I pray and wish it were so, it simply isn't. Sometimes it seems like I don't belong anywhere."

"I didn't know you felt like that," Beatriz replies. "I wish I had. I miss how things used to be. I miss how close we were, even if we spent more time bickering than anything else. I miss you."

"I miss you, too."

"I know what you mean about not belonging anywhere." She hesitates. "I found something when I went to visit Rosa. She had these pictures at her house from when she and our mother were younger. From Cuba. But there were a few other pictures in there—"

"From Barcelona," I finish for her.

"Yes. How did you know?"

"Because I came here looking for you, and I was trying to find some clues as to what might have happened to you. I searched the closet, knowing it's one of your favorite hiding places, and there was a picture of me sitting with our mother and a man I've never seen before at the café downstairs."

"So that's what happened to it. It must have dropped when I was packing. I was in a hurry, and I wasn't thinking clearly. I'm worried, Isabel—I—I think the man in the picture is my father."

chapter fifteen

Since we were girls, Beatriz was always the adventurous one, the romantic, the imaginative one. I was too practical, too logical to see beyond the unassailable reality of things, but Beatriz looked at the world differently, saw beneath the surface. Maybe that trait drew her to espionage. Maybe it's part of what makes her good at it.

"Think of the timing," Beatriz says. "Based on your age in the photograph, Alejandro and I couldn't have been born much later. What if I have a different father? What if that man in the photograph is really my father? What if that's why Alejandro was always her favorite? Because his father was her true love?"

Of all the thoughts that ran through my mind when I saw the photograph in Beatriz's closet, the question of her parentage never occurred to me. There are physical similarities we all share as siblings, a resemblance to our father—and our aunt Mirta for that matter—that has always been clear.

"I think that's a big leap to make off a photograph, Beatriz. We just don't know who that man is or what their relationship was."

"She was in love with him."

"You don't know that. Not off a photograph."

"I do. I know how you look at a man you love, and that expression on her face—that's love. Have you ever seen her look at our father that way?"

"I don't know that you can judge their relationship off what we've seen as children. Marriage is complicated. Who knows what goes on between them behind closed doors? And that picture, maybe it's a different kind of love than the one you're envisioning, Beatriz. She was married. Have you met our mother? What makes you think she would engage in an affair after how much she has drilled the importance of propriety into us?"

"You're always defending her. You're always taking her side."

"I'm not. This isn't about taking sides. But you are jumping to conclusions without any proof. It's a long leap from looking at a photograph that doesn't make sense and concluding that this man in the photograph was someone important to our mother. That they had an affair. That he fathered children with her."

"Did you ask her about the photograph?" Beatriz counters.

"I did."

"And what did she say?"

I hesitate. "She denied that I had ever been to Barcelona."

"Oh, come on. There you have it. Why deny it? Obviously, we have proof that she's lying. Why would she deny it if the photograph has some innocent explanation?"

"There are lots of reasons. Not all of them mean your theory is true. Did you ask her about the photograph?" I ask Beatriz.

"No."

"Why not?"

"Because there's no point. You may have a different relationship with her, she may confide in you, but she has never been like that with me. She's more likely to tell a stranger her secrets than to tell me."

The hurt in my sister's voice is unmistakable, and I long to take a step forward and wrap my arms around her. With a family like ours, there are so many personalities to account for, so many complicated relationships; so much of the past weighs us down.

"She loves you, Beatriz. Maybe not in the manner you'd like, maybe not as well as she should, maybe she doesn't understand you as you wish she did, but she loves you."

"She has a strange way of showing it. And for her disapproval over my relationship with Nick, for her condemnation of me, what if she's no different? Did she have an affair of her own?"

"Is that what this is about? Your anger and hurt for the way she handled your relationship with Nicholas Preston?"

"I just want to know the truth. If our father isn't really my father, I deserve to know. For me and for Alejandro. He would have wanted to know, too."

"You're a Perez, Beatriz. You always have been. We all look alike. You look like our father, like our aunt Mirta. I think you're wrong."

"And if I'm not? If it were you, wouldn't you want to know?"

"Honestly? No, I don't think I would. I don't think I could take another change in my life. Have we not been through enough with problems finding us? Why go looking for them?"

"Well, I'm not you."

"No, you aren't. Did you ask Rosa about the photograph when you found it?"

Beatriz nods. "She clammed up immediately. Said she didn't know anything about it or how it got there. It seemed like she was covering something. You know how they are—they're close, they always have been. No doubt they're holding each other's secrets."

"Or maybe you're reading too much into it."

"I need to know," Beatriz says, and it's the unspoken plea in her voice that undoes me. "I need to know who my father is."

And even though she doesn't say it, I know her well enough to hear the words she doesn't say:

I need to understand who my mother is, too.

"I know you came here because you were worried about me, but even though you found me, you told Thomas you might be gone for a week. It would be nice for us to have this time together. Let's try to be sisters again, to move past the differences between us. We were close in Cuba. We shouldn't let all that's happened since then divide us."

There's something so earnest in her gaze, and for so long I never thought we'd have this kind of a chance again, that I can't resist.

"I'd love that."

I'm too afraid to risk a phone call to Thomas, worried that he'll demand that I return home, so instead I leave a message for him with his secretary saying that I've found Beatriz, but I'll be in Barcelona for a few more days.

"How did it go?" Beatriz asks as she sashays into the sitting room in a green cocktail gown with a daring neckline that has her flawless décolletage on perfect display.

"I left a message with his secretary." I shrug. "He won't be happy about it, but I'm not sure what else to do. I'm surprised he even allowed me to come," I say, more as an aside to myself than anything else.

Her perfectly penciled brow rises. "Allowed you? Are you his wife or his child?"

Technically, with the age difference between us, I am young enough to be either.

"I'm here now," I reply, ignoring her jab. "For several days, at least."

"We should make the most of it. I'm going to a party tonight. For work. Come with me."

"Diego mentioned that you work at the consulate here."

"Yes, as a secretary. One of the diplomatic staff members is hosting some esteemed guests tonight for cocktails."

"You work as a secretary?"

I can't envision Beatriz sitting over a typewriter pecking away at the keys.

She smiles with a flash of perfect white teeth. "My position at the consulate is eminently useful in the work I do."

So not just the consulate, then.

"I'm sure it is. If it's all the same to you, I think I'd rather just stay inside this evening. The past few days have been stressful enough with me jaunting all over Spain in search of you, and unfortunately, I left my cocktail dresses at home in Palm Beach."

I already wore the nicest dress I brought with me two nights ago in Marbella with Diego.

"So, borrow one of mine. We're practically the same size. You need to get out. You need to have some *fun*. Do you remember when we used to sneak out of the house in Miramar and go to parties our parents never would have approved of? Do you remember how good it felt to let our hair down, to have a reprieve from the pressures of being a Perez, from all the expectations of what was ladylike and not?"

"I'm a married woman. I think my sneaking-out days are behind me."

Beatriz shrugs. "I didn't say you had to have a passionate love affair—although I wouldn't condemn it, either—but I wouldn't discount a little champagne, some music, and maybe a dance or two. Borrow one of my dresses. Have some fun, Isabel. It'll be like old times, before everything, when we were sisters who enjoyed spending time together. It'll be an adventure for just the two of us."

With each word falling from her lips, I warm to the idea, Beatriz's powers of persuasion always impressive. As tired as I am, I am drawn to the idea of going to a party where no one knows or cares who I am, where I don't have to make my husband or my parents proud, where I can just be myself, maybe dance for a song or two.

There's something about being on my own, even if it's only been a short time since I left Palm Beach, a magic about being around Beatriz again, that transports me back in time to when we were young girls with the city at our feet and the world spread before us. I've aged a lifetime in the five years since the revolution, and I'm so disconnected from that girl that she seems a stranger, but the glimpse I'm seeing of her now that I'm with my sister again is like a whisper in my ears taunting me to take a risk when I'd usually play it safe.

"Show me your dresses," I say, my eyes casting downward to the pair of discarded sandals still in the living room. "And I'm taking back my shoes."

The dress on the hanger and the dress on my body are two very different things. The rich red color looked beautiful and sumptuous in Beatriz's closet, but wearing it at the embassy party now, the shade is a flashing beacon drawing more attention to me than I'd like. It doesn't help that I'm entering the party with Beatriz, who turns heads whether she's in Havana, Palm Beach, or Barcelona, or that I have a solid two inches on her, showing more leg than normal.

Beatriz links her arm through mine, and she flashes me a smile I've seen countless times before, and I can read her thoughts as surely as though they're my own:

Here we are, the Perez sisters, all eyes on us, the men casting admiring looks our way.

I learned the lesson back in Havana when the revolution came, but it seems Beatriz hasn't quite taken it to heart: It isn't good to be a source of envy of others, because the higher you rise, the harder you fall.

We've only just arrived when a group of Beatriz's friends and colleagues descend upon us. From what I gather, most are surprised to learn Beatriz even has a sister, and I can't quite blame them for assuming she just miraculously arose from the foam of the sea à la Aphrodite or some other goddess.

After the early introductions are done, Beatriz is pulled onto the dance floor by one of her coworkers, giving me an opportunity to grab a glass of champagne from one of the waiters passing them around and to take a spot near the corner of the room where I can watch the party from my vantage point, keep an eye on my sister, and listen to the jazz music pouring through the room.

I'm so caught up in the sound of the music that I don't even notice him approaching until he's standing in front of me, a highball in hand.

"I take it this means you are staying in Barcelona for a bit," Diego says in greeting.

"A few more days."

"Did you make up with Beatriz?"

A laugh rings out across the room, saving me from answering, and we both turn, catching sight of Beatriz dancing with an older gentleman, her head thrown back as though the moment has simply overtaken her. If you didn't know Beatriz well, it would be easy to think that she was having the time of her life, but her laughter is louder than it naturally should be, her eyes taking in the room rather than filled with genuine mirth.

"In a manner of speaking," I reply, my gaze still on my sister. Is this her attempt to get over the heartbreak she's nursing, or is her presence here and her behavior part of some espionage scheme?

"Was your husband upset to hear that you would be gone for so long? He must miss you."

The word "husband" catches me off guard, the image of Thomas here in this smoke-filled room so incongruous that I give a little start, the champagne rocking inside my glass. Thomas would hate a party like this, would dismiss the people around us as too fast, too foreign, too different.

"His business interests keep him occupied in Palm Beach," I reply.

"Must be some business interests. Would you like to dance?"

"With you?"

He laughs. "I had lessons as a child, I promise. My mother made sure of it. It's been a while since I danced with a pretty girl, but that doesn't mean I've forgotten how."

The instinct to beg off with some excuse about how I am not much of a dancer is there, but the truth is that I have always loved to dance, and I've missed the opportunity to do so since I left Cuba. Before I married Thomas, our social invitations were sparse, and unlike Beatriz, I never felt the desire to draw attention to myself at the various occasions we attended, considering how clearly unwanted we were. But here—well—no one knows me, and the desire to let go is enough to have me taking Diego's outstretched hand, allowing him to lead me to the makeshift dance floor that has been created in the center of the room.

Beatriz's eyes widen slightly as her gaze rests on us, but her mouth parts into a sultry smile and she turns her attention back to her partner.

Diego draws me closer, placing his hand at my waist, raising our joined hands so they rest against his chest. I hesitate, and I lay my palm on his shoulder lightly, my fingers barely grazing his suit jacket, careful to keep a respectful distance between our bodies.

Soon, it becomes obvious that he didn't lie—he is a good dancer, quick on his feet all the while his hand pressing into my waist gently steering me through the dance. I've always had a hard time letting a man lead when I dance; it's so much easier to follow the music on your own than to adjust to the rhythm of another, but in this, too, he seems to adapt to my improvisations, and it's easy to enjoy the moment without thinking about my dance partner or anyone else.

We don't speak, the music too loud to allow it, the laughter of others occasionally crashing over the sounds of the song playing. When the music ends, another song begins, and we continue as though we never heard the transition, and he pulls me a little closer and I let him, grateful that the proximity between us has me looking over his shoulder, eye contact and conversation a difficulty to entertain.

It's been some time since I danced with anyone, but it comes back to me slowly, my feet remembering basic steps, acclimating to a familiar beat, and he's such a good dancer that my mind drifts as I watch the people passing us by, as I study the couples wondering whether they are married or lovers, thinking that I would like to paint this scene, this moment in time, making the colors hazy and fluid, a veil over the entire affair. There's an ephemeral quality to the evening, as though this is some sort of dreamlike night as Diego spins me around, and around, and around.

Partners change out on the dance floor, but still we continue on, the room growing warmer, a thin line of sweat trickling down my back. I've long since gotten over any discomfort over dancing with Diego, have little care for who leads me around the room.

I don't even realize I'm laughing until it spills forth from me like some closely guarded secret, and there's a hitch in Diego's stride, as though the sound has startled him. Beatriz looks up from the corner of the room, too, a smile on her face, and I incline my head in a little nod, an acknowledgment that she was right, that what I needed was to put on a pretty dress and have a fun night.

We dance on and on, my laughter turning into a permanent smile, a thrill each time he dips me, our moves growing more daring with each song that passes. There are so few men of my acquaintance that enjoy dancing; in Palm Beach it's all shuffling feet and polite smiles, that there's something exhilarating about having a partner who is as enthusiastic as I am. Only belatedly do I realize that we've carved out a space for ourselves on the dance floor, others watching us avidly.

"Do you want to take a break?" Diego asks me, his voice in my ear causing me to jolt. "Get some fresh air?"

We must have been dancing for an hour at least, and now that we've paused, I realize my feet hurt, my makeup and hair likely disheveled.

It feels wonderful.

"Sure," I reply, realizing I'm more than a little out of breath, unused to such diversions.

I follow Diego's lead, winding through the rooms of the apartment, each one filled with people, the party larger than I initially gathered, or perhaps it's grown since we began dancing. In the corner near a set of floor-to-ceiling glass doors that open to a wrought iron balcony, a group of men and women are having a heated discussion about politics; a few feet away from them a couple kisses passionately beside them with little care for the fact that they are surrounded by onlookers. It's the sort of party I never get to attend in Palm Beach, and exactly the soiree I imagine Beatriz adores.

There's a bar set up near the balcony doors, and Diego leans down, snagging a bottle of liquor and two glasses.

Diego opens one of the patio doors with his free hand, motioning for me to walk ahead of him, and the skirt of my borrowed dress brushes against his suit pants with a swish of taffeta as I step out onto the narrow balcony, the cool air a welcome relief.

He closes the door behind us, walking to the side opposite me so there's some distance between us. He sets the bottle and glasses down on the table, giving both of us a hefty pour.

I take the proffered drink from him wordlessly, turning my back to him and staring out at the city.

We walked a short distance from Beatriz's apartment earlier in the evening, but I've yet to get a sense of Barcelona or where I even am.

I take a sip of the alcohol.

"Are we still near Las Ramblas?" I ask him.

"We are. A few blocks from Beatriz's apartment. You should ask your sister to show you around Barcelona. It's a beautiful city despite . . ." He doesn't say the remaining words out loud, merely gestures at perhaps the futility of everything in a way that I can all too easily relate to.

"Thank you for the dance earlier. I can't remember the last time I had so much fun. I hadn't danced in so long that I didn't really care who I was dancing with; it just felt good to be out there—"

Diego laughs. "Please. No more for my ego." He places his hand against his heart as though I have just wounded him, but the smile on his face belies the sincerity of the gesture.

"I didn't mean it like that."

"Why is it that I find myself constantly humbled by you?" he asks.

"It's not intentional, I promise."

"Maybe I care too much about what you think of me," he replies.

"You shouldn't."

"Shouldn't care?"

"No."

"Because you're married?"

"Yes."

"If you weren't married, if we'd met at a different time, if you were free, would I have a chance with you, Isabel?"

It's a bold question, and one I'm certainly not prepared to answer. Is he handsome? Yes. But the world is full of handsome men, and that on its own is hardly an impressive feat. There's something about him, though, maybe those same qualities of daring that I admire in my sister and have never seen in myself. He is brave, and he is kind, and being in his presence makes me feel—

Would I be attracted to him if things were different, if we had met in a different time?

How would I not be?

"You know I can't answer that. And you know why I shouldn't answer it. You probably think me incredibly naive. It's not that I don't understand that these things happen. I suppose I've never understood the 'why' behind them happening, how people can risk so much and put themselves in such foolish situations for such little reward."

"You don't believe they're simply swept up in the moment, that passion rules them until they give in to their desires?" he asks.

"I don't. I believe that it is a choice when one enters into a dalliance, and if you want to use passion as an excuse or a justification that is certainly your prerogative, but it removes a sense of agency from the equation that seems dishonest, as though one is hardly accepting the consequences for their actions, but instead twisting their decisions into a convenient excuse that leaves them entirely blameless."

There's that smile again. "You've clearly thought about this."

"No—I haven't—not really."

"You have. It's nothing to be embarrassed about. I think I like this world according to Isabel. It's honest, at least."

"I'm not saying I don't stumble," I add, not wanting to give the impression that I somehow think I am above such folly. I have certainly made my share of mistakes, and will no doubt continue to do so. "But there is comfort in following the right path, in trying to do the right thing. There is security in making decisions that are in your best interests. There's safety there."

"And when life comes at you unexpectedly? When all those choices you've made fail to protect you? What do you do then?"

"I don't know. I didn't say it was a perfect strategy; I didn't say it kept me from being hurt, or hurting others, only that I try to follow it, that I try not to make the sort of mistakes I can't come back from. You're right: no matter how hard you try, no matter what you do, life can throw you some unexpected curves that you will struggle to recover from. I never thought my life would turn out the way it did, never imagined I'd leave so much behind, that I'd lose so much. Enough problems come to find you. The last thing I need is to go looking for them."

"Then why try so hard? Why twist yourself up to please others, why deny who you are, if at the end of the day none of this is up to us, if fate or God is going to step in and sweep us up in their path?"

"Because the other way is to suggest that we have no control over this life, that we are simply stumbling our way through the world, peril at every corner. How can you survive a world like that? Why would you want to? If there's not a path to follow, a set of guidelines to aspire to, the world is an absolutely terrifying thing."

"I suppose I think the world is already an absolutely terrifying thing with or without the path," he replies.

I can't disagree with him there given everything I've seen and lost, but there's a stubbornness within me, an inability to reject the precepts of life that have taken me this far, that give me a sense of security when the world is simply too much to bear. It's easier to believe that playing it safe gets you through those unexpected moments, even if the truth is that you're telling yourself little more than a fairy tale.

I tear my gaze away from him and look through the glass balcony doors at the party still going inside.

There is a part of me that envies the lovers who have now moved to the couch, the woman straddling the man; there is a sliver of me that wonders what it would be like to speak freely about politics as the group continues to do, when all I have seen from our time in Cuba is that doing so can all too often have deadly consequences. There is a part of me that yearns to be different, but it seems as though we are the sum of our life experiences, that we have been indelibly shaped by the things that we have survived, and I have come out the other end as this version of myself, even if she often feels like a watercolor substitute for an oil on canvas life.

"I should go find Beatriz," I say.

Diego looks as though he wants to say something else, but he merely nods, walking toward the door and opening it for me, following me as I wind my way back through the path we took, looking for the main room where I last saw Beatriz.

I find her perched on a piano, regaling the entire room with song, which is an incredible feat considering Beatriz has never been able to carry a tune. But the smile on her face is so bright, her partner at the piano looking at her with such an intense expression of adoration, that it's clear no one cares how the song sounds, only that they're enjoying her performance.

When she's finished, she jumps down from the piano with an apology for the audience that has gathered around her. Her gaze drifts from me to Diego and back again.

"Is everything all right?" Beatriz asks. "You disappeared a little bit ago and I wondered where you went."

"I'm fine. It was warm, and we got some fresh air after all of the dancing." I struggle to keep my expression as blank as possible to dissuade Beatriz from whatever salacious thoughts she might have. "I'd like to leave if you don't mind. The jet lag is catching up to me, and I'm ready for bed."

Beatriz nods. "I'll get our coats."

"I can give you a ride back to your apartment," Diego suggests.

"You shouldn't have to leave on my account," I reply. "If you were enjoying yourself, I wouldn't want to stop you from continuing to do so."

"With the two of you leaving, the party just became much less interesting. Besides, I have an early meeting tomorrow, so it's best if I turn in myself."

We follow him from the party, his car parked on the sidewalk. He holds the doors open for me and Beatriz. I choose the back seat.

Another smile from Diego.

Beatriz slides in in front of me, next to Diego, and we're off, the windows cracked slightly, cool air filtering into the car. Up front, the two of them talk about friends they know, the party itself, all sorts of things I barely try to keep up with as I look out the window, Barcelona passing me by.

I've always felt that cities have their own character, a personality shaped by their histories and the people that call them home. Barcelona is a city of whispers and secrets.

Despite the novelty of my surroundings, at some point the need for sleep gets the best of me, because the next thing I know, I am waking up the following morning in the guest bedroom at Beatriz's wondering who carried me up several flights of stairs.

chapter sixteen

When I wake after the party at the consulate, it's light out, the clock near the bed indicating that I slept well, the early afternoon already upon us. There's a phone in the bedroom, and I reach for it, placing a call to Thomas at his office. It's morning in Palm Beach, the dawn not yet having made an appearance, but Thomas has always chosen to spend most of his time at work rather than home.

He answers immediately.

We go through the pleasantries rather quickly, and just as I can tell that he's ready to hang up, eager to get on with his day, I confess that I went out on my own with Beatriz while he was home alone in Palm Beach.

When we're both in Florida, we tend to go our separate ways when it comes to social functions—Thomas prefers evenings with his friends and business associates whereas I gravitate toward spending my time with my family—but this feels different, as though I have changed the unspoken rules between us somewhat when I danced with Diego. But if I expected jealousy or concern, I get neither, just an impatient sigh and an attempt to rush me off the call.

After we've said a quick good-bye, I hang up the phone and go in search of Beatriz, only to find a note waiting for me on the kitchen counter, no sign of my sister.

Sorry, had to dash. Work came up. (It's an emergency—really!!!) I'll be back later. There's not much in the refrigerator, but the food at the café around the corner is quite good. Enjoy Barcelona.

I make a quick meal out of some fruit Beatriz has in her kitchen. After I eat, I shower and dress quickly, slipping on a skirt and blouse I brought with me from Palm Beach over my undergarments. I'm just putting the finishing touches on my makeup when a knock sounds at the door.

I'm reluctant to answer, considering all manner of things Beatriz could be involved in, so I settle on walking over and glancing through the peephole to see who it is.

Diego looks back at me, dressed in a fresh suit, his arms full of shopping bags.

I open the door.

"Good afternoon. How are you feeling today?" he asks me.

"Better, thank you." Embarrassment fills me as I remember he must have carried me up the flights of stairs to Beatriz's apartment last night. "I'm sorry I fell asleep in the car last night. I'm not normally like that."

"No apology needed. It's been a busy few days with all the travel you've done not to mention the time difference. You look like you got some sleep. I hope I didn't disturb you. I thought about visiting earlier, but I didn't want to wake you if you were resting. May I come in?"

"Sure, but Beatriz isn't here if you're looking for her."

"No, I figured she would be out, considering how rarely she is at home," he says with a wry smile. "I wanted to see how you were faring after last night. And I brought you a present."

I open the door wider, stepping back so he can cross over the threshold. I lock the door behind us and lead him into Beatriz's living room.

"I thought you might want to paint while you are here," Diego says, gesturing to the bags in his hands. "The city is beautiful. I thought an artist might appreciate it."

Surprise fills me.

He bought an array of supplies, clearly from a good art store in Barcelona.

"This was kind of you. Truly."

A ghost of a smile plays at his lips. "I've been known to be kind a time or two. You don't have to sound so surprised."

"I'm sorry. I didn't mean to sound surprised. It's just more than I ever expected."

"It's my pleasure to help welcome you to Barcelona—properly, at least, now that Beatriz is safe and sound and you have one less worry on your mind."

"Would you like to stay for a drink? Beatriz doesn't have much in the way of food, but—"

"No, but thank you. I just wanted to drop this off. I have a meeting I'm running late for. Enjoy your painting, Isabel."

After I show Diego out of the apartment, I sit at the vanity in Beatriz's guest bedroom, staring at the blank canvas in front of me. He brought me oils and watercolors, brushes, a sketch pad, and a couple larger canvases, and I select one of the canvases to begin.

I never know what I'm going to paint beforehand, simply follow my mood, letting it guide me. Often, it's like I am emptying my emotions onto the canvas, finding some unknown or previously unacknowledged piece of myself in the swath of colors and the image that begins to appear. There's something about confronting your emotions when it's just you and a blank canvas, no one's opinion or judgment to influence how you express yourself. I don't worry about being perfect, or good enough, or if I'm pleasing those around me when I paint. It's just for me, and the freedom in that may be my favorite part of all.

Each work is like being stripped nude, each layer being cast aside until I have reached the most vulnerable, intimate piece of me. Only then is the painting complete, once my tears have mixed with the oils, once I have painted until the pain or joy is wrung from me. Then I can sit back and stare at it with a sense of satisfaction as though this, too, is another thing I have wrangled, a part of me that has been put into submission so that I can carry on with my day.

And more often than not, I paint Cuba.

When I paint my home, I focus on the textures of my memories—the sharp, tangy taste of fruit, the sensation of the sand beneath my feet, the hot sun warming a spot on my back between my shoulder blades in late summer, the musky scent of the sea calling to me from my bedroom, luring me outdoors.

It wasn't until I painted my twentieth or so picture of Cuba that I realized there were never any people in my paintings, not even dots in the landscape. It's easier to mourn a country than it is to face the loss of the people you love who still live in it.

There are some who would say I should move past this, that I should be grateful for the fact that I have this opportunity to start over. And I know it could be worse. But it's not as simple of a thing as telling myself to forget Cuba or the life I had there, to forget that my brother was killed, and even if I could by some sheer force of will turn my back on the past and keep my gaze firmly centered on the present and future, those experiences have left their mark on me.

The sensation that everything around me is temporary, that one day I will wake up and it will all be gone, is one I cannot shake. When you have lost everything in one sweep, it is impossible to believe that it will not happen again; you mistrust whatever happiness you might find as transient, subject to the whims of whatever calamity may befall you.

No matter how hard I try to be different, I am too marked by the things I've experienced to go through life any other way. But it's hard to explain that to those who haven't lived it, and I often sense Thomas's impatience with me, his desire for me to embrace this spirit of impenetrability he and so many others around him seem to adopt with ease.

Today when I pick up the brush, I don't dip it in the blues I typically favor when I paint the ocean, the pinks and golds that make the sky; instead I go for a deep red, the color of the dress Beatriz lent me last night.

At first the red is just a shape, a splash of color on the canvas, and then it becomes a dress, in motion, a dancer twirling the skirt as she moves with the beat of the music. I add more colors, the small canvas coming to life.

When it comes to the girl in the dress, I hesitate, my inexperience drawing people nearly getting the best of me. Places are easier. Cities have their secrets, their character, their history, and as difficult as it can be to capture all those things in an image, so much of what we see in the world is done through our own lens, so really the way we view things is a reflection on us more than the object itself.

But with people, there are more angles to take into consideration, both how we see and how we wish to be seen, and it is an ever-changing dialogue between artist and subject, a push and pull I never quite master.

The girl in the red dress, spinning around, becomes both me and not-me, a version of myself that might have existed in a different life, a version of myself I yearn for. I pause when I get to Diego's part of the painting, starting first with a hand at the girl's waist, and then an arm, moving up—

For hours, I work, the sun going down, my stomach growling from how little I've eaten that day. I get up from my makeshift work space and walk around Beatriz's apartment, turning on lamps, trying to get the lighting just right.

The sound of a key turning into a lock startles me just as I'm putting the finishing touches on the painting. Paint is smeared across my face, my hands stained, the small canvas now filled with the image of a girl dancing in a whirling frenzy of color and emotion, her partner gazing down at her with longing in his gaze.

I've never painted anything like it.

To her credit, Beatriz's eyes only widen slightly as she walks into the bedroom and is confronted with the mess I've made of her guest room, as her gaze runs over my appearance, at the paint smudged all over me.

"I had no idea you're an artist," she says.

I spend two days in Barcelona painting, the supplies Diego brought me bringing me an immense amount of joy. I've stopped working long enough to eat and shower, catch up on sleep, and I'm back at it, temporarily converting Beatriz's apartment into my own personal art studio.

For her part, Beatriz hardly seems to mind. She's gone more than expected, my hopes of us spending time together as sisters somewhat dashed by the reality of Beatriz's life in Barcelona.

In a way, this week away from Thomas seems incredibly indulgent. To take time for myself, to focus on myself, to just be in this lovely little bohemian apartment Beatriz has created is without question a luxury, and I didn't realize how badly I needed it until now. I envy Beatriz the peace of having this place to herself, and where I once chose marriage over the fear of the unknown and a life alone, I can now see the benefit to living on your own terms in a way I never did before.

That evening Beatriz comes home with bottles of wine, and we sit on the couch, painting our nails like we did when we were girls in Havana, our bedrooms next door to each other. We used to sneak into each other's rooms long after we were supposed to be sleeping and stay up late, telling each other secrets, giggling under the covers until inevitably we fell asleep.

"So, this painting thing?" Beatriz asks as she applies a slick coat of red paint across her toenails. "Is this a new habit you picked up after you married?"

"No, I started a little before that. After we arrived in Palm Beach, after you moved out of the house, after the engagement."

"Why?"

"I felt—once you were gone, after our fight and the disaster at the Bay of Pigs—I felt like I needed something. I was drowning, the walls were closing in on me, and no one was around to throw me a line. I couldn't sleep, I couldn't stay in the house, and so I'd go out during the day and I'd walk around, and I found this little shop that sold art supplies. I'm not sure why I bought them—a whim, I suppose—but once I started painting, I couldn't stop."

"The painting—does it help you?" Beatriz asks.

"It does. At least, I think so. It gives me something to focus on when the world becomes too overwhelming."

"That's what work has been for me," Beatriz replies. "I know it's hard to understand why I would get involved with all of this, why I would risk my safety, but I was just so angry for so long and I needed somewhere to focus that anger. I suppose I wanted to honor Alejandro's memory in a way that might make him proud of me. He was always fighting for what he believed in, thought we all had an obligation to do better. I wanted to be like that."

"When you put it that way, I can understand," I confess. "I worry about you, but I can relate to that restlessness and the fear that your life has no purpose or meaning. It's hard to get through each day without passion in your life."

"Is that what the painting is? Is it something you do for fun or is it something more?"

"What do you mean, 'something more'?"

"You're good," Beatriz replies. "I may not be an artist, but I know beautiful things, and those pictures in the guest room are beautiful. You're talented. You should do something with it. Show people."

Beatriz isn't one to give false praise, but I'm surprised to hear that she likes my artwork and that she thinks my paintings are good.

"Like what, try to sell it to an art gallery?"

"Sure, why not?"

"I don't think I'm good enough to be an artist. It's not like I've had professional training or anything."

She rolls her eyes. "Stop right there and take 'good enough' out of your vocabulary. If you don't think you're amazing, no one else will. Your paintings are beautiful, and more than anything, they're a part of yourself that you can share with the world. The ones you did of Cuba—it's a way of remembering where we come from and all the things that have shaped us." She pauses. "Have you ever painted him? Alejandro?"

"No, I'm not good with people. I never get the essence of them right."

"I saw the painting of the two people dancing that you did. It seems like you got the essence of that one right."

I flush.

"I would love to have a painting to remember Alejandro by. I think about all the family photos that we couldn't take with us when we left Cuba, all those memories waiting for us back home. I worry I'm going to forget what he looked like."

Tears fill my eyes. "What was it like? I heard you went back."

"I was there for such a short time, but it was the same as I remembered, and wholly different. It hurt in a way, because it felt like as tightly as I've held on to this memory, Cuba has moved on. It was one of the things that made me realize that as hard as it is, I have to move forward, have to accept that there's a life for me that might not include going home."

There's a knock at the door.

I glance over at Beatriz in surprise.

Her hand has stilled in midair, the nail polish brush dangling from her fingers. She slides the brush into the bottle, twisting the cap tight. She sets it down onto the coffee table and puts her finger to her lips, motioning for me to be quiet.

Another knock at the door, more insistent than the earlier one.

"Go into the bedroom," she whispers.

"What's going on?" I ask, careful to keep my voice low.

"I don't know. Just go into the bedroom."

"What are you going to do?"

"Take care of it." She strides over to her purse sitting on the dining room table and pulls out a small revolver.

"Are you going to shoot someone?!?"

"Not unless they try something first."

She hurries over to the door, her pistol still in hand, and peers through the peephole.

"It's Rosa," she whispers.

"Rosa? Cousin Rosa? What is she doing here? I thought they were traveling."

Rosa was a professor at the University of Havana for many years, but her husband's diplomatic work eventually brought them to Spain.

"It's complicated."

"Beatriz, what's going on—"

She opens the door and Rosa rushes in as though trouble is on her heels, and Beatriz closes the door quickly behind her, flipping the locks.

I can do little more than stare at both of them, feeling as though I am caught up in the middle of some drama that has already been unfolding for quite some time, Beatriz and Rosa clearly familiar with their roles whereas I have no idea what is going on.

"I need help," Rosa says, bypassing all pleasantries. If she's surprised to see me despite the years it's been since we last saw each other in Havana, she makes no indication, her focus entirely on Beatriz, fear in her eyes. "They've recalled him back to Cuba."

An hour later, we sit in the living room of Beatriz's apartment, waiting for Diego to arrive. I was hesitant to involve someone who isn't family in what is obviously a delicate matter, but Beatriz insisted, and between the two of us I am so clearly out of my depth that I was in no position to argue with her.

The story comes out in pieces, and it is evident that neither one of them wishes to share too much, and the more I listen to their plans, I don't think I want to know more than I absolutely must. The Cuban government has unexpectedly recalled Rosa's husband from his diplomatic posting in Spain to Havana, sparking all sorts of concerns that he has angered Fidel.

"That's who you were meeting at Camila's in Marbella, isn't it?" I ask, realization dawning.

"Yes. They want to defect," Beatriz whispers to me when Rosa excuses herself to go to the restroom. "They know I work at the consulate, that I have ties with the Americans, a handler at the CIA, and they asked me for help when I saw them a few weeks ago, when I found the picture of our mother at their apartment. They have information, are privy to things through their diplomatic position that they can pass on to the Americans, and they're afraid Fidel will try to keep them from defecting. So I told them I'd help connect them with the Americans. But they're under scrutiny and it's a dangerous situation. Now that Fidel has recalled—"

There's another knock at the door, this one quieter than the first.

"Beatriz!" I hiss.

"Don't worry. I'm sure it's just Diego."

Rosa walks out of the bathroom, her eyes wide as her gaze darts from us to the front door.

"And if it isn't Diego?" I ask.

"Go into the spare bedroom," Beatriz orders Rosa. "Don't come out until I tell you it's safe."

Rosa doesn't hesitate, and I'm struck by the trust she places in Beatriz and the realization that my sister has likely been in these sorts of situations before.

"You, too," Beatriz whispers, picking up the gun she had earlier from its resting place on her end table.

I don't move.

"Isabel."

"I'm not leaving you out here—if it isn't Diego—maybe I can help."

Beatriz curses.

"It's Diego," a voice calls out from the other side of the door. "Let me in already."

Relief fills me.

He sweeps into the apartment with the same sense of urgency as Rosa, barely sparing a glance for me.

"We need to talk," he tells Beatriz, his voice low. "Someone has been following you, trying to, at least. They were behind us when I took Isabel to Marbella, and I thought they might be there because of me, but it turns out they're tailing you."

"I know." She looks at me and back at Diego. "Let's go talk in my bedroom," she urges him.

"I'll go," I volunteer. "I'll keep Rosa company. You two stay out here and talk. I don't think I want to know what you're planning anyway. You keep putting yourself in danger, Beatriz, and one of these days it's going to get you killed."

"You don't understand. I have to do this."

"Do you? That just seems like something you tell yourself to excuse the fact that you do it because you like it."

I don't bother waiting for her response.

I sit with Rosa while Diego and Beatriz argue in the living room, their conversation mostly unintelligible except for the fact that sometimes I can hear Diego's voice over Beatriz's, whatever they're discussing clearly sparking his ire.

"I shouldn't have brought you both into this," Rosa says from her place next to me on the bed in Beatriz's guest room. "It's too dangerous. If your mother knew I put her girls in jeopardy . . ."

I reach out and squeeze her hand, her fingers icy to the touch. In all the times I've seen her in my life, I've never seen her as scared as she is in this moment, or as out of sorts as she seems. Her fear for her husband, for herself, is clear.

"You did what you had to so you could protect your family. I think she would understand that better than anyone."

Rosa hugs me. "Thank you. If Fidel knows we're trying to defect, if we have to go back to Cuba, I couldn't—"

The door opens, and Beatriz walks into the bedroom, her gaze darting to Rosa first before settling on me.

"I need to talk to you. I need a favor."

Diego strides in behind her. "You don't need to do this, Isabel."

"What could you possibly need from me?" I ask Beatriz.

"I am being followed by a group of Cubans. They work for Fidel's intelligence service."

"You said you weren't involved with Cuba anymore, Beatriz."

"I'm not. This is different. This is personal. They're not following me because of my activities. They're following me because of Rosa and her husband. Because they want to defect." Beatriz takes a deep breath. "I need you to pretend to be me."

"Pardon me?"

"This is too much, Beatriz," Rosa protests.

A curse falls from Diego's lips.

"I need you to go out with Diego," Beatriz says, her gaze on me. "I need them to follow the two of you so I can get Rosa and her husband to the Americans. I need you to help draw their attention away from me."

"It's a terrible idea," Diego snaps. "It's dangerous and Isabel hasn't the training or experience."

"It is a terrible idea," I agree. "I'm sorry. I want to help, but I don't see how this can possibly work. We look similar, but is that really enough to fool them?"

"You look like me, from the right angle, from the right distance."

"I'm two inches taller."

"They aren't going to pull out a measuring stick. Besides, Diego is taller than both of us, so it's not like they'll notice. You could put on one of my outfits, wear the famous sandals you're so upset that I borrowed. If they see you leaving my apartment, if they see you with Diego, if they see what they think is me, it might be enough to distract them, to trick them into following you so that I can get Rosa and her husband to safety. They want to come to the United States, want to be with the rest of the family. We have to help them."

I glance at Rosa. Her face is pale as she watches both of us, and in her eyes, I see the fear that is all too familiar, the worry that you may lose someone you love because of this danger that seems to forever hang over our heads. I know what Rosa and her husband will face if they return to Cuba and are branded traitors by Fidel.

"Look, I know you want no part of this," Beatriz says. "I know you don't agree with what I do. But I can't not help them. Fidel is throwing people in prison. He's executing them—"

"I know what Fidel is capable of."

"Help me," Beatriz says. "They're family. Help me save their lives."

chapter seventeen

The second I step outside of Beatriz's apartment dressed in a cocktail dress of hers that's the color of eggplant, I'm convinced our ruse is going to be discovered. Diego tenses beside me, his jaw clenched as his gaze sweeps across the crowded street.

"I'm sorry she put you in this position. This isn't your fight," I say.

"It's fine. This comes with the territory for me. She shouldn't have put *you* in this position."

"I'm all right," I reply, even though I'm not, not even a little bit.

Growing up, my mother and Rosa were inseparable, and I think that as much as she always cautioned us to avoid danger at all costs, my mother's loyalty to her family would dictate and she would want us to do what we could to help Rosa and her husband as so many others have helped us in exile, a community of Cubans joining together.

If I am going to risk my life, at least I am doing it for the people I love.

"Just promise me, if there's any sign of trouble, you'll run away," Diego says.

"And what, leave you behind?"

"If that's what it takes—yes. It's not worth you getting hurt."

We walk down the street together, our movements slow, as though we're two friends out for an evening stroll. I'm careful to keep my head ducked lest anyone get a clear look at my face and realize I'm not Beatriz.

"Do you think they're following us?" I ask.

"Let's hope so," Diego replies, his voice grim.

We walk to a nearby restaurant for dinner, choosing our table carefully so that my back is to the street, Diego with a clear view of anyone passing by.

We've just ordered drinks when he says in a low voice, "They're here."

This time, I fight the instinct to look, my gaze carefully trained on the menu. I don't realize I'm trembling until Diego takes my hand, linking our fingers, squeezing.

It's so unexpected, so jarring, that I forget all about the men following us.

"Take a deep breath," he urges. "It'll help. Trust me."

Our hands remain linked as I take a deep breath, and another, and another.

"Better?" he asks.

"I am, actually. Thank you."

"I'm not going to let anything happen to you. I promise."

"Is that why you were so angry at Beatriz when she suggested this earlier? Because you didn't want to be responsible for me?"

"I'm angry at Beatriz because it's clear that this isn't something you want to do, but at the same time, you'll do anything for your family. I worry that she's taking advantage of that. And yes—I'm afraid she's putting you in a dangerous situation."

"It's fine. She's right—it's the right thing to do."

"I just don't want you pushed into something you're not comfortable with."

It's on the tip of my tongue to ask him why he cares when the waiter returns and takes our food order. Once he's gone and we're alone again, I ask Diego—

"Are they still there?"

"Yes."

"At least I hope Beatriz was able to get Rosa and her husband out safely."

We linger over dinner as we promised Beatriz we would, Diego sharing stories of his childhood in New York. He seems reluctant to talk about himself, but the longer we sit here, the more he opens up, and somehow, impossibly, I almost find myself forgetting why we're here and that we aren't two friends out to dinner.

When we're finished eating, Diego pays the bill, and we get up from the table and begin walking back to Beatriz's apartment.

It's been almost two hours since we left, and Beatriz said it would only take an hour to get them to the Americans, our plan for the three of us to rendezvous back at her place.

A block away from her apartment, Diego puts his arm around me, moving me out of the way of two men walking toward us.

I stumble, tripping over an uneven patch of the sidewalk, and beside me Diego stiffens.

There's a popping noise, and Diego lurches beside me. People start screaming, and somewhere off in a distance, someone yells—

"They have a gun."

The two men take off in the opposite direction, leaving us alone.

"Come on," Diego hisses, pulling me along as we slip through the chaos of the crowd.

It isn't until we're climbing up the steps of Beatriz's apartment building that I realize Diego has been shot.

I pound on the door and Beatriz opens it immediately. We run through the open doorway and Diego stumbles to the couch.

"What happened?" Beatriz asks, closing the door behind us.

"I was shot in the arm," he replies. "The Cubans were following us like we planned. They thought Isabel was you. I think we can safely assume they didn't want you getting to Rosa and her husband. One of them pulled a gun. I pushed Isabel out of the way—"

He winces.

"I'll get help," Beatriz says. "I'm sorry, I— Isabel can look after you until I get back."

"Beatriz," I interject. "Someone shot at us because they thought I was you. Someone tried to kill you. You can't go out there."

"I'll be fine. Right now, the Cuban agents are probably planning to leave the country. They can't afford a diplomatic incident. Our work is done in secret for a reason." She grabs a dark trench coat from her closet and slips it on, tying the belt tightly at the waist. She shoves the revolver into her front pocket. "Keep him calm and alert. Diego will be safe here. Just try to make him comfortable. Don't let him lose too much blood, and I'll come back with a doctor and one of Diego's friends to help."

"Why do you have to leave the apartment? Especially this late at night. Why can't you call someone?"

"You never know who is listening on the phone line, and this is one call I don't want anyone else to hear. I'll be back soon."

"Wait—Beatriz—did it work at least? Were you able to get Rosa and her husband out safely?"

Beatriz nods. "They're with the Americans now. They'll be on a plane to the United States soon."

I t's been an hour. Beatriz hasn't returned.

She never specified where she was going or how long she'd be gone, but it's been sixty minutes since she left Diego in my hands, and I'm becoming increasingly concerned that he needs real medical attention other than the blanket I've used to cover his body and the glass of water I've offered him, which he has thrice declined.

For a spy, Beatriz keeps a surprising lack of medical supplies on hand, and besides watching Diego apply pressure to the wound with one of the hand towels I scrounged up in Beatriz's bathroom, I've done little in terms of medical care, my nerves growing more and more with each moment help doesn't come.

Is Diego paler than he was when we first arrived? He seems like it. There's a faint sheen of sweat on his brow, too.

Worry fills me.

"Would you like some water?" I ask.

"Please don't offer me any more water. Does Beatriz have some brandy? Something strong, perhaps?"

"I'm not sure alcohol is the best thing for you right now. What if it makes you pass out?"

"Believe me, in my current position, I think I'd welcome the loss of consciousness."

"I'll see what she has," I reply against my better judgment, heading toward the bar cart in Beatriz's dining area.

I find a bottle of scotch and pour him a drink. He takes it from me without a word, downing the contents quickly before handing me the empty glass.

"I'm not getting you more. Not yet."

"So stern, Isabel." He grimaces before closing his eyes and collapsing back on the couch.

I can't take it anymore—the suspense of where Beatriz is and if she's been able to find help, the sense of helplessness, my worry that something will happen to him—so I walk back into Beatriz's bathroom and recheck her supplies.

Still nothing.

A groan emanates from the living room, and I abandon my fruitless search in the bathroom, grabbing the only thing I can think of—a washcloth, which I dampen—and walk back to check on Diego.

"How do you feel?" I ask him.

"Like I've been shot."

"I really wish you would let me call a doctor. We don't know how long Beatriz will be, and I'm sorry, but I'm not equipped to handle something like this. I can't even tell how bad it is. A gunshot wound is no small thing. You could die."

"Are you really apologizing for not knowing how to treat a gunshot wound? You don't have to rescue everyone, Isabel. I hardly expect it, nor should anyone else. It's enough that you're here with me, although I'm sorry to have put you in this position."

An unladylike oath falls from my lips in Spanish, and where I'm used to speaking in my native tongue and Thomas having no clue what I'm saying, Diego's eyes widen slightly, a pained smile crossing his lips.

I reach out and press my hand to his brow.

"You're warm."

Feverishly warm.

I wipe the dampened cloth against his face, dabbing at the sweat pooled on his forehead, glancing at the clock once more.

"I'm sorry," he says.

"Are you apologizing for being shot now?"

A faint smile crosses his lips, and he flinches. "Not for being shot, no. That part was entirely outside of my control. For making you deal with me being shot, I suppose. For you being there. This was what I feared. If they had shot you—"

"It's fine," I say, even though it absolutely is not. "I'm sorry Beatriz dragged you into this in the first place."

"It's not fine," he says, that hint of a smile making another appearance. "You don't have to lie. You're pretty terrible at it. And you shouldn't apologize for your sister. I knew what I was getting myself into."

"Just promise me you won't die. I have no idea how to dispose of a dead body, and I have no desire to learn now."

"Wouldn't think of it. I'd hate to be your first dead body."

"You wouldn't be my first," I reply, absentmindedly, my stomach clenching at the memory all those years back in Havana.

Diego's eyes widen slightly, but he doesn't press me on the matter.

I glance back at the clock, frustration filling me.

"Have you ever been shot before?" I ask, struggling to keep my voice casual.

"Are you asking to see my scars?"

"No. I'm wondering if it's necessary for the bullet to come out, and if so, if I'm going to be the one forced to do it if the doctor takes any longer to get here. There are some utensils in the kitchen; perhaps if I could heat them that would sanitize things and—"

He laughs, the sound coming out raspy.

"Please don't. I think if it comes to that, I'd rather take my chance with the bullet. My friend will be here soon. He wouldn't leave me like this."

"You trust your friends that much?"

"I have to trust them to be willing to fight alongside them. After all, without trust what are we doing here? They could turn me in for my work to overthrow Franco and his regime. Many in Spain would have. So, they've earned my trust for not doing so." His gaze meets mine. "Who do you trust, Isabel?"

"My sisters. Myself some days. Not as much as I'd like."

His eyes flutter closed.

"No. You can't fall asleep. That much I do know."

"That's for concussions. Gunshots are a whole other beast."

"*Have* you been shot before?"

"No, this is my first time. I wouldn't recommend it."

"You're getting drunk," I say, realizing he's beginning to slur his words.

"Not drunk enough. Trust me. Will you sit with me?" he asks. "Please. I promise I'm not trying to seduce you—I just don't want to be alone right now."

"I don't think you'd have much success trying to seduce me in your condition," I tease, trying to keep things light between us, trying to distract him from the pain.

"You'd be surprised," he wheezes.

I take a seat beside him on the couch. I don't realize I'm fidgeting until he reaches out and places his hands over mine.

"You're scared."

"I'm scared. All the time," I add belatedly.

"Of what?"

I laugh. "I think an easier question would be to ask what I'm not scared of. That list is shorter."

"What aren't you scared of?"

"Spiders. Snakes. Alligators. Singing in public."

"That's a good list. Singing in public absolutely terrifies me. Beatriz does it often, and she's awful at it."

My lips twitch. "She is. You're humoring me."

"Not at all. I can't think of much that's braver than boarding a plane by yourself and crossing an ocean to save your sister. You didn't know what you were getting yourself into or what danger lay ahead, but you did it. Where I come from, that's pretty brave."

"I was terrified the whole time. Even the littlest thing—traveling by myself, without my husband—scared me."

"It's the bravest thing of all to do things when you are scared."

"I used to be fearless. I think we all did. Life was easier. I envy that girl, the one who worried about such trivial things."

"What are you afraid of now?" he asks me.

"Something happening to my family. To my parents, my sisters. Never seeing Cuba again. I'm afraid that I'll always feel this way."

"What way?"

"Like I'm going through the motions of my life, a shadow of my former self. That the girl who danced at parties in Havana died there, too. I miss her every day. I keep waiting for her to reappear like an old friend who has been gone for a long time and I may never see her again."

"I think you will. I think I would have liked to meet that girl. I probably would have asked her to dance after I'd worked up the courage myself. As much as I would have liked to meet that girl, though, I'm glad I got to meet this Isabel, too." He grins. "The one who was ready to stab me with her beauty scissors in the car, who will risk everything to find her sister. I know you miss who you were in Havana, and I've no doubt she was utterly spectacular, but this version of you is, too."

"How did you know about the beauty scissors?"

"Don't you realize by now? I've been paying attention."

"You're kind."

His cheeks redden slightly.

"I missed that in the beginning. I thought Beatriz was friends with you because you're an adventurer like she is, but you're a good man. I'm glad Beatriz has found friends like you in Barcelona."

I take a sip of my drink, and I can't help but take pity on him because he looks embarrassed by the whole conversation.

"What are you afraid of?" I ask him.

He gazes up at the ceiling as though he is considering my question. "Flying in an airplane. Speaking in front of a crowd. Telling a woman I love her not knowing if she loves me back. Large dogs with loud barks. A fascinating woman telling me I'm kind."

He looks back at me, a smile on his lips.

"Are we friends now, Isabel? We've shared our fears. It almost seems like we are."

"I don't make new friends easily," I reply, flustered by the strange direction this night has taken.

"That doesn't surprise me."

He says it so quickly, I reel back, and his expression changes.

"No. I'm sorry. I didn't mean that like it sounded. Only that you seem like you're careful about who you let into your life."

"I am. I—I don't trust people easily."

"Do you trust me now?" he asks.

"I do. I didn't thank you earlier for saving me. I didn't even see the gunman, didn't realize what was happening."

"I told you I wasn't going to let anything happen to you. Besides, you helped get me back to Beatriz's apartment. Sitting with me now, distracting me—"

"It's the least I can do considering you took a bullet for me. It's the least I can do after all you did to help me and Beatriz. I just don't want anything to happen to you."

"It'll be fine," he whispers. "I promise. I'm not going to die and leave you to deal with this mess."

"It's not that—I don't want you to die under any circumstances—I just hate being so helpless. I'm sorry. I'm tired, and I'm nervous, and I'm cross, but you shouldn't bear the brunt of it, especially when you're injured."

"Please stop apologizing to me, Isabel. I like you better when you're being yourself, not who you seem to think I want you to be." His smile deepens. "The other night, for instance. It was nice to see you let go, to see you enjoy yourself."

"I probably let go a little too much. I can't remember the last time I danced like that."

"You were extraordinary. Most beautiful thing I've ever seen."

Our gazes meet, and—

The sound of a key turning in the lock makes me jump. We both turn as Beatriz swings the door open, a stranger at her side. They close the door quickly behind them.

"How is he?" the stranger asks me.

"In pain, but otherwise fine," Diego answers.

"He has a fever," I interject as I move out of the way to let the man examine him.

"Are you all right?" Beatriz asks, pulling me aside.

I nod. "How about you?"

"I'm fine."

"Can you walk?" the man asks Diego.

"I can."

"Let's go. There's a doctor waiting for you at my house."

The man puts his arm around Diego, helping to support his body weight.

Diego gives me a little salute with his uninjured arm on the way out. "Thank you for rescuing me, Isabel."

chapter eighteen

Two days after Diego was shot, I'm putting the last touches on a new painting when there's a knock at the front door of Beatriz's apartment. Ever since Beatriz said she would like a painting of our brother, Alejandro, I've been playing more with capturing images of people in my life. I haven't yet tried to paint Alejandro from memory, am not quite ready for such a reckoning, but with each attempt—Beatriz smoking near the open window in her apartment, Maria on the beach, Elisa playing with her son, Miguel, at their home—my confidence grows.

When I open the front door to Beatriz's apartment, the suggestion on my lips that perhaps she should hide a key somewhere she's likely to find it, it isn't Beatriz standing on the doorstep, but instead Diego stares back at me, his hat in hand, his color returned since I last saw him when he was pale and bleeding all over Beatriz's velvet couch.

I've wondered about Diego, worried about him, since he left Beatriz's apartment. My sister and I have been like two ships passing in the night, but she's kept me updated on his health, letting me know that he has recovered from the shot.

"How are you?" I ask.

He doesn't answer me right away, his gaze raking me from head to toe.

"Better. I— You look—" He shakes his head, his gaze dropping to the floor before returning to me once more. "Can I come in?"

"Sure." I take a step back as he enters the room. "I'm sorry. Beatriz isn't here. I don't know when she'll be back, but I'll certainly tell her you stopped by."

"I didn't come here to see Beatriz. I came to thank you." He flashes me a rueful grin. "I don't know that I would have gotten through it without you."

"I didn't do anything extraordinary; I just did what anyone would do."

"You were kind. That's not such a small thing. Brave, too. You didn't ask to get involved with this mess, but that didn't stop you from taking care of me, from helping out."

"You look better than I expected. I asked Beatriz and she said that she had heard you were recovering nicely, but I will admit I have no idea what that means as it relates to a gunshot wound to the arm."

"They got the bullet out, stitched me up. You can barely notice it."

"Are you in pain?"

"Only a little. They gave me some medication to help."

"I'm glad you're better."

"How much longer will you be in Barcelona?" Diego asks me. "I confess when I came here, I worried you'd be gone already and I wouldn't have a chance to thank you properly."

"I'm here for a few more days."

"And how have you found the city? Have you been able to see many of the sights?"

"I haven't seen much of it. I've spent most of my time in Beatriz's apartment. I went out one day by myself, but I just sat at the café downstairs for a little while and people watched."

"Let me show you around. Just for a few hours. You can't come all the way to Barcelona and not get a taste of the city."

"That's very kind of you to offer, but no. I couldn't. I'm sure Beatriz will be back soon and she can show me the city. Besides, shouldn't you be resting? A gunshot wound is no small thing."

He waves me off. "I'm hardly going to go on a miles-long trek uphill, and besides, it was a graze, really. And the injury is in my arm. I've rested more than I care to. You and I both know Beatriz could be hours before she's back. She's not one for schedules and plans. I owe you considering how much you helped me after I was shot."

"I did very little. And you already brought me the art supplies, which truthfully have kept me happily occupied since I arrived here. Not to mention the help you gave me when I first arrived. I was so worried about Beatriz, and I don't know what I would have done if I'd faced her absence alone."

"You would have been fine. You didn't need me at all. When I was injured you were magnificent, Isabel. You kept me distracted. Better to be in conversation with you than dwelling on a bullet in my body. Come to think of it, you're right—I did bring you the art supplies, and I drove you to Marbella. So really you owe me, and I can't think of anything I'd rather do than spend a day in Barcelona with you."

In the end, I can't say why I agree to go with him. Maybe it's my curiosity about Barcelona and the fact that I'm leaving so soon and will likely never get a chance to see the city again. Or maybe, if I'm being honest with myself, it's because I enjoy his company.

Whatever the reason, I agree to accompany Diego on a short tour of the city.

"Well, you have me now, so where are you taking me?" I ask after we both get into his car.

"I thought I would show you art Barcelona style."

The whole city is a living piece of art, from the architecture on the buildings to the energy on the streets. I never considered myself one for travel, always thought I would be happiest putting down roots, but the more I see of the world, the more I meet people, the more I am curious about what else is out there. In Cuba, our life was limited to the social circle our parents allowed us, to the friends who were the children of their friends, families with equally prestigious last names. We all rebelled in our different ways, but I am struck by how insular it all was, how so much of my life has been shaped by others' expectations for me rather than my own passions and desires.

For a while we drive around, and Diego points out the sights to me, throwing out different pieces of history about each locale.

"It's a shame you aren't here for longer," he shouts over the sound of the wind coming through the convertible's open top. "There's so much to see."

Diego parks the car, turning off the engine and coming around the side to open the door for me. We walk side by side until he stops abruptly in front of what looks to be a church.

"What is that?" I stare at the enormous edifice, the towering spires, the bright colors, the whimsical style unlike anything I have ever seen in my life.

"That is Gaudí. It's called La Sagrada Família."

The Holy Family.

"His work is all over the city, but this has always been my favorite of his. As an artist, I thought you might enjoy it."

"I am hardly an artist."

"If you create something, you are an artist. You act as though you are embarrassed of your accomplishments, as though you don't want people to know the real you. Why hide who you really are rather than sharing it with the rest of the world?"

It's a very personal statement to make considering how little we know each other, but it still lands somewhere that makes me a tad uncomfortable, because he is right: I have yet to learn to live boldly. Some of the difficulty stems from the role I always played in our family as the peacemaker, some of it is probably my personality, but mostly it is the fact that I am afraid.

"Tell me about the church," I say, my voice shaky.

Diego takes a step closer to me, his hands in his suit pockets, his eyes on the church in front of us.

"Gaudí believed this church would inspire people to follow the faith."

"That's a lofty goal for an artist."

"You don't think art can change the world?"

"It seems an audacious thing to imagine it could."

"I have to disagree with you there. I do not paint or write poetry, but I cannot deny that I am moved by it, that in the stories of others I find myself looking at the world differently, that it inspires me to want to fight for what I believe in, to want to fight for my country."

He says the last part quietly, but I can't help but think that these whispers aren't out of reverence for the church, but because he is a man living in a dangerous political situation, who is tempting fate through his activities.

"George Orwell wrote *1984* after his experiences in Spain during the war," Diego says. "He saw the dangers of a government creating their own reality, shaping and distorting truth to fit their narratives. What is that if not art changing the world? What is the point of living if you don't fight for what you believe in? If you don't take risks, if you don't have things in your life that you love to the point of dying for them?"

We're speaking in whispers now, our heads bent toward each other, and I shift my body toward his, our gazes locking.

"For me, the cost is always too high; there is too much to lose," I reply. "I love my family. I would do anything to keep them safe, especially considering how close we came to ruin.

"When we first arrived in the United States, we were all in mourning. We were more fortunate than most that my father had some money outside of the country, but we'd just lost Alejandro, and our lives had been upended.

"I left my fiancé back in Cuba. His family didn't want to leave so soon—thought things would improve. But more time passed, and Fidel strengthened his hold over Cuba, and the Americans we thought might help, well, we all saw how that turned out.

"Thomas knew people. He was as connected as my family could hope for given how everyone looked down their noses at us because we were Cuban, because we were different, because nearly all of our money and power was gone, and even though my parents never would have considered someone like him in Cuba, it was the best hope for us to gain a foothold in this new country that was to be our home. Beatriz's affections were elsewhere, and Elisa was married, Maria too young, and Thomas had remarked on how pretty my eyes were."

"You do have beautiful eyes," Diego says, his expression solemn.

"Don't—please. Don't think that I am asking you to feel sorry for me, or that I somehow regret the choices I've made. I walked down the aisle with my eyes open and I chose Thomas. I don't regret that. I did the best thing, the right thing for my family. I suppose that's what I am the proudest of. You said that you feel defined by the things you love, by the things you would risk your life for. My family is that for me. I am proud of what I have done for them."

"But what about you? Are you to martyr yourself for your family's happiness?"

"That's the same argument Beatriz and I have been having for years, but what Beatriz fails to understand, perhaps because she doesn't want to, is that she enjoys the freedom she has because one of us had to do what was best for everyone else. It just so happened that was me."

"You're wrong, you know—I don't feel sorry for you. I was just thinking that you are incredibly brave, that to put your family first as you have, you must be deeply loyal. But I already saw that in you from the beginning. You don't give yourself nearly enough credit. Beatriz told me you're the one who keeps the family together, and that's hardly surprising considering you got on a plane simply because you were worried about your sister."

"I'm the eldest. It's my job."

"I don't think it's that. It's who you are, Isabel. It's a beautiful thing."

"My family is all I have," I reply. "How could I not care for them?"

"I think I envy you the big family. The bond you have. They're lucky to have someone like you in their lives."

"You don't have any siblings?"

"No. You are fortunate to have family so close, to have connections to other people, a place where you belong," he says.

"I am. Truthfully, though, for all that I love my family, it can be difficult, too. We were all expected to act a certain way, and share their beliefs, and never argue, never disagree, never develop our own view of the world and our roles in it. With my brother, Alejandro, he was supposed to inherit the family business, but he wanted no part of it, thought my family and others like it were what was wrong with Cuba. He became estranged from the family—from our parents, at least.

"I regret most, I think, that I didn't stand up for him when the estrangement happened, that I didn't do enough to tell him that I admired his courage and convictions. When he was a baby, I used to try to help take care of him. We all loved him so much. And I can't help but worry that in his final moments he felt abandoned by his family."

A tear slips down my cheek, and then another.

"I'm sorry," Diego replies. "It's hard when families are fractured by war, when friendships are divided. It is one thing when war happens far away, when you're fighting an unknown enemy, but there is something painfully personal when the fighting happens on the streets where you live, when you are driven from your home, when the person you are suddenly told to hate is someone you've known and loved your whole life. My mother struggled in exile in the States, missed the friends and family that remained behind in Spain, felt untethered as she was cut off from her homeland."

I wipe at the tears on my cheeks, more than a little embarrassed for him to have seen me lose composure in this manner. "Sorry to be so emotional in front of you. You didn't sign up for that when you agreed to give me a tour of Barcelona."

"Ah, but you nursed me back to health when I was shot, so I'd say we are more than even. In fact, I might owe you another outing. Would you like an ice cream?" he asks. "There's a vendor up ahead."

"That would be lovely, thank you."

"What would you like?"

"Strawberry if they have it, please."

We walk toward the vendor together, and when we reach the cart, Diego orders for both of us.

"My wife would like the strawberry," he says easily. "I'll have vanilla."

Surprise fills me, but I take the ice cream from him wordlessly. Only when we are alone once more, eating the ice cream, do I ask him—

"Why did you—"

"Call you my wife?" Diego finishes for me.

I nod.

"The ice cream vendor might have thought nothing of it, but sometimes it's better to be careful than to court trouble."

"I thought we agreed on cousins," I counter.

He grins. "I think we're past being able to say we're cousins. Not when I look at you the way I do."

We walk a little farther, our ice creams in hand, Diego pointing out various sights as we go. It's a lovely day, and despite my trepidation over agreeing to let him show me Barcelona, I enjoy myself thoroughly, so much so that when he asks me if I would like to go to the beach the next day, I can't help but say, yes.

chapter nineteen

Beatriz doesn't respond at first when I tell her Diego and I are going to the beach, and when I ask her if she'd like to join us, she only smiles and says she has other plans, a knowing look on her face.

"It's not like that," I protest.

"Of course it isn't. Still, if I did come, I would only be in the way; three's a crowd and all that."

"We're friends. That's all."

"Sure."

"Fine. I'm not going. If you're going to make this into something it's not, I'm not going. The last thing I need is for people to get the wrong idea, for Diego to get the wrong idea. If you think it's inappropriate for me—"

"Isabel, relax. I was only teasing. I'm glad you're getting out, that you're having fun while you're here. The truth is, no one needs it more than you do. So, enjoy your day at the beach and think of me when I'm hunched over a typewriter going over meeting notes or something dreadfully boring."

"You could come, you know."

"Do you really want me to come?"

"He makes me nervous," I admit.

Her eyes narrow. "Has he done anything to make you uncomfortable? If he's been inappropriate . . ."

"No. It's nothing like that. He flirted a bit with me in the beginning, but that's all."

"Just in the beginning?"

"I told him it wasn't a good idea, that I wasn't looking to have"—my voice drops to a whisper—"an affair."

Beatriz grins. "Do you know that I have *never* seen you like this. I'm sorry, I just have to take a moment to savor it. Isabel Perez flustered over a man."

"Stop. It's not funny. When we're alone together, I feel . . ."

"What? Desire? Passion? Longing?"

"I'm not going. That's it."

"Oh, you're going. You're going, because if you don't, you will spend the rest of your life wondering what would have happened if you did."

"I'm married. Nothing is going to happen. I know you think I'm silly, but that's a line I'm never going to cross."

"I know it isn't. You forget I know you, Isabel. Maybe better than anyone. You can go to the beach with Diego, and you can stay faithful to your husband. I have no doubt both of those things will be possible."

"Why put myself in this position? Why play with fire?"

"Because you aren't letting yourself live. You haven't figured out what you want, haven't taken a chance to even figure out who you are. Look at how brave Alejandro was. And do you think Elisa has followed the mighty Perez rules or do you think she had an adventure or two somewhere along the way? I've certainly had more than my fair share of adventures. But you've not allowed yourself any of that. It's a day at the beach. Just go."

"That's it? That's your great advice—'just go'?"

She grins. "That's it. Be brave, Isabel. See where it takes you."

"Please come with me."

"Diego would kill me," she jokes before sashaying out of the room. "Wear the sundress I set out for you on the bed. And that red bathing suit," she calls over her shoulder before leaving me alone in the apartment, nerves filling me.

The dress Beatriz left me to borrow is the perfect sort of compromise, the white fabric dotted with bright red flowers. It's whimsical and fun, and exactly the sort of dress Beatriz would buy for herself. The bathing suit is the same color of red, a bolder shade than I'd normally gravitate toward, a daring design.

I dress quickly, finishing the ensemble with a straw hat with a matching red ribbon and shoes from my sister's closet just as there's a knock at the door, no time to check my reflection in the mirror or to change my mind and put something else on.

When I open the door to Beatriz's apartment, Diego stands in the hall dressed in an elegant beige linen suit.

He whistles. "That's some dress."

"It's Beatriz's."

"You can tell Beatriz I wholeheartedly approve of her taste in clothes." He grins. "At least when you're wearing them."

"I thought we weren't flirting."

"Sorry, I didn't mean it that way, merely as a statement of fact. You look stunning."

"You're still flirting."

"Let's try this again. Good morning, Isabel, it's a beautiful day outside. Are you ready for the beach?"

I bite back a smile. "I am."

I follow him out of the apartment, into his speedy convertible, and we're off, music playing from his radio, the top down on the car.

We slip into a companionable silence as we drive, and I occupy myself with gazing out the window, taking in the sights of Barcelona, until the scenery changes and we reach the beach.

It's a beautiful day, the April sun shining bright and strong. I stroll to the water's edge, Diego trailing behind me silently as I kick off my sandals, feeling the sand beneath my toes.

We walk for a little while, and Diego points to a spot near a cluster of rocks. We stop and he lays out a big blanket. Diego places the food basket on the ground and shrugs out of his jacket, setting it on the sand.

I sit down while he rummages through the contents of the basket, producing a bottle of wine, two glasses, and containers filled with meat, cheese, bread, and olives. He tells me more about his childhood in New York while we eat.

"So, you were somewhat of a troublemaker," I tease.

He grins. "Total hellion. But my mother always saw the good in me, no matter how many rosaries she probably prayed for my immortal soul."

"She must have loved you very much."

"She did."

Once we're both finished eating, we strip down to the bathing costumes we wore and wade into the sea, laughing and splashing around until we return to the beach and lie back on a pair of loungers set apart from the rest of the beachgoers.

I look up at the sky, studying the clouds there.

"How old are you?" I ask, casting a sidelong glance at him. In this friendship we have developed, we have skipped around, missed some things about each other.

"Twenty-seven."

I lean up on my elbows. "I'm older than you."

"I figured you were. Beatriz and I are nearly the same age, and you mentioned that you're the eldest of the Perez siblings. Well, how much older are you?" he asks, his tone teasing.

"Two years."

"An older woman."

I give him a little shove in return, but as my hands connect with his uninjured shoulder, he reaches over, taking one of my hands in his, and holds it there in place for a beat, two, before tugging it toward him so that our clasped hands rest together over his heart, his bare skin warm beneath my fingers.

A preternatural stillness fills me, the sensation that if I move a muscle this moment between us will be shattered, and so my body is frozen there on the blanket, with the sun beating down on me, the sound of the ocean waves crashing around us barely registering over the roaring white noise in my ears.

It is such a small intimacy—the heat of his palm against mine, the rumble of his heart—and yet I am bared before him, as if we have taken an undeniable step forward together when all logic suggests we would have been better served to take a leap apart.

What now? I want to scream at Beatriz's voice in my head. I came, and it was just supposed to be a day at the beach, nothing more, *just go*, she said, and what am I supposed to do with these emotions twisted up inside of me, this feeling that is so big and so bold winding its way through me?

I can't look at him, can't look anywhere but up at the sky, at the clouds.

I can't take it anymore, and I wrench my gaze from the sky, turning my head so that I can just make out his profile, his eyes closed as though in prayer, his chest rising and falling softly, our hands linked together.

"I should go soon," I say.

Diego's eyes open with a soft fluttering of lashes, but he doesn't face me—rather, he looks skyward—and I think that if I were a braver woman, if I weren't so tightly wound, if I let the desire unspool inside of me as I wish it could, I would reach out and press a kiss to his brow, would slide my fingers over the planes and hollows of his face, would stroke his soft, full lips.

Desire is a sharp, piercing sensation inside of me, and in my imagination, in the dreams that will surely come from this encounter, I can see myself doing all those things.

But of course, here on earth, in reality, I do none of them, and when I tug my hand from his grasp, he lets me go, and as I return it to the blanket, to myself, the sunlight glints across my gold wedding band, and a wave of shame engulfs me.

"I should go," I say again, and that beautiful mouth of his quirks into a pained half smile.

He sits, propping himself up so he is on his elbow, mimicking the position I was in earlier, and he turns his body so his gaze runs over me, and despite the warm air around us, a tremor runs through my body like a string being plucked on a bow, the vibration settling in my bones in its aftermath.

"We should go," he agrees.

"If I were weaker, I would find myself in trouble with you," I say, the words little more than a whisper. Tears of frustration fill my eyes, pricking me. "I'm sorry."

"There's nothing to be sorry for."

We don't say anything as we walk back to the car, but as he opens the door for me, before I slide into the passenger seat of his convertible, I can't resist answering the question he asked me when we danced at the party at the consulate, even if the words come out as a whisper, only audible because he is standing right behind me, a breath away—

"Yes. If I wasn't married, you'd have a chance."

chapter twenty

The apartment is empty when we return, Beatriz still out for the day, the lights off, slivers of sunlight coming in through the drapes as the golden hour descends on Barcelona.

"Thank you for taking me to the beach today."

"The pleasure was all mine."

"Would you like to come inside? Beatriz should be home later."

"I would like that. I would also like to see these famous paintings I've heard so much about."

"I don't think so."

"Why? If you make something beautiful, if you put a piece of yourself into it, why wouldn't you share it with the world?"

"I don't know. I suppose there's always the worry that if you show a part of yourself to the world, to the people you care about most, and they don't like it or understand it, or see it for what it is, then it's like you're giving a part of yourself to someone only for them to discount it—and you—entirely."

"But how will they ever know you if you don't share the most important parts of yourself? How can they ever love you if they only love an idea of who you think they want you to be rather than who you are?"

"It's easier that way, I suppose. The idea of sharing my art with someone—it's like being naked in front of them."

"I would very much like to see your artwork, Isabel," he replies in such a deadpan manner that I can't help but laugh, which was no doubt his intent in the first place, the twinkle in his eye easing the nerves inside of me.

"Come." I lead him to Beatriz's guest bedroom where the paintings I've done since I arrived in Spain lie.

Diego follows behind me, and the apartment has gone so silent that I fear he can hear every hitch in my breath, the thudding of my heart.

I step aside and he walks up to the largest of the paintings, propped up on the vanity, the first one, the one I did after the night we went dancing, the colors bleeding together as the dance went on, the one I painted of the two of us.

He doesn't speak as he looks at it, and then he glances at me, and the expression on his face—

I turn away from him, unable to meet his gaze, a lump forming in my throat and something I'm afraid to name thrumming in my blood.

No one has ever looked at me like that. Not my fiancé in Cuba, not Thomas, not anyone. I fear no one else ever will.

The silence between us stretches on until a point where I can almost no longer bear it, and he moves, the sound of his footsteps on the carpet filling the room.

Diego stops, inches between us, my back to his chest, and it would be the easiest thing in the world to lean back into the curve of his body, but I don't; instead, I stay where I am, and when he sets his hand on my shoulder, his fingers touching the bare expanse of skin above the neckline of my dress, I shudder.

"Isabel."

When he turns me gently so I face him, I don't protest, and this time I force myself to meet his gaze.

"They're beautiful," he says. "They're passionate and honest. They're you."

It's the tenderness in his voice that undoes me.

"I can't do this."

"Isabel."

"He's not a bad man, Thomas. It would be easy to excuse my actions if he were. He married me knowing what he was getting—that I am not prone to deep emotions, that I do not share my feelings, that I was never looking for a grand love match—I'm getting greedy now, and I have only myself to blame."

"You're not greedy to want those things, to hope for more."

He takes my hand, and the instinct to pull away is there, the knowledge that this is a selfish, stupid, dangerous thing, a scream inside me bursting to get free.

But I don't pull away, do I?

Diego's hand is warm against mine, his palm smooth, the pads of his fingers skating across my skin.

"This is foolish," I whisper, even as I allow myself another moment of my hand in his, and—

"I'm afraid."

I say it quietly, because it is my most selfish, secretive confession. That while so many of my countrymen are struggling so profoundly, while I am much more fortunate than most—I am simply tired of fighting, of worrying, of waiting for everything to end. I am tired of the grief that has become a companion to me; I am tired of the sensation that I am always living on borrowed time, of hoping for more, of believing in the possibility of it only to have it taken away from me. Sometimes, I wonder if it is some defect in my character, some part of me that is lacking, that made me so unable to carry the things others do seemingly so effortlessly.

If Beatriz is passion and fire, I am surely made of meeker stuff.

"I'm not who you think I am. I think sometimes that you look at me and believe we are similar. That because we have been through similar struggles, because our families have known exile, we understand what it is to lose things we should not lose, for our existence to be threatened, that I am a fighter like you. That I dream of political change and revolution. But I'm not like that at all. I am not brave. I'm scared all the time. I'm not Beatriz trying to push my way through the world and make it conform to my standards. Most of the time I wish I could make myself so small that I could disappear."

"Isabel."

His breath is inches from my lips, and I know that if I leaned forward, my mouth would be on his, his breath becoming my breath, the flame nearly consuming me.

I move away from him. "I can't. I'm sorry. I—"

"I know. We can be friends." His smile twists into something self-mocking. "The very best of friends."

"We should not be friends or anything close to it. It's probably for the best that we'll likely never see each other again."

"No, we probably shouldn't. If only you had come to Spain earlier, or you had met your husband a few years later, if somehow we had met in another life . . ."

My life has been ruled by a series of "if only . . ."

"That sounds very romantic." My voice sounds faint. How can I rebut such a sentiment? Perhaps there are people who live in such a manner, who believe it is possible to fall in love in a flash, but I have never been such a person. What kind of people fall in love in a moment? Not me. If I have an impulsive bone in my body, I've yet to meet it.

I can't say when things changed, when Diego went from a handsome stranger to something more, when he snuck up on me and caught me by surprise, lodging some piece of himself inside of me. I can't say when this shifted from an idle curiosity to know more about him, his life, to a thrumming inside of me that won't be ignored. Maybe he had to sneak up on me; maybe if I had seen it from the first, I would have placed barriers between us, would have done everything in my power to stop this from happening. Maybe I was in denial all along.

"I thought you were beautiful that day we met," he says almost casually. "But that wasn't what I noticed most about you."

Don't go down this path . . . don't make this mistake . . . don't say things you can't take back . . . don't admit things you might regret . . .

"I admired you more than anything. Your courage, your loyalty, your convictions. You might not think you're brave, but I wish you could see yourself as I do. You're extraordinary."

Is this what it was like for Beatriz when she fell for Nicholas Preston? Did she have this same sense of longing while knowing that what she wanted, needed, would forever be just out of her reach?

I consider putting my arms around him and hugging him, but I can't ignore the warning bells in my mind that we've already come too far, things forever altered between us.

So instead, I let him go, closing the door behind him, locking it with a decisive click, and I sink down on the couch in Beatriz's living room, the one he bled on the night he was shot, my legs momentarily giving way beneath me. I am flashes of myself—New Year's Eve learning Batista fled the country; my brother's body lying on the gravel in front of our family home in Havana; walking through Rancho Boyeros Airport, my head held high as I lose myself to exile; standing in a church marrying a man I will never love. The most important events in my life have come down to timing. If I had been born in a different country, in another moment in history, if I lived on firm ground instead of a country ruled by ever-changing political whims, who would I have become?

It's easy to imagine what it would be like if things had been different, if I had been allowed to follow my heart. It's easy to imagine that if I had my choice, I might have chosen him.

The next day, I change my ticket and am on the first flight to Palm Beach.

chapter twenty-one

Alicia

1937

BARCELONA

I need help," I say once I am safely ensconced in Nestor's office at the clinic where he works, the door closed behind us.

When Consuelo told me of her fears that she was pregnant, I didn't know what to do, until Nestor's earlier promise to help if I ever needed it came back to me.

"What's wrong?" Nestor asks me.

"I need to tell you something, but if I trust you with this—my parents can't know. Not yet, anyway. I know how close you are to my father, how much you admire and respect him, and I don't want to jeopardize that or put you in an uncomfortable position—"

"Whatever you need, I'm here for you. I promise. You can trust me."

"Consuelo thinks she might be pregnant."

* * *

It's been thirty minutes since Consuelo went in to be examined, and with each passing minute, I become more worried. I wanted to go in with her, but Consuelo said she was fine on her own, but now as I wait for her, I question whether I should have insisted—

The door opens.

I already know the answer by the look in Nestor's eyes.

A nurse exits the room behind him, not meeting my gaze.

"She's pregnant, isn't she?" I ask him once the nurse has left us alone.

"Yes. I'm sorry. I know you're worried about her. As far as the pregnancy goes, she's in good health. I think she would like to see you." He takes my hand. "If there's anything I can do to help you, I promise I will. And I won't say anything to your parents, but you will probably want to tell them soon. She said she's been wearing looser dresses lately, but very soon she won't be able to hide it anymore."

I nod. "I didn't start showing until late in my pregnancy with Isabel. It sounds like Consuelo is the same."

"Do you know who the father is? I asked her, but she didn't tell me."

"No, but I'm going to find out," I vow.

Consuelo is sitting by herself on an examination table. Her cheeks are stained with tears.

"I'm pregnant," she whispers.

"I know."

"What am I going to do?"

"I'm going to be here beside you for this. You won't be alone. I promise."

"Thank you. I don't think I could do this by myself, Alicia."

"You won't have to. You can count on me for anything. How far along are you?"

In my worry for my sister, I forgot to ask Nestor.

"Five months."

Shock fills me. I never thought she would be that far along considering she's not showing yet, and for her to have gone this long—

I think back to the times she has been ill, to the times she has been quiet, and I chalked it up to her worries over the war, but now—

"Have you suspected for some time?"

"Yes. I hoped I wasn't, but with each month that passed, well—"

"I'm so sorry, Consuelo. I'm so sorry you've been alone with this. You must have been so scared and so worried."

She's not much younger than I was when I had Isabel, but still—she is alone, whereas I was a wife and had Emilio's support. I cannot imagine how frightened she must be.

Or how our parents will react.

"What did Nestor say about the baby? He told me you were in good health, but I know you haven't been feeling well lately."

"The baby is fine. He said I just had some normal sickness. I felt the baby kick the other day," she whispers, her hand drifting down to her stomach. "It was the strangest sensation. These little flutters, and I—it became real."

I know exactly what she means; I remember the first time I felt Isabel move inside me and how scared and excited I was as I realized I would never, ever be the same again.

"It's going to be fine," I say, even though I have no such certainty. "The most important thing is that you are healthy and that you stay calm. I'm here for you. I promise you; we'll figure this out together. You don't have to go through this alone. Who is the father?"

"He's a man I met. We fell in love."

Maybe there's a way to solve this so Consuelo can still find happiness. Maybe he's a good man, and he really loves her as she says he does. Maybe they can be married.

"How did you meet?" I ask gently.

"I was walking down the street on my way to music months ago, a day when you had to stay with Isabel because she was ill, and we bumped into each other. I dropped everything I was carrying, and he stopped to help me pick up my things. He was kind, handsome, and charming, and he asked if he could buy me a drink, and it just felt like I was never going to have a chance like that. A chance to meet someone that wasn't arranged by our parents especially now with the war going on. I snuck out when I could to meet him. Please don't be mad at me. I know it was wrong, but he told me he loved me, that there was nothing wrong if we loved each other. That we would be married when the war was over."

With each word falling from her lips, anger builds inside me, worry filling me, because his honor sounds questionable at best, considering she is a young girl he seduced.

"Does he know you're pregnant? Or that you suspected you were?"

"No, I haven't had a chance to tell him."

"How long has it been since you've spoken with each other?"

"I haven't heard from him since the end of January. We were supposed to see each other a few weeks later, and he never showed up."

"You said he told you that you would get married after the war—so he's a soldier?"

"He came here to fight with the International Brigades. He's a war hero. He's a good man."

I offer a prayer to the heavens that this is all some misunderstanding, that he is a good man, that he is somehow worthy of Consuelo despite all the evidence to the contrary accumulating before me.

"He's Cuban," she says. "Like us."

It's such a small thing when she says he's Cuban. There are plenty of Cuban men with the International Brigades, fewer in Barcelona, but still. It is not unheard of. And yet, there's a memory in the back of my mind.

When Rosa's husband came to Spain to fight with the International Brigades, he stopped by our parents' house to see me, to pass on some things Rosa asked him to bring me. I met him outside the house, having to cancel our original plan to eat together, because Isabel was sick.

I see it in my mind, see it all unfolding, handsome Gonzalo, swaggering Gonzalo, charming Gonzalo, Gonzalo who somehow managed to convince Rosa to marry him, exactly the sort of man who would sweep a romantic, sweet girl like Consuelo off her feet. Gonzalo who I disliked from the beginning; Gonzalo who died in Jarama in February.

I close my eyes. "What is his name?"

That night, after Consuelo has cried herself to sleep, I sit at the small desk in my bedroom, my own tears wet on my cheeks, and write the most difficult letter I've ever had to send.

chapter twenty-two

Two weeks have passed since Nestor confirmed Consuelo's pregnancy, and as he predicted, she's beginning to show, our ability to keep it secret from our parents waning with each day.

When Consuelo no longer feels well enough to attend her music lesson, I take Isabel on my own, and afterward we go to the café for a sweet and a treat. Isabel has grown so much since we first arrived in Spain, her transformation from baby to little girl startling me. Each time I look at her, it's like another change has occurred, as though if I blinked, I'd miss something important.

When I write Emilio letters now, I tell him about Isabel's growth, my guilt over all he is missing filling me with each day that passes. His letters in return are terse—expressing concerns over the situation in Spain, threatening to come to Barcelona himself. He writes of his desire for Isabel to return to Cuba, but he always refers to it as though it is a familial obligation that we are together rather than an emotional need to see his daughter and wife.

Nestor often stops by to say hello during our trips to the café.

He's become a favorite of Isabel's, bringing her little treats and carrying her on his shoulders throughout the neighborhood.

One day, Consuelo joins us for some fresh air and takes a picture of the three of us sitting at the café, and in the late evenings I find myself looking at the photograph, at our happy smiles, imagining what might have been if Nestor had reciprocated my feelings, if I had never married Emilio in the first place.

It is a fantasy, nothing more, and each time I feel myself drifting to the past, wishing things had turned out differently, it's Isabel that brings me back to the present and reminds me that had I never married Emilio, I never would have had my daughter.

I slip the photograph into a drawer just as I hear a shout followed by more yelling.

I rush downstairs.

Consuelo is crying in the sitting room, our parents pacing. She looks up as I enter the room.

"Alicia—please—you have to tell them—"

My mother whirls on me, fury in her voice. "How long have you known?"

I walk over to where Consuelo sits and put my arm around her. "Yes, I know. I went to the doctor with her."

My father's face turns impossibly redder. "The doctor? Who was it? Was it one of my colleagues? Was it Nestor?"

I don't respond.

"He was married," my mother snaps. "The father—she had an affair with a married man."

"She didn't know he was married. He deceived her. She's innocent in all of this. If there's blame to be had, it lies squarely with him," I argue.

"Do you think that matters, Alicia? Do you think she will have an easy time of it in this world as an unwed mother at her age? In this country, with a war going on? Your sister may be young and naïve, but you should know better. We are refugees. We came here from Cuba with nothing, were lucky we even found a home, had a chance to start over. How are we supposed to protect her? And if the Nationalists are victorious, if anyone ever finds out who the father of this baby is, that he was a soldier in the International Brigades? What happens then?"

"They want me to go to a convent in the country to have the baby," Consuelo interjects, her gaze pleading. "They want me to give the baby up for adoption, to let the Church find a family to raise it as their own." She grabs my arm. "They can't take my baby from me. Please."

Horror fills me. "How can you ask that of her?"

"What else is there to do?" my mother asks. "What would you do if it were Isabel in this predicament? Consuelo will be ruined. I can't allow that. She will have no future, no prospects, be ostracized for this mistake. The cost is too high."

"There may be another option. There's still time before she's due, for us to come up with a solution that doesn't involve Consuelo losing her child. I've written a letter to Gonzalo's family telling them about the baby. His brother Felipe is coming from Cuba. His ship should dock at the port of Bilbao in the next few days, and hopefully, he'll be in Barcelona soon.

"Don't do anything rash, please," I beg my parents. "Give us a chance to find a way to make this right."

"You are thinking with your heart, not your head," my mother replies. "One day when Isabel is grown, you will be forced to make difficult decisions you can never imagine yourself making. You can judge me for this, but I am doing what's in Consuelo's best interest.

It is my place to protect my daughter. One day, you will know how difficult this is—the choices and sacrifices we make for our children. The world will not be kind to her if she raises this child on her own, Alicia, not in this war. Better she realizes that now than when it's too late."

"You are putting respectability over Consuelo's feelings, over her heart," I say. "She loves this child. She doesn't want to lose it. You're not acting in her best interest; you're acting in yours because you're scared of the trouble this will bring."

"Yes, I am afraid. For your sister, for you, for all of us."

"For me?"

"When you came to Barcelona to stay with Isabel, I allowed it because I felt sorry for you, because what Emilio did to you was wrong and I thought that the time and distance apart might be good for your marriage, that you could heal from his betrayal, and that you would eventually return to Havana. I thought you would make the best decision for yourself and for your daughter. But the longer this separation stretches on . . . Sometimes you must make sacrifices—as a wife, as a mother. You'll learn that lesson the hard way one day."

"I will never make decisions for Isabel out of fear, will never tell her that our reputation is more important than her heart."

"'Never' is a strong word, Alicia. You have no idea what life will throw your way or how you will respond to it."

chapter twenty-three

Rosa
1937
HAVANA

March drifts into April, and we settle into a routine of sorts. I avoid the rest of the family as much as possible, my days spent at political meetings or at the university, my evenings spent dining alone. A few times, Felipe has knocked on my door at night, but I've ignored him, choosing instead to sew in my room or write.

The printer's office remains shuttered, and there are rumors that he's simply disappeared, so for now I keep the pages I write tucked under the mattress in my room.

The nights are the hardest for me, the moments when I am supposed to be asleep, and yet, I cannot relax for all the thoughts running through my mind. When I do fall asleep, I am plagued by memories and nightmares.

I dream that they are fighting in Spain, and while I've never seen a war, have no idea if my dream is even accurate, it feels so real that I wake in the middle of the night with a jolt, my last image that of Gonzalo walking toward me, blood dripping down his face, his hand clutched to his stomach, his body doubled over in pain.

I think about his last moments often, wondering what it was like for him: if he knew death was imminent and had made peace with it or if he was caught off guard by the whole thing, if he never saw it coming.

I wish I knew.

It's still dark out, daybreak hours away, but after the dream I just had I can't imagine falling back asleep anytime soon.

I get out of bed, grabbing a robe draped over the arm of the chair. I slip it on, tying the belt tightly around my waist, and head downstairs to the kitchen in search of whatever food might be left over from dinner. As I near the base of the stairs, I spy a light emanating from the downstairs study, the door ajar. I pray it is Felipe's father working late and not Felipe himself.

"Can't sleep?"

I freeze, the desire to gather my robe in my hand and scurry back up the stairs overwhelming, even as I know this reckoning has been coming for a long time now. Instead, I square my shoulders and walk into the study, taking my time before allowing my gaze to settle on Felipe, sprawled in an elegantly appointed leather chair in front of an immense wood desk, a half-empty glass of rum in front of him, an opened envelope lying next to the bottle.

The first few buttons of his shirt are undone, exposing several inches of tanned skin. His hair is ruffled, far from the elegant style he normally sports.

In the hall, the clock chimes some hour past midnight.

"I was asleep," I reply. "A dream woke me up."

"To think, I once would have given everything to know your dreams."

As far as shots across the bow go, his is a warning that tonight he will not deal fairly with me, that the cease-fire that has settled between us will not be allowed to stand, and even as I dread it, there is another part of me that has been waiting for this confrontation that has been building like those ominous moments before the storm, something electric in the air.

Haven't I imagined countless times what I would say to him if I had the opportunity to speak freely?

My back to Felipe, I walk over to the bar cart, my fingers trembling slightly as I reach for the decanter, removing the heavy crystal top, pouring the liquid into one of the empty glasses. I can feel his gaze on me as I take the first sip of the drink, the rum burning its way down and leaving a warm glow in its wake.

I turn slowly, drink in hand, and Felipe is exactly where I left him, sprawled in the chair, staring at me.

I refuse to speak first, just as I refuse to look away, to cede this battle to him. He's not the only one who has reasons to be angry.

But where I've come spoiling for a fight, I suppose, Felipe surprises me by starting with a topic I don't expect.

"Why did Gonzalo go to Spain? Why didn't you stop him?"

I open my mouth to answer him, but no sound comes out, the liquid courage doing little to untangle the conflicting emotions gnarled up inside me.

Instead, I approach the desk, taking one of the two open seats across from him.

I set the highball glass down on the desk with a little thud, the amber-colored liquid swishing near the top of the rim.

"You give me too much credit if you think I had any sway over your brother."

"Didn't you?"

"You knew him better than I did. After all, what is a few months of marriage in the face of a lifetime of brotherhood?"

"You were married 167 days and 167 nights before he left for Spain."

It takes a moment for me to catch my breath.

"Do you think I didn't keep count, Rosa? That I didn't lie awake and imagine you in my brother's arms?"

"You go too far."

"Do I?"

"Lower your voice," I hiss. "Do you want to wake the whole house?"

"You left," I say.

I didn't think saying two words could bring me to tears, but it's impossible to choke back the sob, impossible to know if I'm crying for the girl who had her heart broken well over a year ago or the woman who now at twenty-two finds herself to be a widow. Life doesn't prepare you for a thing like that, for starting out with so much promise, so much hope, and ending up in this place alone. "You went to New York for your family's business, and I didn't know when you would be back. You told me nothing of your feelings, gave me nothing to hold on to while you were gone."

Felipe pushes the chair back abruptly, rising from his seat. "He was supposed to keep you safe," he says, and I can't tell who he is angrier at: me for loving his brother or Gonzalo for dying. "I could live with the fact that you were his wife, if I thought that he could make you happy. That he could give you a good life. He ruined all of that."

"He's in excellent company. He's hardly the first Aguilera to break a promise to me."

"I didn't make you any promises," he replies, his words filled with regret.

"Then I suppose he's just the second Aguilera to break my heart."

He reels back as if I've physically delivered a blow to his chest, and as ugly as it is, it feels good to strip away the armor he wears so well. That was always the thing about Felipe—you never knew exactly where you stood. Gonzalo wore his heart on his sleeve, but with his elder brother there was always an impenetrable layer that was impossible to pierce.

"I didn't—" Felipe catches himself mid-sentence, as though he realizes the futility of arguing with me, the plain truth of it written on my face. "You didn't wait for me," he says instead.

"Wait for you? What was there to wait for? You said it yourself: you made me no promises. You spoke nothing of your feelings, of your heart. You left and you went to New York City without any commitment. I wanted to wait for you, but the more time that passed, the more I felt as though I was a fool for doing so, for trusting you, for believing in you. You didn't even write to me."

"I did write to you. I wrote you constantly. I told you—" He breaks off. "Never mind what I told you. It doesn't matter anymore. None of this matters. You were already otherwise engaged. *You married my brother.*"

"I didn't know he was your brother. If I had known, I never would have married him. But you told me so little about you. Our courtship, if you can even call it that, was walks around the University of Havana. We spoke of so many things, but so little about our lives. I knew your favorite books, but nothing of your family. You never even kissed me."

My cheeks burn as the words fall from my mouth, as though he can hear in my voice how badly I had wished it were otherwise.

"You could have asked me."

"And yet, you never volunteered it. Why?"

He sighs. "It's complicated with my family. Surely, you can see that. When I was with you, there wasn't any pressure to be the Aguilera heir. You didn't know my family was wealthy, that they were powerful, and it felt good for once to know that you enjoyed being around me because you liked *me*, not because you wanted the advantages that came with my family's name."

"I can understand that. But you must realize—it left me feeling as though I knew so little about you. It was easy for doubt to creep in. And you're right, I suppose I could have asked you more personal questions, but the truth is that when I was around you, I was so nervous all the time that it was difficult to string the requisite words together for all the feelings inside me.

"I never received any letters. Not one. I waited for them eagerly. You said you would write. But when none came, I just assumed that our time together had meant more to me than it did to you. That you had found someone in New York who held your interest more than I had. I was devastated," I reply, unable to meet his gaze as the confession springs from my lips.

"After we married, after I realized you were brothers, Gonzalo told me about you, about how you were with your women, how you had such impossible standards that no woman was good enough for you, and I realized that I was just a diversion for you, something that kept you entertained while you were bored, that your family never would have allowed you to seriously consider someone like me."

"My women?!? If I was such a womanizer, I damned sure would

have kissed you, considering how badly I wanted to. And as for no woman being good enough for me, that's utter nonsense. I never thought of any other women. I only thought about you. But why would I expect otherwise from my brother? Gonzalo was capable of twisting the truth whenever it suited his purposes."

"What is that supposed to mean?"

"That whatever Gonzalo told you was a lie. That there were no women; there was always only you. And I did write to you."

"If you wrote me so many letters, what happened to them? It's not like they would have just disappeared—"

I remember what he told me about the staff, about his parents when he gave me the letter from Alicia.

"Do you think your parents' staff was intercepting your mail when you were in New York?"

"Now I do. The night before I left, you see, my father and I came to an agreement. I told him that I had met someone. I told him that I loved her, and I was going to marry her. That I would go to New York and do what he wanted me to do, but that when I returned to Cuba, I wanted to be able to marry the woman of my choosing. Because I wanted to marry you."

His words quite simply steal the breath from me.

"You never spoke of any of this to me."

"I didn't want to make you promises I couldn't keep. I knew my parents had their own ideas of the wife they wanted for me, and I knew that it would be difficult to change their thinking, but I believed I could try. In hindsight, when my father gave so little objection, when we made the agreement we did, I should have realized that he had another plan in place. I should have realized that they were probably having the staff intercept our letters when I sent them out to be mailed and when I never heard from you. I thought you'd moved on, and then when I learned you had married my brother, well—"

"I didn't know you were brothers. I promise. Not until we had already married, and Gonzalo brought me to the house and sat me down in your father's office and I saw the pictures behind his desk. I didn't do this to hurt you. I *never* would have married your brother had I known you were related."

"I believe you." He's silent for a beat. "But Gonzalo knew."

"What do you mean, he knew?"

"He saw us together once. At the university. He asked me about you, about who you were to me, and I tried to play it off because I didn't want him anywhere near you. I thought that was the end of it, until my father wrote me in New York to tell me Gonzalo had married you. He didn't realize what it meant to me when he shared your name in the letter, when I realized my brother had married the woman I loved. I wanted to come back to Havana. I wanted to confront you, him. I was angry and heartbroken, but what could I do? You were married, and I hoped at least you were happy. As angry as I was, I couldn't wish you ill.

"I made mistakes with you. I know that. If I had handled things differently, if I had been able to stand up to my family, maybe none of this would have happened. I'm sorry for the hurt I caused you. I'm sorry for the hurt we all caused you."

"How could he—" I can't even finish the words. I am going to be ill. What kind of man does such a thing? What kind of man did I marry?

"Gonzalo was always competitive with me. I think he resented the fact that I would take over the family business because I was the eldest.

"And if I'm being honest, I always resented him. My parents

expected so much of me, held me to an impossible standard because our family's legacy, our future, rested on my shoulders and an Aguilera is not to be anything less than the best. But with Gonzalo, our parents were willing to look the other way at his political leanings, at the trouble he was causing in Cuba. They funded his lifestyle and let him play the revolutionary with his antics all while he lived in the privilege that my hard work afforded him. When he married you—" He's silent for a beat. "It broke my heart."

There are so many things I wish to say, more than anything a desire to close the distance between us and wrap my arms around him, giving him somewhere to put this pain that he has directed at me. And at the same time, I lost that right a long time ago when I married his brother, when everything we had simply fell apart.

"There's something else you should know," Felipe says. "I'm going to Spain."

Shock fills me. "Why? Are you going to fight with the International Brigades as well? After we lost Gonzalo, why would you risk your life doing the same thing?"

"I'm not going to fight. Things in Spain are complicated."

"Complicated, how?"

"There are some family matters that need to be addressed. Some of Gonzalo's affairs that need to be settled. It's best if I am the one to handle them."

"Family matters? Pertaining to Gonzalo's life in Spain? Why wasn't I notified about that? He was my *husband*. This entire family seems eager to simply remove me from the process, as though I have no claim to him, as though my feelings, my grief, don't matter in all of this—"

He's silent, and then, with aching gentleness, he says to me:

"There's a child, Rosa."

"What do you mean 'there's a child'?"

"Rosa."

Felipe slides his glass to me across the desk, my own empty, the amber liquid swaying in the heavy crystal.

I focus on the drink, unable to meet his gaze, steeling myself for the inevitable. I take a long swig of the rum, and another, a fire licking its way down my chest, curling in my belly, settling next to the rage and misery stirring there.

I wish I'd never met either of them.

I look up and meet his gaze, knowing at least that while he thoroughly shattered my heart, he won't lie to me.

"Gonzalo has a child in Spain?"

"I'm sorry. There's a woman, and she's pregnant. I didn't want to be the one to tell you. And I didn't want anyone else to tell you, either. Gonzalo was my brother, and for that I tried my best to love him as brothers do." His jaw clenches. "But as a man—my brother made many stupid mistakes. Most of all, the way he treated you."

"That's rich coming from you."

"Do not compare us."

"Why shouldn't I? You both betrayed my trust in different ways. Gonzalo had some woman in Spain. You lied about everything else."

"And you married the first man you met without trusting me enough to give me a chance."

"What chance was there to be had? The first time I sat in this office with Gonzalo and saw your picture, when I saw the way your father looked at me, the shame he felt at the idea that his youngest son would marry someone from such a low background, I realized even if I had never met Gonzalo, your parents never would have accepted me for you."

"Maybe I loved you enough that it didn't matter. I would have found a way for us to be together."

Something flares at me as he says the word "loved," some nearly indescribable pain. I can't speak, all the implications of what this means hitting me in waves, the realization that while I prayed for my husband off in Spain, while I missed him, while I mourned him, he was unfaithful to me.

Minutes go by, and neither one of us says a word, as though Felipe knows that I need this time to process everything, to wrap my mind around a betrayal I never envisioned. Finally, when I do speak, I ask—

"Did Gonzalo write to tell you about the baby before he died? About the mother?"

"No. He didn't know about the baby. I received a letter. They're in a precarious situation. The mother is a few months away from giving birth. There's some complication with her family. She's only eighteen. Apparently, Gonzalo made her promises, told her they would be married. She believed him."

I want to take one of the glasses on the desk, one of the bottles sitting right there, and throw it against the wall.

"Be angry," Felipe urges. "You should be angry. What he did to you— He should have protected you, loved you, cherished you. He should have woken up every day and considered himself the luckiest man in the world to be able to call you his, to be yours. If I were your husband—"

"What? If you were my husband, what would be different?"

"If I were your husband, I never would have left you in the first place. If I were your husband—"

"Don't say things like that." I rise from my chair and step forward, my fingers curling into little fists as I walk into the curve of his body, my hands trying to erect some sort of barrier between us, to push him back, to show him as I fear I can't adequately do with my words that there is no place inside me for this, that I cannot entertain such conversations, that each word he says sends another dart of pain through me.

I must be a masochist to have my heart broken twice by men in the same family.

I open my mouth to tell him to stop speaking, to tell him to stop picking at a wound that never quite scabbed over, but instead all that comes out in a gasp is—

"I loved you," which now seems as much of an indictment as anything.

"I know."

He says the words so quietly I barely hear them, even though the regret in his voice comes through loud and clear.

"How could you have married him when you loved me?" Felipe asks me.

I don't have an answer for him, don't have an explanation to give that can describe the vagaries of the heart, that I was angry and hurt, and that I wanted to forget maybe for a second all that we'd been through together, how he had wound his way so tightly into my heart that I could not remove him, and maybe on some level, some shred of ugliness I did not know I possessed, perhaps I wanted the news to eventually drift to his ears, maybe I thought about Felipe seeing me walking down the street with Gonzalo, imagined him knowing that in not wanting all of me, in deciding that I did not fit into his life, he had lost me entirely to a man who wasn't afraid to claim my love.

Except, of course, now I know that wasn't the reality at all, that Gonzalo was never worthy of the love I gave him.

How could I marry Gonzalo when I loved Felipe? I do not know, only that I did. And while my regrets may be legion, they are also behind me, and I will not apologize for the mistakes I've made, not when Felipe has had his fair share, too; when he never told me how he felt about me.

Felipe hands me the letter sitting on his desk. "You should read this."

It takes a minute for it to register that the handwriting is familiar to me because it is Alicia's. It takes a moment to absorb the blow, over and over again, that not only was Gonzalo unfaithful to me, but he used the time I sent him to see Alicia in Barcelona to set this whole thing in motion.

Alicia's letter is full of apologies and sadness, but I can barely absorb the words written there. I have left my body, and I am somewhere else entirely looking down on this disaster, like a part of me has died and will never be recovered.

How could Gonzalo have acted so dishonorably? How could I have been so wrong about him? How could I have believed myself to be married to a good man, an honorable man, and ended up with this?

"So, he lied to this girl. Lied to everyone."

"Yes."

"What will you do when you get to Barcelona?"

"I don't know. Help however I can. The baby will be born soon, and the war there is intensifying. I have a responsibility to her, considering everything Gonzalo put her through. This baby is an Aguilera, and it deserves more from this family than my brother gave it. So does she. So do you."

"When do you leave?"

"I secured passage on the next ship headed for Bilbao. From there I'll get to Barcelona. It leaves tomorrow."

"I know you have to go; I know it's the right thing, but—"

The words break off with a sob, tears running down my face, the emotions of everything that has happened hitting me full force. How could Gonzalo have done this to me? How could I have been such a fool?

"Rosa. Please don't cry."

Felipe walks toward me and wraps his arms around me, pulling me closer to him so that my head fits under his chin, my cheek resting against his heart beating through the layers of his clothing.

Now that I've started, it seems impossible to stop, all the emotion that I've kept inside me since Gonzalo died bubbling to the surface and spilling all over any hope of calm I could claim.

My tears wet Felipe's shirtfront, his hands at my back stroking me while he whispers in my ear, his words full of his pain at seeing me sad, at his anger toward his brother, at his regret for how things have ended up. The words he offers flow through me as quickly as the tears, until all I can focus on are the sensations filling me, the release of emotions I've been clinging to for so long.

"There's a war going on," I whisper.

"I'll be fine."

"Will you? Gonzalo thought the same thing."

"I am not my brother." Felipe releases me, taking a step back, his gaze searching. "I know the timing is horrible, that you're dealing with more now than anyone should have to bear. But I made the mistake last time I had to leave you of not making things clear between us, of not telling you how I felt, and I lost you. I won't make that mistake again.

"I love you. I have always loved you. Even when you were my brother's wife, even when I stayed in New York long past the time when I should have because I couldn't bear the idea of seeing the two of you together, couldn't stand facing the fact that I had everything I ever wanted when I had you and I threw it all away.

"I want to spend my life with you. I want you to be my wife. I know that might be a long time away, I know it's a lot to ask considering you were my brother's wife, I know my family will never accept us, that most of society will probably condemn us, and I don't care. I would walk away from all of this if that's what you wanted. I will walk away from it if it means that you will let me be yours."

He steps forward, pressing a kiss to the top of my head, and it takes everything in my power not to reach out and hold on to him as he walks away, leaving me alone in the study, grappling with how much my life has changed in the space of an evening.

In the end, it's the letter from Alicia that does it. While she wrote directly to Felipe and the Aguileras, asking for help for her sister, she also enclosed a letter for me where she wrote of her sorrow and her fears for Consuelo, who Gonzalo so horribly deceived.

I read the words repeatedly, unable to sleep, unable to clear my mind of them—

Rosa,

I don't even know how one starts a letter like this, so I'm just going to tell you. You've often heard me speak of my sister,

Consuelo, in the letters I've sent you. She's just turned eighteen. It has come to my attention that Consuelo was involved with a man who has left her pregnant and alone.

When I asked her who the child's father was, she began telling me of a man she had met one day outside her home—a Cuban man fighting in the International Brigades. She told me his name, and I realized it was your own Gonzalo. I think they must have met the day he came by the house in Barcelona to give me the gifts you sent me. Rosa, I'm so very sorry.

There is nothing I can say to make this situation better for you, nothing I can do to alleviate the shame I have for my part in inadvertently bringing them together, for the pain I know this will cause you. I cannot imagine what you must be going through, how betrayed you must feel, and I will never understand the pain life doles out, how so many losses can be directed toward someone who deserves so much better.

I know we are not to speak ill of the dead, but he was unworthy of you. What a horrible, wretched man. That he betrayed your trust and Consuelo's is an abominable thing. She is so young and scared, and I fear ill-equipped for the path that is in front of her.

Consuelo is heartbroken and says she loves the baby, that she cannot give it up, but our parents fear for her and the situation in Spain. I have offered to take the baby myself, but with my separation from Emilio, it is a difficult situation. Our parents want her to give the baby up for adoption, and she won't hear of it. I cannot imagine how hard it is for you to read of her after the hurt you have experienced, but Rosa, she is so young and so innocent in all of this. She had no idea he was married, thought he loved her and that she could trust him, and now her life has

been ruined. I have written to the Aguileras at her request, in
the hopes that they can help intervene, and perhaps would be
willing to take the baby.

She needs help.

I am so sorry, Rosa.

You are ever in my thoughts and prayers, and more than
anything, I wish we could be together, that I could be there for
you in your time of grief.

I love you.

Alicia

That next morning, just as Felipe is getting ready to leave for
Barcelona via Bilbao, I walk downstairs, my suitcase in hand.

"I'm coming with you."

chapter twenty-four

Isabel

1964

PALM BEACH

After the freedom I enjoyed in Spain, it's strange to return to Palm Beach where I am once again both wife and daughter subject to everyone's expectations and observations. In such a short time, I got used to being on my own, Beatriz's lifestyle appealing in its independence, in the ability to do as one pleases without having to answer to another. I miss her apartment and the time I spent there. I miss Barcelona and the version of myself I was able to be in the city.

Now, when I paint, it isn't Cuba but Barcelona that I recreate over and over again, the subject of my images, two figures lying beside each other on a nearly empty beach, or a café near Las Ramblas, or Beatriz's sun-soaked apartment.

I try not to paint Diego.

For the first week I am back, I nearly succeed. But I have no photograph of his face, no way of remembering him since I left the painting of us dancing and all the others in Beatriz's apartment, and with each day that passes I worry I am forgetting him—the sound of his voice, the look in his eyes, the feel of his hand in mine.

In the end, I can't resist.

I paint Diego as I remember him—on the streets, in Beatriz's apartment. I paint him as though doing so can exorcise this part of me, that if maybe I capture his image enough I will not see his face at night when I dream, will not hear his voice, will not replay our last days in Barcelona together.

I am a fool.

A week after I have returned from Spain, my parents come to our house and join us for dinner.

Before I left Barcelona, I promised Beatriz I would speak with our mother about the photograph we found, but with my father in attendance, tonight hardly seems the appropriate evening for it, and as much as I've tried to talk to her since I returned from Barcelona, she's been evasive and unreachable.

For most of the evening, my mother and I are quiet while Thomas and my father speak of business and their mutual acquaintances.

We're nearly on to dessert when my mother turns to me and says, "Do you have some news to share with us?"

Confusion fills me because it's such a simple, innocuous question, but there's an undercurrent I'm intimately familiar with there, as though I have forgotten to do something important and will now be left with her disappointment because of it.

I wrack my brain trying to think of what she wants me to say—it certainly can't be about my trip to Barcelona. That, she barely acknowledged, and Beatriz herself is perpetually a difficult subject between us. I am almost ready to plead confusion when she sighs.

"Honestly, Isabel, your father and I thought you invited us to announce that you were expecting. What wonderful news that would have been."

My eyes narrow, for there is no chance that's what she really thought. There was nothing in my tone, nothing in the invitation or even our manner of formality this evening, that suggested this was a special occasion. But whatever impression I gave doesn't really matter, because while she says it as an aside to me, she makes sure Thomas cannot help but overhear her comment.

I open my mouth to interject and shift the focus off me at the same moment Thomas says—

"As it happens, I couldn't agree with you more, Alicia. It's time Isabel found something to keep her occupied during the days besides that silly painting."

He says it casually enough, nothing in his tone to belie anything other than the impression that he is amused by the entire business, but as he speaks, our gazes lock across the table, and I realize he has seen the pictures I've painted of Diego, and more than that, he wants me to know that he's seen them.

I look away from him, my cheeks heating both at the insult over my paintings and the realization that I have been careless, and as I do, my gaze connects with my mother's, her eyes alight with fury.

I set the diamond earrings Thomas bought me on the heavy wooden dresser, surprised to see that my fingers are trembling, the jewelry hitting the surface with a thunk, scattering haphazardly, one of them falling to the floor.

I bend down trying to locate it in the dim room, the bodice of my dress tight against my torso, the seams digging into my stomach. There's a knock at the door just as my fingers seize over the earrings, the prongs scratching the inside of my palm, my heart beating madly, the world spinning out of control thanks to the alcohol I've drunk and the surreal nature of the whole evening.

"Come in," I say, already dreading the conversation we are to have. Will Thomas confront me over the paintings now? Have I pushed my husband to his breaking point with my careless actions? I'm not even sure what I will say to him, how I will excuse myself. On the one hand, the entanglement between me and Diego hasn't traversed into the physical, but on the other hand, in my heart I know that there is a wrongness to this, that I have crossed a line I cannot come back from.

I am not the sort of person who does things lightly, who breaks vows, who willingly hurts others, and yet somehow I have become that person, pulled in two by my attraction to Diego and the life I vowed to have with Thomas.

And even as guilt fills me over the foolishness of my actions, another fear enters my mind—

Will Thomas wish to resume our relations as man and wife?

But when the door opens, it isn't my husband ready to confront me or take his place in my bed. Instead, it is my mother, still dressed in her gown from earlier this evening. My parents left our house an hour ago, so for her to have returned to speak with me—

She closes the door behind her with a soft click.

There must be a particular parental skill to the ability to reduce your grown offspring to children with a single look.

"What have you done? Thomas is clearly upset with you."

This is the tone she adopts when talking to Beatriz, one I have heard her employ but have never had directed at me.

"You are a fool. I swear to you if you ruin this marriage, I wash my hands of you and your siblings. After all your father and I sacrificed for this family, after all we have done to give you a better life, for you to throw away your chance at happiness with Thomas—"

"It's been nearly three years," I say, surprising us both, I think. "We aren't happy. We aren't going to be happy."

There's a plea in my voice, a need for her to understand, to accept that I am trying as hard as I can, that I have done my best to please them, but that I am hurting, that maybe, just maybe I have made a terrible mistake.

"Is there someone else, Isabel? Is that what this is? Is this Beatriz all over again? You don't think I noticed that you went to see your sister in Barcelona and you came back completely different? You don't think I can tell when something is wrong with one of my daughters?

"You can only push a man like Thomas so far. Whatever he wants from you—if it is a child—give it to him and make him happy. If you're lonely in your marriage, a child will change that. It will give you something to bind your family together.

"Don't throw everything you have away because you are restless. Do you think you are the only woman to be unhappy in her marriage? Do you think you are the only woman to be married to a man who doesn't respect her and who will never understand her?"

How long have I heard such sentiments? Since I was a little girl, old enough to understand them? This was what Beatriz heard and Elisa. It's the lie that Maria will hear. My mother's mother likely told her the same thing, as did my aunt Mirta's mother, so many generations of women in my family believing that their only worth was through marriage.

I was taught that love is earned rather than given freely.

"Do you not understand how precarious things are for us?" she asks. "Do you not understand how much you risk? Your husband will start to notice things are amiss."

"There's nothing amiss. My marriage is as it ever was."

Where did that bitterness in my voice come from? What has happened to me? I can't say that I was forced into marrying Thomas, that I protested even once when my mother suggested that he was the best I could hope for, when I greedily sought to guard my heart.

"Good. I suggest you keep it that way. Don't allow yourself to be swayed by passion; don't make the same foolish mistake your sister has."

"I don't think Beatriz would view falling in love as a mistake."

As a child, I saw a different side of my mother than my sisters and brother did. Alejandro might have been her favorite, but I was the one she relied upon, the keeper of the peace, responsible for looking out for my siblings when my parents simply couldn't be bothered to do so. And so, perhaps for that reason alone, she treated me less as a child at times, but more as a trusted confidante, showing me the cracks in the facade when her grief or troubles were too much to bear.

After my brother was murdered, I acted as the unofficial go-between, shuffling from her room to the others in the house when she didn't wish for everyone to see her in the throes of loss.

It's hard to be angry with her when I have been the one to hold her as she cries, our roles temporarily reversing as I stroked her hair and told her everything would be fine.

And perhaps, because we are the most alike, women determined to do our duty, to survive by locking away any passions or emotions that might threaten the impregnable fortress we have built around us, I understand the toll it takes on her.

Does she ever wish to give it all up, or is that too great of an indulgence for her to contemplate?

"Beatriz humiliated this family," my mother snaps.

"These things happen. Life happens. We aren't all perfect. We can't be. Maybe we shouldn't be trying to pretend we are, working so hard to give the illusion that we are untouchable. Maybe that's what got us in this mess in the first place."

"Do you think any of this is easy? Do you truly not understand how unwelcome we are here because we are different? Do you not see the looks we get when we speak Spanish in public? The whispers behind our back. Do you know the things they say about us? The only way we can survive here where we are not wanted is to be better than those around us. Prettier, smarter, more successful, wealthier. The only way to thrive here is if we elevate ourselves to a position where we are not worthy of their scorn, where they have to accept us because to do otherwise would be at their peril."

"Is that why you wanted me to marry an American man? Because you want me to be like them? Because you want me to fit in here?"

"Better to fit in than to be ostracized here or dead back in Havana. You aren't a child anymore, Isabel, and I won't treat you like one. You know what was at stake for us back in Cuba, know what we lost when your brother was killed. This is not a game we're playing. This is literally life or death."

"How am I supposed to live my life feeling as though I am carrying my family's honor on my back, as though our legacy will only survive if I have the life you've chosen for me? And why is our legacy, why is our honor so wrapped up in success, in money and power and what it can buy us? Where does happiness rank? What is the point of all this, what is the point of living, if not to aspire to something more?"

Is this to be the legacy of the Perez women? Beatriz perpetually single, Elisa married but mourning the possibility of the life she left behind in Cuba, me in a loveless marriage with a man who despite the passage of time still feels like a stranger, who shows no interest in getting to know me better, in having a real marriage based on affection and respect, say nothing of passion? I think of our little sister, Maria, and I pray for better for her, that one day she will find a man who loves her, that she will follow her heart rather than duty, guilt, and expectations.

"I'm not happy," I say again, as though if I say it enough, perhaps she will hear me, perhaps she will care.

"I don't care if you aren't happy. None of this is about happiness. Your happiness doesn't matter. This family matters, and you will do everything you are asked to in order to protect the family. Your children can be happy perhaps, when we have gained a foothold here, when we have a chance at more."

"When will it ever be enough? When will we stop working to-ward things, when will we stop looking to the past or the future, when will we simply be as we were intended to be? I'm like a ghost here, walking through memories and fear, and I don't want it to be like this anymore. I can't keep going on like this, living half a life."

"You have no idea what you are talking about. What it is to suf-fer. I lost my son. Do you think I have time to think about my hap-piness? Do you think your father has ever wondered if I am happy in this marriage, if I love him? Do you think he has ever even cared?"

"Why do you stay with him if you are unhappy? Why did you

marry him in the first place? Because you wanted someone to take care of you?"

There has always existed a tension in my parents' marriage, one that even at a young age, I understood was best left to the adults to sort out. For a long time, I assumed that was how marriage was to be, but now, looking down the stretch of spending the rest of my life with someone I do not love, I realize how foolish I was to choose this, to throw my chance at happiness away because I was afraid.

And because I'm angry, because she's pushed me past the boundaries where I'd normally tread, I can't resist asking—

"You can deny it all you want, but I saw a picture of us in Barcelona. I know we were there." I have no doubt she is prepared for this, that Rosa has warned her Beatriz has been poking around and asking questions. "Who is the man in the photograph with us? Were you lovers? Beatriz thinks you looked at him as though you loved him."

She pales, and I worry she isn't going to answer me, that I have pushed her too far.

"You don't know what you're speaking of. Your father was the one who didn't love me."

Surprise fills me.

Was my father unfaithful somewhere along the way? Does he have a mistress now? It is a strange thing to think of your parents as people with their own desires, to imagine that they may be ruled by their passions, but I never considered the possibility that there could be someone else—or rather, I never allowed myself to consider the possibility.

"I'm sorry."

"It's no matter. The days of me being a young girl, naive and wearing my heart on my sleeve, baring all in the hope that he would love me back, are long since gone. You cannot trust love, Isabel. It ebbs and flows. It is not reliable, and it is not constant. You should put your faith in security and the tangible things that provide it. You should guard your heart and be careful not to give in to your impulses.

"I've never had to worry about that with you. Beatriz always felt like she was a ticking time bomb walking around, ready to blow up the world and remake it in a fashion she deemed up to her standards, but you have always been smarter than that, more cautious."

It is unspoken, but I hear it anyway:

You have always been scared.

She reaches out, her palm brushing my cheek, the diamond bracelet on her wrist glinting in the lamplight.

"Don't disappoint me, Isabel."

chapter twenty-five

After the dinner with my parents, Thomas and I speak little, the tension in the house reaching a fever pitch. I spend as much time as I can in Coral Gables with Elisa or walking on the beach near our home with Maria, doing everything I can to tiptoe around the problems in my marriage, an effort that's easier said than done considering how much it's on my mind.

When we first married, Thomas expressed little interest in being a father, and that was fine with me. Given my own experiences within my family, taking care of my siblings, motherhood was never a dream of mine, and the idea of bringing a child into a marriage of convenience rather than one of love was hardly appealing. But now, Thomas has changed everything on me.

Sometimes, I think painting is the only thing that keeps me sane, the artwork I create an escape from all the problems I don't want to face. Beatriz decided to visit from Barcelona, her presence a welcome distraction, too. Since our time together in Spain, the awkwardness that existed between us has dissipated, and for the first time in a long time, we are sisters again.

I'm finishing up a portrait of Maria that she sat for earlier in the week when Beatriz calls me from Elisa's house in Coral Gables, her voice filled with excitement.

"One of your paintings sold," she says in greeting, bypassing all pleasantries. "I just spoke to the gallery in Spain."

"What do you mean one of my paintings sold?"

"The ones you left in Spain, that you didn't take back with you when you all but fled Barcelona. I asked around looking for an art dealer, and I found a gallery that was willing to take your work on commission. I didn't tell you because I knew you would protest that you weren't ready to show them to someone in the art business. But he thought they were good, Isabel. Really good. He said you had talent."

It's the pride in Beatriz's voice that does it for me. A tear trickles down my cheek, and another.

"He's sending you your portion of the sale."

She names a figure that astounds me. To someone like Thomas, it would hardly be anything, but the idea that someone has paid money for artwork I created is still staggering. For so long, I thought my worth was entangled in my ability to blend into my surroundings, to keep from courting scandals as my siblings did, to behave as others wished me to, that it's an extraordinary thing to comprehend that in choosing to do the opposite, in these bold paintings I created from some part of my soul I never even realized I had, someone wanted them enough to pay money to hang them on their walls.

And perhaps, more than anything, it is the realization that as grateful as I am for the money, I didn't paint them for others.

I painted them for me.

"He also wants to know if you have any more work to send him.

I told him you have loads. Maybe I should be your agent," she teases.

"Beatriz—I—thank you. You're right: I wouldn't have done it without you pushing me, and I can't tell you how much it means to know that someone bought one of my pieces. I honestly never imagined it."

"We're sisters. It's what we do for each other."

And it occurs to me—

"The picture—which one did he sell—"

"The one you did of me in the apartment."

Relief fills me. I remember the picture clearly, Beatriz lounging in a chair near the window in her living room, the sun shining through as it began to set in the sky.

"You look beautiful in that painting. I'm hardly surprised someone would want to buy it. But listen, I need you to save one for me. There's a picture of a girl dancing in a red dress—"

"Oh no, I didn't sell him that one. That one has already found a home."

A lump forms in my throat. It's silly to care who gets the painting, but I can't deny the wave of grief at the idea of that moment being forever lost to me.

"You aren't the only one who thought it was special, and since the poor guy had already had his heart broken by my sister, I gave him the painting as a consolation prize."

"You gave the painting to Diego?"

"I don't know that I as much gave it to him as I didn't disagree with him when he insisted that I not sell that one. He had rather strong opinions on that subject. He offered me anything for it, but I knew you wouldn't take his money. It didn't seem right all things considered. It's hanging in his apartment."

"How was he? The last time you saw him?"

"Honestly? He seemed sad. Like he missed you. Like he wished things could have turned out differently. I think he understood, though, why you had to leave."

"Are you all right?" she asks when I don't say anything.

"I will be."

"Good. You should have the money from the painting soon, and I'll be in touch about how you can send more of your work to Spain. He thought your Cuba pieces would be of particular interest." She's silent for a beat. "The portrait you did for me of Alejandro." Her voice cracks. "I don't know how to thank you. You captured the essence of him perfectly. It's the greatest gift you ever could have given me."

Tears fill my eyes. "I'm glad. I'm glad it helps."

"I love you, Isabel."

I smile. "I love you, too, Beatriz."

With the news that the canvas sold, I'm more inspired to paint than ever before. I begin experimenting with new subjects, challenging myself in ways I previously wouldn't have. I'm grateful to my sister for the impetus, filled with the realization that I need to take more chances with my artwork, the desire to hone my craft as much as possible. For the first time in as long as I can remember, I am filled with hope.

Elisa calls early in the morning, just as I am finishing up another canvas.

"We need to talk about Beatriz," she announces.

"What's wrong?" I ask Elisa, the early-morning phone call catching me off guard. "Isn't she with you? I just spoke with her a few days ago and she was fine. We talked about meeting for a day of shopping."

"Have you seen the newspaper this morning? The society page?"

"No, Thomas usually takes the paper with him when he goes to work. Why? What's wrong?"

"Nicholas Preston has gotten engaged."

An oath escapes.

"My thoughts exactly," Elisa replies.

"I'll be right there."

When I arrive at Elisa's home in Coral Gables, I'm greeted not by her housekeeper, but by Elisa herself, the house strangely quiet for the normal bustle that occurs with my exuberant nephew.

"Where is everyone?"

"I sent Miguel and Juan off together and dismissed the staff."

"How bad is she?"

"Quiet, mostly. She hasn't cried, but I think at this point tears might worry me less. She's just so subdued. Very un-Beatriz."

I follow Elisa to her favorite room in the house, a beautifully lit sunroom that overlooks the back grounds and pool area. Beatriz is perched on the couch in an aqua-colored gown, hugging her legs to her chest, staring out the window.

Beatriz turns at the sound of my heels, and our gazes connect across the room, and despite the fact that we are grown women so far past our childhood years, something flashes between us, and in a moment, we are playing outside in our backyard in Miramar, are giggling and shushing each other after nipping a bottle of expensive champagne from our parents' stock, are holding each other tight outside the front entrance of our home, our brother's dead body at our feet. At once we are a line of Perez girls walking through a crowded airport in Cuba, sorrow etched in our hearts.

I close the distance between us, taking a seat next to her on the couch while Elisa hovers behind us.

"Beatriz."

"It's silly, I know, to let it affect me so. He asked me to marry him last year. I was the one who turned him down. I was the one who told him that he needed to find someone who could fit with the life he wanted. I was the one who did this. Silly that it should hurt so much now."

"Not silly at all." I reach out, taking her hand and squeezing it, trying to infuse her with some of my strength.

"I saw the announcement on the society page," she says. "And I just—I didn't know what to do. I couldn't face being by myself, couldn't stand being alone with my thoughts, couldn't stare at that picture of them together, couldn't live with the decision I made."

"You don't have to live with it," Elisa interjects, taking a seat in the armchair next to us. "You could still have the life you want. You're both healthy and alive. You have a chance to undo this. There's nothing worse than losing the person you love and not being able to do anything about it, but in this instance, you have the possibility to change things."

"Do I? They look happy in the picture," Beatriz replies. "*He* looked happy."

"Beatriz."

"I love him," she says, a smile on her face despite the tears swimming in her eyes. "I will always love him. And because I love him, I want that for him. I want him to be happy. I want him to have the life he deserves. I want him to do the good he needs to do in this world that so desperately needs men and women like him. I'm happy that he's found someone to be by his side for all of that. I just wish it could have been me."

"I know," I reply. "If it's any consolation, I think you're incredibly brave to choose the hard decision, to make the choice that hurts now because you want what's best in the long term. And I admire you so much for knowing who you are, for always being unapologetically yourself and for living life on your own terms. It's not easy to do so coming from a family like ours, it's not easy to do so considering where we come from and what we've lost, but I admire your courage and your passion more than you'll ever know." I smile. "Basically, I want to be like you when I grow up."

Beatriz laughs, wiping at the tears falling down her cheeks. "Don't be ridiculous. We're not so different. We're both survivors. I found that taking up as much attention, being as bold as I could possibly be, helped me get through everything we went through in Cuba and after. And you've found that in retreating from the world, in silence, you feel safe. You've been surviving, Isabel. There's no shame in that. You shouldn't wish to be anyone other than yourself."

There's a wisdom to Beatriz that's so easy to miss if you aren't looking for it. For all her impulsiveness, it's easy to discount her, but she'll say something so wise it makes you think. Perhaps Beatriz is right; maybe love is about meeting people where they are, not where you would wish them to be.

"Are you happy?" Beatriz asks me.

"We're not here talking about me."

"Maybe we should be," Beatriz counters. "Take it from your little sister. You don't want to be here like me. Are you happy? Did leaving Barcelona give you the peace you sought?"

"I really don't—"

"We need champagne," Beatriz interjects. "We're going to talk about you."

"How on earth does this call for champagne?" Elisa asks. "I'd hardly call this a celebration."

"There's no rule you can only drink champagne when you're celebrating. If we're going to commiserate I'd much rather do it with champagne than anything else."

Elisa smiles, some of the worry leaving her eyes. "I can't argue with that logic. I'll get us the good stuff," she adds, turning on her heel and exiting the room.

"Thanks for coming," Beatriz says when it's just the two of us. "Somehow, I knew you would."

"Always."

"Let me be there for you, then. Are you happy, Isabel?"

"Happy enough, I suppose," I lie. "Today isn't supposed to be about me. I'm here for you. I know what you said earlier. I know that you're brave. But it's understandable to also be a little unsure of yourself. Do you regret it—the choice you have made?"

She's silent for a little too long, certainly long enough for me to wish I hadn't asked the question, an unmistakable, awful sensation that I have overstepped filling me.

"I'm sorry, I—"

"Sometimes I regret it," she replies. "Perhaps you could even say often. But it wasn't fair to pretend I could be someone I'm not. To ruin his life and all his potential with the baggage I carry with me. Exile—it stays with you. It changes you. And you can't go back. If things were different, if I could be different, I would love nothing more than to spend my life beside him. Then again, if things were different, if Fidel had never taken it all away, we never would have met. So, I suppose fate has a sense of humor after all.

"It was the right thing to do. For both of us." She looks at me. "You didn't just ask because you're worried about me."

I am afraid to admit that I see parallels between my situation and hers, that part of me wonders if Diego is meant to be my Nicholas Preston, if I am headed down the same path of heartbreak and disappointment—even more so, because I am a married woman, my heart not mine to give as freely as Beatriz gave hers.

"Do you care for him?" Beatriz asks.

I have the distinct impression that she's gentled the word somewhat, that what she's really asking is another four-letter word she knows I can't bear to hear.

"I might. I don't know. It's too fast. Too unexpected. I didn't ask for any of this. I didn't want it."

She laughs. "Do you think people schedule falling in love, Isabel? That they write it in their calendar and make a plan? It often is unexpected. And yes, sometimes it can be fast. Sometimes you can meet someone and feel seen in a way that you never will again. That's the whole point, that's why people write poems, and songs, and paint pictures about it. Love is supposed to move you."

"What if it isn't love? What if it's just passion?"

Easier to blame it all on passion, to equate this attraction between us to the physical because presumably that is a need that can eventually run its course and be satiated. Harder still to consider the possibility that this thing between me and Diego is more than that, that perhaps in him I have found something I was looking for and might never find again.

"You'll never know if you turn your back on it. What will you do?" Beatriz asks.

"Nothing. What is there to do? I'm married."

"Happily?" Beatriz's tone makes it clear that the question is more rhetorical than anything else, for there's no chance she believes it to be true.

"I made a vow. I can't break that. I can't give my word and have it mean nothing."

"No, I suppose you couldn't. Not you. If you want some advice from your little sister, here's what I'd tell you. If you want Diego, if you love him, if you think you could love him, hold on to him and don't let go."

She makes it sound so easy, but the truth is, for me, marrying Thomas was easy. These emotions inside me, the way Diego makes me feel—that's the hard part.

"Don't let who go?" Elisa asks, returning with a bottle of Dom and three flutes.

"Can I tell her?" Beatriz asks. "After all, Elisa's the only one of us who is actually happily married. She might have some advice."

Elisa's eyes widen slightly at the caveat "happily." I'm sure she's suspected that things between me and Thomas aren't the same as they are for her and Juan, but there's a difference between suspecting and hearing outright that your sister isn't happy in her marriage.

"I'll tell it," I say, and so I do, filling Elisa in on the parts of the Barcelona trip that I never mentioned to her, about how my feelings toward Diego have surprised me, about the painting, and my marriage, and everything.

I don't realize Beatriz has taken my hand until she squeezes it, urging me on.

"I left Barcelona," I say, "because I didn't want to do anything I'd regret. I didn't want to be tempted into breaking my marriage vows. But I think Thomas knows something is off, and more than that, something in me has changed, and I don't know how to go back to the person I was, how to want the same things. And now, Thomas wants to have a child."

"Is that what you want?" Elisa asks.

"It's what I should want. It's what our mother wanted for me. But no, I don't know that I want to be a mother, and even more, the idea of bringing a child into this marriage with Thomas—" It seems wrong to speak of our family, to acknowledge the dynamics that I have protected for so long, and still, I need to. I am realizing how much we have all suffered for the pretense we have maintained, pretending everything is perfect when the truth is so far from it. "We grew up in a household with parents who weren't happy in their marriage, who stayed together because that's what was expected of them, because for our mother there were no other easy options, but we saw the toll it took on them, how their disagreements and discord filtered down to the rest of us. I don't even know that I want to have children, but if I ever did have them, I wouldn't want them to feel as though they were born out of obligation but out of love."

"Do you love Thomas?" Elisa asks me.

"No. I don't. I knew that going into it. He knew that going into it. And I don't even know that he loves me. If he does, he's certainly never said it. I thought that would be fine, that I didn't need to be loved—"

"Everyone wants to be loved, Isabel," Elisa interjects. "It's not wrong to want that. Do you think you could ever learn to love him?"

"I don't think so. We want different things, are different people. And that would be fine, but there's no desire to bridge those things between us. He doesn't understand me or care to try to understand, and part of me thought that would be good enough, that a marriage based on separate lives was all I should expect because that's what

I saw, but now—I want better for myself. I want to be respected, not just tolerated."

"You deserve those things, Isabel. Everyone does. I know what it is to marry for your family's benefit, and I was fortunate that for me, that marriage turned out to be a source of joy. But I had to fight for that happiness with Juan. I had to demand that we have the kind of relationship that was built on mutual understanding and respect. And if your husband isn't willing to give you those things, if you are so unhappy that you cannot make it work between you, there are always other options available to you."

"I'm scared," I confess. "Scared to be on my own, scared to embark on this new path alone. A divorce—what would that do to the family, to our reputation?"

"We'd be the notorious Perez sisters," Beatriz replies. "Nothing wrong with that. Better they find us scandalous than piteous."

"Can I make a suggestion as someone who has experienced what life can throw at you unexpectedly and who loves you and has seen how much you've struggled these past few years?" Elisa asks.

I nod.

"It would be a mistake to live the rest of your life unhappy just because you are doing what you think your family wants you to do. There's no shame in admitting that your marriage was a mistake."

"I chose it, though. I chose it knowing that we didn't love each other. I chose it not wanting to be married to someone who loved me. How do I not live in this mistake I made? How do I not take responsibility for it?"

"Isabel," Elisa says. "There's taking responsibility and there's punishing yourself and everyone around you for the rest of your life. You've always held others to such a high standard, and you've been equally unforgiving with yourself. You have such a strong sense of right and wrong, and that's a good thing to be sure, but you also have to allow for people to make mistakes. You have to give yourself permission to make a mistake and a chance to recover from it."

"I wasn't exactly raised in a house where that was an option."

Elisa reaches out and wraps her arm around me. "Neither was I. There's a cost to trying to maintain the facade that you're perfect, that everything is easy. I understand why our parents felt the need to do it; you and I were raised in the same place, with the same expectations on our shoulders. It's hard not to carry those expectations. It's hard not to pass them down. You have a chance to make different choices."

"You think I should leave Thomas."

"I don't think you should be unhappy. Life isn't some punishment you accept because you must prove you are worthy to other people. Live on your own terms, Isabel. If I had one thing to do over in my life, it's that I would have been bolder, taken more chances, and worried less about what everyone else thought. I'm past the point of do-overs now, and there's no point in regret, but you have a chance."

"I couldn't agree more," Beatriz says. "I think we're ready for that champagne."

Beatriz opens the bottle, pouring the frothy gold liquid into the glasses Elisa holds out for her.

Simultaneously, we raise our glasses up, and Beatriz says:

"To the Perez sisters. Always together in good times and in bad. I wouldn't want to go through this life with anyone else by my side."

She smiles at me, and suddenly, she is the eldest one, giving me the advice I most need to hear—

"Be brave, Isabel."

chapter twenty-six

My hands shake as I pull the suitcase down from the top of my closet, running my fingers over the familiar leather, my gaze resting on the monogram there and the reminder of the fact that I ceased being Isabel Perez a long time ago. It was a wedding present from my sister Elisa.

I set my suitcase down on the edge of the bed, opening it up, methodically placing my clothing inside its satin-lined interior. For much of my life, these sorts of tasks have been done for me by my parents' household staff and Thomas's housekeeper, but I need to do this on my own.

My hands won't stop shaking.

I have never seen Thomas lose his temper, never heard him raise his voice to me, but if I've learned anything in this life it's that you can't predict what people will do when you take something away from them, when you threaten their version of the world as they know it.

I choose the most sensible dresses, some underthings, a few pairs of shoes, the essentials that will get me through this transition. All my things will hardly fit in the smaller suitcase, and it's hard to know what I am allowed to take, what is too much, what will anger Thomas, what is mine and what is his.

I slide my wedding ring off and set it on the dresser.

The door to my bedroom opens without the usual polite rap Thomas uses to let me know he is entering, and I freeze, my hand gripping the edge of the dresser.

Part of me wishes I had gone to my father, or Elisa's husband, Juan, or had not told my sisters I would be fine when they asked if I wanted someone with me when I told Thomas I was leaving, that I had sought more advice on how to go about getting a divorce. There are a few things I can sell—jewelry that came to me before the marriage that won't bring much but should at least help me secure a lawyer as we figure out the dissolution of our marriage. And of course, there is the money that I've made from my painting.

"Are you going on a trip?" Thomas asks me, and his gaze slides down to my bare hand, the wedding ring removed. He's silent for a long, awful moment. "I see. Not a trip."

"No. I'm sorry, but I can't do this anymore." Tears fill my eyes. "It's not your fault, and I should have spoken up a long time ago. I'm not happy. And I don't blame you, because for a long time I didn't know how to be happy or what I wanted. That wasn't fair to you. You walked into this marriage thinking you were getting one thing, that I was fine with the way things were, and I know I'm the one changing things now, but I can't live my life like this."

Thomas sighs, and suddenly he looks as though he's aged a tremendous amount in a short time, and I am sorry for what I've put him through, for my inconstancy. "Can I sit?" he asks, gesturing to the sitting area in my bedroom.

I nod.

"I can't say I'm entirely surprised. I've known you weren't happy for quite some time. I thought it was a phase, that as you got older, matured, you might come to appreciate the advantages of our marriage more. We're very different. I knew we were when I expressed an interest in you, but I thought that with time you would understand what I needed from you, the kind of wife you should be. I thought you would be grateful enough for the opportunities you would have as my wife that it would be enough for you."

There's no condemnation in his voice, merely disappointment, and I can't help but wonder if this is his demeanor when a business deal goes awry.

"I know. It's not enough. I'm sorry."

"So, you want a divorce?"

"Yes."

"Is there someone else? The paintings in your room—"

I can't deny that I have feelings for Diego, but at the same time, I'm not leaving Thomas for another man. I'm leaving Thomas for me.

"I think there's enough of a possibility for me that things might change. But I'm not there yet, am not at a place in my life where I can imagine jumping into another relationship. I need to be on my own. My entire life I have been defined by my relationship to other people. I was someone's daughter, and I was your wife, and now I just want to be Isabel, whoever she is."

Women in my family do not get divorced, but at the same time, I don't want the legacy of the Perez women to be that we sacrificed our happiness to please others. This pressure to be pleasing, to not be disruptive, to do as we are told is an unending cycle that will only lead to unhappiness and discontentment. I don't want to look back on my life and regret the decisions I made or the fact that I didn't have the courage I needed when it counted.

And as I walk away, suitcase in hand, I hear my sister's voice in my head, Beatriz saying,

Be brave, Isabel.

I n the end, it's my aunt Mirta who comes to my rescue by inviting me to stay with her and Uncle Anthony in New York. My parents are, predictably, furious, and while I spend the first week of my life as a soon-to-be divorced woman comfortably ensconced in Elisa's house with her and Beatriz, soon it is time for Beatriz to return to Barcelona, and society in South Florida is too small to give me the privacy I seek.

Now, impossibly, unexpectedly, I am the Perez who is a scandal.

In New York, there is anonymity to be had, and while I speak to my sisters regularly as I sort through the intricacies of this divorce, Anthony's attorneys helping me, it's good to have this space from my family, Mirta there to keep me company when I need it and leaving me to my own devices when I need that, too.

I paint often, gathering the courage to take some of the pieces to a small gallery in the city. When they begin to sell, it's more of a trickle of funds coming in, but it's enough to give me hope that I may be able to live a small, independent life on my own.

I think of Diego often, too, paint him sometimes, and wonder if Beatriz has told him, now that she has returned to Barcelona, that I am divorcing Thomas. Somehow, knowing Beatriz, I imagine she has.

Since we never had children together and I have agreed to not ask Thomas for a financial settlement, the divorce goes relatively smoothly, and despite the angry phone calls from my parents, with each day that passes, I am at peace with the decision I have made.

There are still problems to be fixed—living in the city rent-free at Mirta and Anthony's has given me a tremendous amount of freedom, but it isn't a long-term possibility. The kindness that my aunt and uncle have shown me in welcoming me to their home, though, has meant everything.

One evening in December, seven months after I left Thomas, I accompany Mirta and Anthony to a private event at the Museum of Modern Art to commemorate Mirta's forty-eighth birthday. Many husbands may have waited until a more momentous milestone to hold such an elegant affair, but my uncle Anthony has always loved to make Mirta happy, and tonight is no exception, an opportunity to dress up and celebrate the life Mirta has built for herself.

Modern art isn't my usual preference, but I've been looking forward to this night, curious to see the paintings the museum houses. During this time in New York, I have begun buying books on art, trying to teach myself some of the things that I never learned in school, but instead of picking up on techniques, I find myself lost in the images themselves.

In our house in Havana, my parents had an impressive art collection, built up by generations of Perezes. When I was younger, I used to roam the space, making up stories about each painting, imagining the lives of the people whose eyes peered back at me. I looked at pictures of boats and saw myself sailing on one of them, the salt air blowing my hair around, the sea spraying on my face. The magic of art is that it can carry you away from reality. It can make you forget. It can make you believe.

I didn't paint back then, didn't consider it. I just knew that when those paintings were there, when I could look inside those canvases and escape, I was no longer in a house filled with fighting—my parents' disagreements over my brother, Alejandro, defying President Batista, their parental angst spilling over into marital discord. I was no longer in a house filled with fear or grief. When I saw those paintings, when I lost myself in them, I was free.

And when we left Havana and all those things behind us, I realized the escape I had relied on to maintain my calm was gone, and instead I picked up a brush and created my own refuge in the messy and inexpert canvases that fill me with longing, and sadness, and nostalgia, and also sometimes—hope.

I walk on through the gallery, slipping my clutch beneath my arm, my gaze drifting from piece to piece until it settles on an enormous canvas dominating the wall.

The painting is almost grotesque in its imagery, the colors stark. It's all angry shapes and slashing lines that taken together force a story I attempt to unravel. There's so much going on that it's almost difficult to find one thing to concentrate on, as though each disparate image is its own painting within a larger canvas, each one fairly screaming, *Look at me.*

It is horror come to life before me.

It's not the sort of art I favor, the image howling of anger, pain, and grief in a manner I'm wholly uncomfortable with, but something about it keeps me rooted to the spot in the floor.

It's not the sort of painting that's easy to look away from once it has you in its grip.

I'm not sure how much time passes while I stand there, don't even realize a gasp has escaped my lips until someone says—

"Powerful, isn't it?"

I nearly jump at the question, the familiar voice catching me off guard. For a moment, I felt as though I was in the painting, as though I could hear the bull charging, the people's screams, could feel the flames. It felt as though the painting was alive, as though it could pull the viewer into its macabre world.

I wrench my gaze away from the image on the wall and focus on the speaker—a tall, lean, dark-haired man dressed in an elegant tuxedo, a champagne flute in hand.

Diego.

Neither one of us speaks.

For all the times I have painted his face since our last days together in Barcelona, I wondered if I would ever see it again in person.

"What are you doing here?" I finally ask.

"Beatriz wanted me to drop off a gift for your aunt."

"Beatriz wanted you to fly all the way from Barcelona to deliver a present?"

"No, if I had to guess, she wanted me to come to New York because she knew you would be here. She wanted me to see you. *I* wanted to see you. I had a business meeting in the city, but I'd be lying if I said I had to be there, that someone else couldn't have come in my stead." He takes a deep breath. "I'd be lying if I didn't say that I've thought of you every single day since we last saw each other in Barcelona."

His expression is solemn as he says, "I heard you left your husband."

"I did."

"Did you—"

The words linger between us, unspoken, but I know what he's asking anyway—

Did you leave your husband because of me?

"No. I wasn't happy. And I realized I couldn't continue like that. I want more for myself. I deserve to be happy. I don't know yet what that looks like—but it's good to be on my own. I'm happy now. Getting there, at least."

"I'm glad. You deserve that. You deserve everything."

I take a pause, channeling some of my newfound bravery. "I thought about calling you. So many times. Beatriz told me you took the painting. The one I did of the night we danced in Barcelona."

"It hangs in my bedroom. I'm sorry I took it; I just couldn't imagine anyone else having it, wanted to hang on to a piece of you for as long as possible, wanted to remember that night as much as I could."

"I'm glad you have it. I wouldn't have wanted it to go to anyone else."

There's so much I want to say to him, so much I'm still figuring out myself.

"How have you been?" I ask him.

"Missing you."

"I worry about you—in Spain. I worry if you're safe."

"I am."

"And your arm?" I ask.

"All healed."

"Good," I whisper.

"My heart on the other hand . . ."

I flush.

"I want to kiss you," he says.

I startle, nearly tipping over my champagne.

"Sorry. I didn't mean to catch you off guard." Diego smiles, the look in his eyes rocking me once more. "I'm still figuring out this friendship between us. How honest I should be with you. It's hard to see you and not want to tell you things."

"I'm still—I'm still figuring things out."

"I know. I'm sorry. I don't want to pressure you or come on too strong. We were friends in Barcelona. We can be friendly. Let's look at art together."

"'Look at art together'?"

"It seems like the safest option. Besides, you're an artist. I can't pretend to know much about art, but I want to learn more about the things you're passionate about. I want to understand them better."

I turn my attention away from him and back to the painting, struggling to calm my racing heart.

Art has made me feel so many things, has put a smile on my face, has made me wish to weep, but this is an entirely novel experience. The longer I look at it, the more I notice new things that jump out at me. I almost like that about the painting, the way it hides its secrets in plain view. It's almost as though it challenges the viewer to look deeper, to sit in their discomfort.

Maybe I admire its courage.

There's a small plaque beside the painting with the name of the work and the artist's information.

Guernica. Pablo Picasso.

"I'm not familiar with his work," I admit, turning back to face Diego, a little embarrassed considering Picasso's stature in the art world. "It's not my usual style. Modern art, I mean."

"Are you familiar with the history behind the painting?"

I shake my head.

"Picasso was asked to create a piece for Spain's pavilion at the World's Fair. The Germans had just bombed the Basque city of Guernica, and Picasso read an eyewitness account that inspired him so much he gave the world *Guernica.*"

I glance back at the artwork on the wall across from me, the background offering a fresh perspective. The colors and brushstrokes are more powerful now, leaping off the page.

Its sheer size is staggering, the images looming, and I struggle to put my emotions into words. It shows humanity at its worst in an unflinching light, as though daring the viewer to look away from the horrors of war.

"It's honest," I say. "Unflinchingly so. It's an indictment, isn't it? As though Picasso wanted to say, 'Look upon what you have wrought until you cannot look away.'"

"For many in Spain, this painting has been a form of resistance, a source of hope. Prints secretly hang in homes while Franco keeps a tight grip on the country."

That's the thing about the time we spend together—there is something so easy about talking to Diego, an understanding that passes between us. There is a part of myself I can share with him that Thomas has never understood or taken an interest in understanding. Thomas lives in a world where society is suited to accommodate him, in a country where his ability to speak, to exist freely without fear, is held to a paramount. We interact with the world so differently that it is difficult to understand each other on a fundamental level.

"I—" I take a step closer to Diego, my body moving of its own volition, and I reach out to take his hand in mine—

"Isabel!"

I whirl around at the sound of my name.

My aunt Mirta hurries toward me, her face pale. "Isabel. I'm so sorry. It's your mother."

chapter twenty-seven

Alicia

1937

BARCELONA

It's been a week since our parents learned of Consuelo's pregnancy, and it's becoming clearer to me that staying in Barcelona
is only getting more difficult, particularly with the growing violence in the country, the news of more children being sent out
of Spain for their safety. The stories coming out of Nationalist-
held territories are filled with atrocities toward women, and I cannot help but fear what will happen if Barcelona falls to the
Nationalists.

Nestor and I spend more and more time together, and I've taken
to helping in his clinic, the need growing greater with each day that
passes.

Felipe's ship is due into the port of Bilbao any day now.

I'm sitting in the café one day with Isabel when one of my parents' maids comes running toward me, out of breath, panic on her face.

"What's wrong?" I ask her.

"Consuelo asked me to come find you. They've taken her."

"What do you mean, 'they've taken her'?"

"They came and took Consuelo to the convent. Your mother waited to do it when you were out of the house. She knew you didn't want Consuelo to go."

"Did my mother travel with her?"

"No, she and your father are still at the house. I think she plans on going later."

My heart pounds. "Where did they take Consuelo?"

"They're headed to a convent in a small town in the Basque region of Spain. Guernica."

I immediately take Isabel to the clinic where Nestor works and beg him to lend me his car so that I can journey to Guernica. He agrees on the condition that he drive us, given the fighting going on around Spain. It's too late in the day to leave safely, but the next morning we set out for Guernica before the sun is up, Isabel in the back seat behind us. I say nothing to my parents of my plan for fear that they will object.

A pistol rests beside Nestor, a stark reminder that despite the beautiful weather and landscape surrounding us, we're hardly going on a scenic drive. Fighting has intensified in the countryside, the Republicans and Nationalists vying for control, the violence in Spain spilling out through the country.

Fear grips me as we drive to Guernica, the signs of war closer to us than ever now that we are no longer in Barcelona. And still, I can't help but remember the promise I made to Consuelo that I would be by her side through this pregnancy, and the idea of my little sister alone in an unfamiliar city spurs me on.

Guernica is bustling when we arrive late in the day. The market is open, livestock to be sold, neighbors sharing news of the events in Spain.

On the one hand, people are socializing and buying things, clearly eager for this bit of normalcy in these difficult times. On the other, refugees from nearby towns have poured into Guernica, and they carry uneasy expressions on their faces as though they've seen the worst and know that it can happen anywhere.

The weather is pleasant enough, hardly a cloud in the sky, a light breeze in the air.

There are several convents in town, and we stop at two of them and ask if Consuelo is there with no success until we reach the third one.

One of the nuns hesitates. "I don't know her name, but yes, a young girl came from Barcelona. She is pregnant."

"How is she?" I ask, relief filling me.

"She is fine. She's resting in one of the rooms."

"Take me to her, please."

I follow the nun through the convent, Nestor trailing behind me, Isabel in his arms.

The nun stops in front of a wooden door, and I push it open.

Consuelo lies in a slender bed with white linens.

"Alicia!"

She rises from the bed, rushing to greet me, and I throw my arms around her.

"I told you I wasn't going to leave you. Everything is going to be fine. Gonzalo's brother, Felipe, is coming. His ship will be at the port of Bilbao soon. We'll figure this out. I promise. I'm not going to let them take your baby away."

I hold Consuelo while Nestor speaks with the nuns, convincing them that Consuelo is his patient and needs to be in his care.

When we leave the convent, the atmosphere has changed. Many of the shops have pulled down their shutters. Smoke rises over the hills from a battle nearby. The fighting is so close, and if not for Nestor agreeing to accompany me today, I don't think I'd have made this journey.

Perhaps I should have left Isabel at home in Barcelona with my parents.

The church bells have been ringing on and off all day, and each gong and clang rattles my nerves.

A low-flying plane buzzes past us.

It's late in the day as we drive out of the city, the four of us piled into the car. Nestor parks near the hillside to look at a map and get our bearings before we journey to Bilbao.

Bells ring out once more, the direction coming from the convent we visited. This time the ringing doesn't stop like it did earlier; it just continues on and on.

A siren squawks.

People run from the city, heading toward the hills.

"What are they—"

My words are cut off by a low humming in the sky, a plane off in the distance.

Beside me, Nestor stills.

The plane flies over the town of Guernica, coming closer to us, closer still. It turns, and as it does, Nestor grabs me and Isabel, yanking my body toward him.

"It's a German plane. We need to get cover, now," he urges.

It was so crowded today, excitement in the market, children laughing, families smiling—

Beside me, Consuelo screams.

The explosion from the first bomb the plane drops over Guernica nearly sends me to the ground, but for Nestor's arm wrapped around me, holding my body tightly to his, Isabel crushed against his chest. He drags me away from the car, my daughter in his arms, Consuelo beside us, pulling us behind a large rock.

Another explosion. Then another, my ears ringing. I open my mouth to cry out, but he puts a hand over my lips, silencing me.

"The car . . . they'll use it as a bombing target. We need to get to safety before they see us."

I take Isabel from him, holding my daughter to my chest, trying to quiet her tears, stroking her hair, doing anything I can to calm her.

Terror fills me at the sound of more explosions over the town, the humming of more planes, the screams.

With each explosion, my sister shakes beside me, her mouth open in a soundless scream.

My limbs are sluggish, my mind struggling to reconcile the images before me, to comprehend that this is real, not a nightmare, that I need to *move*.

Nestor pulls us toward the woods on the mountain above Guernica, and I lengthen my strides to keep up with him, the weight of Isabel making it harder to run, my lungs burning with the exertion, my legs pumping madly. I almost think I'm going to fall, but I keep a tight hold on my daughter, Consuelo just behind me. When we reach the edge of the woods, I glance over my shoulder.

The sky is filled with low-flying planes dropping bombs over the city of Guernica.

The sound of gunfire fills the air.

"Are they shooting?"

"They're going after anyone trying to leave the city now," Nestor answers, his face ashen.

For what must be over an hour, planes unrelentingly bomb Guernica. There are no tears. Whatever fear I might have felt has fled my body. There are no words to describe what I am seeing, no way for my mind to process it. I am here, crouched down in the dirt and in these woods, one hand clutched in my daughter's, the other in my sister's, and at the same time, I am somewhere else entirely. Time is little more than a blur, and maybe that is a blessing of sorts, maybe this is my mind's way of protecting me from this, by erasing and dulling the sharpness of my impressions to something infinitely more bearable. Finally, blessedly, the airplanes leave, the only sounds filling the night sky the echoes of cries from the town.

I rise from my crouching position. There will be injured, an untold number who will need assistance. Beside me, Consuelo and Isabel remain still.

Nestor tugs on my hand, unceremoniously yanking me to the ground.

"Wait."

"The people in the city—they'll need help—" I protest.

"Wait. Give it a while longer."

"They've left."

His mouth is in a grim line. "Let's hope so."

We stay like that, hidden in the woods, his arm around me, holding me in place, and just when I'm ready to insist that all is clear, that we go toward the town to help, I hear it again:

The sound of airplanes.

Hope fills me that it is the Republicans come to defend the city, but it instantly becomes obvious that this is something else entirely.

These planes are flying much higher in the sky than their predecessors. These planes leave fire in their wake, the battered city of Guernica aflame before our eyes.

The next bombs come in whispers, exploding in white flames that eventually turn into blazes all over the city, the explosions conjuring up smoke and dust, creating an inferno.

"Why would they—was bombing the city not enough?" I whisper.

"This was a message—and a test. They didn't want to just bomb the city; they wanted to destroy its people and their will. To fire-bomb innocent civilians—" I think Nestor's going to cry. He clears his throat. "If this is the world the Germans and their allies wish to bring about, we are all doomed."

It's nearly dark, the red glow of the burning town illuminating the night sky.

The car Nestor borrowed to take us to the city has been bombed, and so we walk together, hand in hand, toward Guernica, following a stream of people emerging from the woods and the surrounding areas to check on their loved ones.

Bomb craters litter the ground around us. The town is engulfed in fire and smoke, the streets we just walked down, the buildings we saw now destroyed.

Bodies fill the plaza where a busy, joyous market took place just hours before. Animal carcasses are strewn next to human ones, burned beyond recognition, the stench overwhelming, and still the fire rages. The heat emanating from the ground warms the soles of my shoes. The fires only seem to grow stronger, larger, as everyone races to put them out, to save people crying for help from beneath the rubble.

Beside me, Consuelo leans over and retches.

I pull Isabel to me even tighter, trying to keep her gaze averted from the horrors surrounding us.

I pray that she is too young to remember seeing this, that she will forget all these horrible things.

Around us, people run carrying stretchers, crouched on the ground tending to the wounded, to the survivors. Nestor and I immediately jump in and begin helping.

A crash sounds off in the distance, and I flinch, remembering those planes soaring above us, the sound of the bombs, fearing that they have returned, but no—it is only the sound of a building falling to the ground.

chapter twenty-eight

Guernica has been destroyed by the bombing.

People are out searching for their family members, their friends, their loved ones. So many missing. So many dead. The dead are barely recognizable.

In the late evening and early morning, firemen and police arrive from the nearby town of Bilbao. Trucks and trains are used to evacuate women and children from Guernica.

"We need to go," Nestor says. "We don't want to be caught here if the fighting spreads to the ground."

The urge to stay here and help is overwhelming, but he's right—in the aftermath of the bombing, we are surrounded by utter chaos, and after the destruction that rained from the skies, the thought of being caught on the ground if the planes return or soldiers arrive is even more terrifying. Consuelo looks like she's about to collapse, her pregnancy clearly taking its toll. Isabel doesn't speak, hasn't spoken since the bombing began, her head buried in the crook of Nestor's neck as he carries her.

We walk toward Bilbao, the roads crowded with people.

We are surrounded by silence, the occasional cry, but more than anything it as though a miasma has settled around everyone who just witnessed an unbelievable atrocity. Nestor keeps hold of my hand and doesn't let go, my arm around my sister. The farther we walk, the more my limbs ache, my heart heavy, exhaustion setting in.

In Bilbao, they are ready for us, the news of the bombing already having traveled far.

We shelter in a barn with other families who fled Guernica.

Someone brings a radio into the barn, and we all crowd around it. We listen in horror as the Basque president announces Guernica has been bombed by the Germans at the Nationalists' invitation.

Hours later—as though we have not seen the truth with our own eyes, heard it with our own ears, Radio Nacional broadcasts that there is no German or foreign air force in Spain, never mind that there *is*, that they bombed a Spanish city to ruin, that we all watched it happen.

Anger mixes with grief and a stunned disbelief all throughout the barn.

What the Germans did here seems like a horrible harbinger of what's to come—an experiment, a place where they thought the world would turn their backs if they waged the kind of warfare they desperately wish to.

We sleep fitfully in the barn, the straw rough, the night cold, the surrounding noises loud, the images of what we saw too horrible to allow for peace.

Isabel sleeps in my arms, Consuelo beside me. Each time I close my eyes, I am transported back to that moment when the planes came, am plagued with worry for Consuelo and Isabel.

I pray for the people of Guernica and all they lost.

When I wake in the morning, my sister and daughter still sleeping, Nestor is already up, sitting apart from the pallets where we slept the night before, his back to me.

I rise from my position next to Consuelo and Isabel and sit down next to him.

He doesn't look at me, his gaze trained on the others in the barn.

"I fell in love with you when you were eighteen."

My breath hitches.

"I remember because it was your birthday," he continues, "and your parents had me over for dinner. It was one of the last times we saw each other before your parents left Cuba, before your engagement to Emilio was announced. You probably don't even remember, but I told this awful, silly joke, and no one at the table laughed, but you smiled, and I thought to myself, 'I don't care if I make a fool of myself in front of every single person here as long as I'm able to make her laugh.'"

"I remember," I reply softly. "I remember everything about that night. I wore a blue dress because it was your favorite color, and I knew you would be there."

"I should have said something to you that night. I should have told you how I felt, but it was so new, so fast. You were like family to me, someone I cared for deeply, someone I loved, and I looked at you and I realized I didn't love you like family at all. That what I felt for you was something more. It terrified me. You terrified me." He turns toward me. "Now, knowing how Emilio has treated you—I wish I had done things differently. I wish I'd had the courage to tell you that I love you. That I've loved you for so long. And that I'm sorry we never had a chance to see what might have been."

I want to weep at his confession, at all the possibilities that pass me by in an instant, but the last day has wrung the emotion from me, and so all I can do is reach out and take his hand, our fingers interlacing, as we sit beside each other in the barn, my sister and daughter sleeping behind us.

"I've been talking with some of the others," he says after a few minutes. "There are ships evacuating women and children from the port of Bilbao. You need to get on one of those boats.

"Things are going to get worse. The Republicans aren't going to be able to hold this threat much longer. The city is running out of food. And if you mean to go back to Barcelona, well—the city's air defenses will not be able to withstand an attack like Guernica."

"I can't leave my parents. I need to go back to Barcelona and get them out, too."

"Consuelo can't take such a journey in her condition, Alicia. You know that. And Isabel has already been through so much. You can't risk their safety by returning for your parents. I promise, I'll go back to Barcelona and do everything I can to help them."

"What do you mean, 'go back to Barcelona'? Why wouldn't you get on one of those ships, too? You said it yourself—it isn't safe here. You don't have to stay here; you could go home, return to Havana."

"I can't. What we saw at Guernica—do you think the war is going to end here? If we don't stop Hitler, if we don't defeat the spread of fascism, Guernica is just the beginning. This is a threat to all of us. I'm a doctor. This is a chance for me to make a difference. To stand up for what I believe in. This is a chance for me to fight, to help those who need it." He hesitates. "Please go to the port. It's your best chance. Felipe is arriving on a ship from Cuba. Let me take you to him so that you can get out of the country. There's a group that's leaving for the port today. We should go with them. I'll wait with you until you're safe. What's happening in Nationalist-held territories, what's happening to women, the violence that we just saw—get out. Get out while you have a chance. Please."

"Are you sure you won't come with us?"

"I can't. I'll see you to the port and stay with you until your cousin's family arrives, but I have to go where I'm needed."

By some miracle, we arrive at the port of Bilbao, and Nestor and I join the crowds for two days waiting for Felipe's ship to pull into the dock, the desperation around us growing with each passing day.

I stand beside Nestor as he attempts to get information about the ships coming in from Havana, as we try to ascertain when Felipe will arrive. Consuelo and Isabel are resting at the hotel room we've secured, our funds running low, the money Nestor brought with him nearly gone.

All I have left to sell is my wedding ring, the gold band Emilio slipped on my finger at the Cathedral of Havana. If Felipe doesn't arrive soon, I'll have to pawn it, but even as I know how desperately we need the money, it feels like I'm giving a piece of history away—

I always thought I'd save it for Isabel, that when I died, it would pass on to her.

On the fourth day, we go to the ticket office. People are shoving and yelling. A woman stands in the corner, tears in her eyes. She's visibly pregnant, a blond-haired man beside her arguing with one of the shipping clerks.

Someone in the crowd bumps into her, and I reach out, putting my arm around her waist and steadying her.

"My companion is a doctor. Do you need assistance?" I ask her.

"I'm fine. We're trying to get on a ship out of here. We lost everything—the soldiers—they came and took everything. We've been waiting for days."

She reminds me of Consuelo, and the fierce determination in her eyes—

I slip the gold wedding band off my finger and hand it to her.

"Take this. You can sell it. It will help you find passage wherever you're going."

"America. The baby's father—my husband—is American." She looks down at the ring in her palm. "I can't. I can't take your wedding ring."

"Take it. For the baby. To get to safety. I'd want someone to do the same for my daughter."

"I can't—I—"

"Alicia!"

I whirl around at the sound of Nestor's voice.

"Felipe's ship is due to get in later today."

Relief fills me.

I turn back to the woman.

She takes my hand, tears spilling down her cheeks. "Thank you."

Nestor pulls me along, and I turn away from her. When I glance back, she's still there, her hand on her stomach, cradling her babe.

I pray they'll make it out of Spain safely.

We get Isabel and Consuelo from the hotel and return to the dock. We watch as people come off the ship, scanning the faces there. I have never met Felipe in person or seen a photograph of him, but I look for a man who resembles Gonzalo, someone I assume will be well-dressed—

For a moment, I think my eyes have deceived me.

Walking next to a tall man, wearing a simple gray dress, is Rosa.

I shout her name, and run toward her, pushing through the

· 264 ·

crowd. Felipe looks as though he's going to move in front of her, as though he would protect her from me if he could, but realization sets in, and I hear her say—

"Alicia?"

I rush into Rosa's embrace.

My voice shakes as I tell them about Guernica, as Consuelo and Isabel stand beside me. Rosa cries, Felipe quiet beside her. There will be time for me and Rosa to speak privately, to discuss all the things that have transpired, all the losses, the grief, but at once Felipe picks up on the urgency of the situation, and after talking to Nestor, he leaves us to arrange swift passage out of Spain for the five of us.

Nestor pulls me aside. "There's a truck carrying men to go help the Republican cause. I'm going to catch a ride on it."

"So, this is good-bye?"

He nods.

"Thank you." I swallow past the lump in my throat. "Thank you for the kindness you have shown me. For your friendship. You didn't have to help me, to risk so much. Many men wouldn't have."

"It was my honor to help you. I only wish I could have done more. I wish things were different."

"I do, too."

I reach out and I take his hand, hardly caring who sees us, linking my fingers with his.

I lean up on my tiptoes and press a kiss to his cheek, his skin warm against my lips, and he turns his head mid-motion, and his mouth captures mine, his hands releasing mine as his fingers wrap around my nape, pulling me closer.

It's a kiss filled with longing, and sadness, too, the unfulfilled promise of what might have been, the unmistakable sensation that this is a good-bye.

He releases me first.

In the wake of all that has happened, in the wake of what we have seen, it seems indulgent to linger on what might have been, to harbor regrets.

"Be safe," I say, the lump in my throat seemingly growing bigger, the impossibility of what I am suggesting undeniable. After seeing the war up close, the horrors of Guernica, I cannot imagine what it will be like for him.

He turns around just as he's walking away and says, "If you ever make it back to Barcelona, I'll meet you at our café. I'll bring you red roses."

I smile through the tears swimming in my eyes, the regret pummeling my heart even as I know there is no other choice to be made. "It's a date."

The journey from Spain is an emotional one, the ship filled with people fleeing the war, the losses so many have suffered simply staggering. I sleep little, the memory of what we saw in Guernica haunting my dreams.

The closer we get to Havana, the more it hits me that I am coming home, and I still don't know what I'm going to do about Emilio.

I've thought about the day I might return to Cuba for nearly a year now. To see Cuba's shores feels like a dream, and it isn't until tears trickle down my face that I realize how badly I wanted this moment, how much I yearn to go home.

chapter twenty-nine

Rosa

1937

BILBAO

On the journey from Havana to Bilbao, we spoke little, Felipe seemingly understanding that it was best to leave me to my own devices, to grieve and to mourn in private. I spent most of the two weeks reading some of the books I brought along, writing in my journal all the thoughts that were going through my head, my anger toward Gonzalo and the entire situation leaving me with more questions than answers, confusion filling me over my feelings toward Felipe and his pronouncement that he wished to marry me, my hurt over Gonzalo's betrayal keeping me up late at night as I imagined him in someone else's arms, wondered what their child would look like.

And somewhere along the way between Havana and Bilbao, I went out on the deck and looked out over the water and realized that I had to make a choice. That I could mourn a man who was not worthy of me, could hold on to this anger for so long that it would destroy me, or I could let go of a short-lived, ill-fated marriage and focus on myself and my future, rather than my past.

And then the words came.

I wrote, and I wrote, and I wrote. I wrote about what it is like to be a woman in Cuba, how much I felt indebted to Gonzalo's family, how I looked toward my future as a teacher to support myself when my husband failed to do so.

Little by little, word began to trickle in, reports coming from Spain that the violence was intensifying, the situation out of control. There was talk of turning around and returning to Cuba, discussions of taking on refugees to evacuate, and soon my worry for Alicia eclipsed all else.

For the return journey, I stay alone in a cabin, Alicia, Consuelo, and Isabel sleeping in the room next to me. Felipe seems content to leave us to our own devices, and while he checks on us daily, I welcome the time and the space I need to grieve, and to decide what I want.

The more time I spend with Consuelo, the less hurt I feel over Gonzalo's betrayal. She is so young, innocent in all of this, and seeing her as she is now, I realize that the man I thought I knew, the man I thought I loved, wasn't who Gonzalo really was after all. I think there is a part of me that will always be angry, always be hurt, but given the scale of the suffering and sadness I saw in Spain, the stories Alicia and Consuelo have shared of Guernica, I am simply grateful to be alive.

"Do you still mourn him?" Alicia asks me one night when neither one of us can sleep.

It seems wrong to speak ill of the dead, to dissect each facet of my marriage when I am the only one left, but I can't deny that I've been wondering what sort of man I married myself as I've run through all my memories with Gonzalo, as I've attempted to understand the decisions I made.

"I think I mourn the idea of who he was. The loss of that illusion. I mourn the life I thought I had even though it was never real, even though it was all founded on a lie. I was a fool."

"Oh, Rosa. I am so sorry."

"I should have known, shouldn't I? Should have somehow sensed it? His letters from Spain became more and more sporadic. I told myself it was because he was busy with the war, because it was difficult for him to send things, that the mail could be unreliable, but now I feel foolish for making excuses for him, for letting him treat me like this."

"He was in Spain; there was an ocean between you. Why do we as women take responsibility for men's mistakes? I have no doubt you did the best you could, that you were a good wife to him. He shouldn't have done what he did."

"I know. And if it were a friend of mine, someone I loved saying this, I would tell them the same thing. But it's harder when it's me, when I am responsible for my decisions. How do you trust yourself to be with someone else again after you've been hurt so badly?"

"I wish I knew," Alicia replies softly. Her gaze turns speculative after a moment. "Is there someone else? Felipe, perhaps?"

My cheeks burn.

"Anyone can see the way he looks at you, how solicitous he is over you. It's clear that all he wants is to be by your side, and yet, look at how much space he has given us, how respectful he's been. You can't paint everyone with the same brush, and you can't expect all men to make the same mistakes. Felipe and Gonzalo are two very different men."

"I know that. In my head I know that. But my heart—my heart can't be hurt anymore."

"And what about your happiness?"

"We were together," I confess. "Before I ever met Gonzalo. Before I knew who Felipe's family was."

Alicia gasps. "Rosa. I need to know everything. Now."

"There's not that much to tell. We met at the University of Havana one day, in front of the Alma Mater statue. Felipe was visiting a friend who is a professor there and I was on my way to class when we bumped into each other. I was carrying some papers and they went everywhere, and he bent down to help me pick them up. We barely exchanged ten words to each other. But the next day when I went to class, he was standing at the Alma Mater statue waiting for me, and we started talking, and every day after that he would be there."

"He waited for you by the statue. That has to be one of the most romantic things I have ever heard."

"I didn't know what to make of it at the time. I was young, and I had spent my whole life in the country, and there was something about him—Felipe had traveled so much, read so many books, seemed so sophisticated, so much older. He never even kissed me, but I was already halfway in love with him."

"How did you end up with Gonzalo?"

When I'm done telling the story, Alicia asks, "Do you still love Felipe? Because there's no point in asking if he loves you. That one is obvious."

"What will people think? He's my brother-in-law."

"He is. But the only thing that should matter is you. Society is going to condemn you for all sorts of things you can't control, because you're a woman and shame is the best way to keep us in our place. You know that better than anyone. Don't let that ruin your life. Do you still love him? That's the most important question you have to answer for yourself."

"I don't know. It's so difficult to know what I can trust anymore. I thought I loved Gonzalo and look where that left me."

"You can trust yourself, Rosa. Don't let Gonzalo take that away from you, too."

chapter thirty

Alicia

1937

HAVANA

As soon as the ship docks in Havana, a familiar silhouette comes into view, the sight of Emilio standing there in a white suit and hat stunning me.

The Emilio I knew would never have waited at the dock for his wife, would have sent someone to recover her and bring her to the immense Perez mansion in Miramar.

But there he stands, his gaze locked with mine as he spies me and Isabel standing on the ship's deck. He doesn't wave, but neither do I.

"What will you do?" Rosa asks from her perch beside me.

"I don't know."

We disembark the boat, and I walk toward my husband, Isabel in my arms.

I stop a few feet away from him, my heart pounding.

Neither one of us speaks.

He reaches out, and I pass Isabel to him as I have so many times before.

Shock fills me at the tears welling in his eyes as he looks down at Isabel.

"She's so much bigger than she was when you left," he says, his voice gruff.

I've never seen Emilio cry, not even when Isabel was born.

A tear rolls down my cheek, and then another.

"Are you ready to come home?" Emilio asks, holding his hand out to me, and I know what he's really asking, the choice I now face.

It's the sight of Isabel in her father's arms that makes the decision for me. It's the sensation of Cuban soil beneath my feet. And it's the memory of the terror I experienced in Spain, the unknown of whether my parents are safe, the responsibility I have to my sister and her unborn child.

I take his hand.

Emilio releases a deep breath, and some of the tension seems to leave his body. He grips my hand even tighter.

"Where's your wedding ring?" he asks me.

I stare down at the bare stretch of skin.

"I gave it to a woman who was desperate to get passage out of Bilbao. She was pregnant. She bought a ticket out of Spain with it."

"That was kind of you."

"If you had seen what it was like in Spain—it was the least I could do."

"Well, you're back in Cuba now. You and Isabel are safe."

. . .

The door to the Miramar mansion opens, and there's a staleness to the air, as though the house has been in stasis, waiting for me to return.

Somewhere behind me, I hear Emilio giving the driver instructions about our bags, Isabel asleep in his arms.

I help Consuelo and Rosa to their rooms, and as I walk by the framed picture of the corsair's wife, I can't help but wonder if the stories about her are true or if the family legacy has taken on a fictional bent. Was her arranged marriage really a love match or is that merely the story we have told ourselves, generations of Perez wives and daughters—that our greatness is defined by how we serve the family? By being obedient? By choosing duty over love? Is that the legacy I'll pass on to Isabel?

I pray one day she will follow her heart when she marries rather than all the expectations laid before her.

In this moment, I think that if I could return to Spain, I would. I would make a different decision standing on those docks, would have never let myself leave.

But of course, instead, I go up to my rooms and dress for dinner, check in on my sister and cousin, rouse a sleeping Isabel and put her in one of her finest dresses, brushing her hair until it gleams.

Dinner is a quiet affair, Isabel silent, Emilio, Rosa, Consuelo, and I struggling to make conversation. My absence to Spain is the elephant in the room, and I know that eventually we will have to confront the fact that I left him and all the reasons I did.

. . .

That night, I wait in my bedroom dressed in a white silk night-gown I bought as part of my trousseau years ago and never got a chance to wear.

Emilio comes late in the evening, and it's clear that I'm not the only one who is nervous, who feels the impact of the nearly yearlong separation between us.

Neither one of us speaks, simply too much between us for words, and then Emilio moves toward me, closing the distance and sitting on the edge of the bed next to me.

In a way, it's as it was when we were first newlyweds, strangers who had grown up adjacent to each other whose parents thought they should marry. There was an awkwardness between us that first night—a lack of knowledge on my part, a lack of experience with each other on both of ours. But what I remember most about my wedding night was that even though neither one of us had any great illusions of love, we both were there because we wanted to be. Because we had made a commitment to each other. A commitment to be a family. And even though his affair and the time I spent in Spain have taken that bond and threatened it, here we both are choosing each other again. Even if it isn't the great love I dreamed of, it is the family I will give my daughter, and the vow I made that I will keep.

"We won't speak of it again," Emilio says gently, and in the earnestness of his gaze, I know that he has regrets, too; that in this we are united.

Afterward, Emilio sleeps naked beside me, and I lie on my side and I offer a prayer to God. If this is to be my life, if this is the choice I have made, I pray he will bless me with more children. A sister for Isabel, perhaps. She's so quiet since we returned from Barcelona, so serious. She shouldn't be so alone in this house. I pray the Miramar home will fill with laughter, with the sounds of my children running down the elaborate staircase, that there will be joy in this house even if I won't necessarily find joy in my marriage.

I pray that my daughter will be strong, that she will be happy, that she will be safe.

I pray I made the right choice.

chapter thirty-one

Rosa

1937

HAVANA

After we dock in Havana, I am overcome with emotion, grateful to have my feet on Cuban soil once more, relieved to be home. Emilio arranges for our luggage to be delivered, and we are off to the Miramar house he shares with Alicia.

"I'm sorry to leave you," Felipe says once I am settled at my cousin's home, "but I should go see my parents and tell them what has happened in Spain."

"Of course."

"If you'd like, I can have the rest of your things sent from my parents' home."

"Thank you." I reach out and lay my hand on his arm, stilling him. My heart pounds. "Will you come back later tonight? So that we can talk just the two of us?"

"Yes."

It's later than I anticipated when Felipe returns from his parents' house, the rest of the household already abed, the evening growing late when there's a knock at the door. I glance through the window and see Felipe standing on the doorstep, my heart pounding as I let him in, nerves filling me at the risk I'm taking, the staff already long asleep.

By the time he arrives I've dressed for bed, and his gaze heats as he looks his fill at the sight of me in my nightgown.

"Would you like something to eat?" I ask him. "We already dined earlier, but there's food in the kitchen."

"No, I'm not hungry."

He seems exhausted.

"How are you?" I ask. "How was it at your parents' house?"

"They're coming to terms with what Gonzalo did. Still—though. The baby will be their grandchild. They're concerned about how they're going to explain the scandal away, but I bet they'll come around. They reminded me that eventually they'll need a legitimate Aguilera heir."

"How can they worry of such a thing at a time like this?"

"I don't even want to think about it right now. I'm too damned tired. I left them with more pressing issues at hand when I told them I had no idea how you felt about children, but if you would have me, you were the only woman I would ever consider marrying."

"That must have been upsetting," I say, realizing how faint my voice sounds.

For as long as we've been speaking, Felipe has been inching closer to me until he's right in front of me, so close that his knuckles graze the fabric of my white nightgown.

"You have no idea," he whispers. "I love you, Rosa. You're the only woman I've ever loved, and I was a fool to lose you the first time. I can't stand to lose you again. If you'll have me, I'm yours."

I tilt my head up, meeting his gaze, my answer there for him to see.

He doesn't hesitate, doesn't even question it. His mouth descends, his lips covering mine.

Whatever he was holding back before, whatever pent-up feelings have existed inside him are unleashed the second his lips touch mine, his hands cupping my face, fingers threading through my hair.

The intensity of his kiss rocks me, the magnitude of how badly he wants me catching me off guard for a heartbeat, and I tug at his clothes, pulling his body against mine.

"Upstairs," I whisper against his mouth, belatedly remembering others are asleep in the house and could walk downstairs at any moment and catch us together. Although after everything we've been through and how long it has taken us to come to this place, I can't find it in me to care about the possibility of scandal. Such things hardly seem important given the magnitude of loss we have just seen.

Felipe groans, sweeping me in his arms and carrying me up the stairs.

I tell him which room is mine as he pushes against the door and strides into the room, depositing me on the bed before closing the door behind him and turning the lock.

We come together in a frenzy, and while I feared that there

would be awkwardness, our past entanglements and hurt an insurmountable obstacle to overcome, what surprises me most is how easy things are between us, how natural it is to be with him.

"I love you," he whispers just as we are falling asleep in each other's arms.

Whatever doubts I had disappear, and I finally say the words aloud that I've felt in my heart for years.

"I love you, too."

chapter thirty-two

Isabel

1964

PALM BEACH

The flight from New York is a blur, my aunt Mirta beside me, holding my hand until we land in Palm Beach. Diego offered to call Beatriz for me, to let her know about our mother. When I arrive at the hospital, Maria and Elisa are already there, their faces streaked with tears.

"What happened?" I ask Elisa when she rises from the plastic waiting room chair to greet me.

"The doctor says she had a heart attack," Elisa answers.

"How is she?"

"I don't know. They won't let her go home; the doctor says she needs to stay here for a few days. If she has another heart attack—" Elisa steps away from Maria, drawing me to the side. "Beatriz is almost here."

"When can we see her?"

"She's resting now, but they should let us see her soon." Elisa hesitates. "I think you need to prepare yourself. She looks bad. It is bad."

I sit next to Elisa and Maria in the chairs, our father joining us for a few minutes before going off to make some phone calls. Seeing him like this—it reminds me of those final days in Havana when we boarded an airplane for the United States. For all the tensions in their marriage, all the times I wondered if they were happy, it's obvious seeing how much he's struggling that my mother anchors him, and now that she's in the hospital, he's adrift.

At some point, Beatriz joins us in our vigil, and we all sit and wait, a line of Perez sisters.

I've nearly given up hope of seeing our mother at all when a nurse comes by and tells us that we can visit her.

I'm unprepared for the sight of her. No matter how much I tried to tell myself that she wouldn't look as I remembered her, to brace myself for all the things Elisa warned me about, seeing her lying in the hospital bed looking so fragile nearly knocks the breath from me.

We surround the bed, Beatriz and me on one side, Elisa and Maria together opposite us.

Tears well in our mother's eyes as she looks at us.

"I'm sorry," she whispers.

"Mami."

It's been ages since I called her that, but the word comes back to me now as though I am the little girl who used to sit on her lap when she braided my hair, as though I can remember the feel of her arms around me, the way in which she used to lift me up and hold me close to her, her heart beating against my chest, the scent of her perfume engulfing me.

"I thought I was doing the right thing by you girls," she says. "I thought that if I told you to bend yourself to the world, it would be kinder to you. It was the advice my mother gave me the night before my wedding. The advice her mother gave her." A tear trickles down her cheek. "I didn't want you to hurt like I did. I didn't want you to know that kind of pain. I wish I had known how to be the kind of mother you needed. I wish I had done more."

"You did what you needed to," Elisa interjects. "You kept us safe."

"I wish I could have done more. I wish—" She's silent for a beat. "You asked me about the photograph, about Barcelona. I lied to you. I lied to you because I didn't want you to ask questions, because I didn't want you to think badly of me, because there are some things that are too painful to speak of."

"What happened in Barcelona?" I ask.

"I took you to Barcelona in the summer of 1936, Isabel . . ."

Did you love him? The man in the photograph—Nestor?" Beatriz asks when our mother is finished with the story.

"I could have. It was complicated."

"But you left him," Beatriz replies.

"I did. It wasn't that simple, though. We had to get out of Spain. It wasn't safe anymore. They were evacuating so many, and I didn't want something to happen to Isabel.

"I made a choice. It wasn't an easy one, and maybe it wasn't a perfect one, but so many of life's decisions never are. I did the best I could at the time with what I was facing. Nestor was determined to join the fight, and while I understood, I was a woman alone in a country that was not my own, in a war, and Isabel needed me. So did my sister, Consuelo, and her unborn child."

"Growing up you always told us that Consuelo's husband—Gloria's father—died in Spain," I say.

"We all made a deal to protect Consuelo and your cousin Gloria. I didn't want my sister to suffer. She and her daughter would have been ostracized. It was easier to lie to protect her, to tell everyone that she was a widow. The Aguileras had relatives in Spain—distant cousins—and given everything that was going on in the country at the time, it was easy to say she had married one of their cousins. Gonzalo's parents certainly didn't want the stigma that would have come to them if Cuban society had known what their son did, so this way they were able to play a role in the child's life, claim Gloria as a relative, without carrying the shame of Gonzalo's actions.

"Consuelo and Gloria lived with us until she married your uncle right after Elisa was born. Your father gave them shelter, protection, cared for them as though they were his own family. I will never forget the kindness he showed them. I needed your father for the help he gave to my sister." Her gaze shifts to me. "You needed your father, too. It wasn't just about me and what I wanted anymore."

It's Elisa who reaches out, taking our mother's hand and squeezing it.

"I understand," she says.

"Is Nestor my father?" Beatriz asks.

Our mother's eyes widen. "No, of course not."

"But based on when we were born, you could have been pregnant—"

"You were twins, Beatriz. Twins come early. You and Alejandro certainly did. You are without question Emilio Perez's daughter. There is no other possibility. I didn't realize you thought that. I didn't tell you about Barcelona because it was too painful to speak of, because I wanted to protect my sister, because when I returned to Havana your father and I agreed that we would put the past behind us, that we would start fresh as a family without the baggage of our mistakes weighing us down.

"You were that fresh start," she tells Beatriz. "You and Alejandro. The first time I held both of you in my arms, I felt something stirring inside of me, as though I was awake after having been asleep for a very long time." Her gaze drifts to all of us. "Later we had Elisa and Maria, and you girls kept me busy. You gave my life purpose. And the revolution—everything we went through, well, I can't imagine not having your father by my side."

She reaches out and Maria takes her hand, burying her face in the curve of our mother's hip as she cries, Elisa stroking her back.

For Maria to lose our mother at this young age—

"I'm proud of you. I spoke with Rosa. She told me what you did for her. How you helped her and Felipe defect. She told me how brave you were. All of you are so brave, so strong. You and your brother are the greatest joy of my life. I'm sorry if there was ever a moment that you doubted that, if I ever made you feel like that wasn't the truth. If I die—"

"You're not going to die," Beatriz interjects.

"I might. If I die, I will at least be at peace knowing that you have one another. That you will never be alone. I wanted that for you desperately. The bond you have is everything. Don't ever forget it."

chapter thirty-three

We walk down the aisle of the church in a row, a line of Perez sisters dressed in our finest black dresses. She would expect and want nothing less.

I am first, and then Beatriz, Elisa, and finally Maria.

A week ago we were all gathered around our mother's bedside, and now she's gone.

There are whispers in the pew, comments on what a tragedy it all is, that she really was so young, some who are more privy to gossip than others remarking that there was once a brother who died in Cuba, that we are a family who has had so much tragedy in such a short time.

I try to keep my gaze straight ahead, to float somewhere above the voices, this moment that is happening. I try to keep my gaze straight ahead, at the gleaming coffin that rests there.

Another heart attack, the physician said. Nothing anyone could have done.

We're told she didn't suffer, and I suppose if there is solace to be had in a moment like this, it is that. More than anything, I try to tell myself that she is with Alejandro now, her beloved son in her arms. I try to tell myself many things to make this pain bearable.

My gaze drifts from the coffin to the front of the church where the family sits. Mirta and her husband came down from New York to offer their support, not that my father has allowed them much of an opportunity to give it. He sits in the pew, his eyes dry, having spent his days shut up in his office. They were married nearly thirty years, and while I never had any illusions that they were a great love match, I cannot imagine what it must be like for them to have gone through so much together and for him to now be on his own. He is not the sort of man who is prone to great emotions, but I keep watching him, wondering if there will be a crack in the facade.

Next to Mirta and Anthony sit Rosa and Felipe, who have settled in Miami since Beatriz helped them leave Spain. Our aunt Consuelo is still in Cuba where she has lived with her daughter, Gloria, since she left Barcelona with our mother, the revolution separating them like so many other Cuban families.

I cannot believe she is gone.

Surprisingly, Thomas sent his condolences and a lovely bouquet of flowers, our divorce nearly finalized. Elisa tells me that there are rumors that he's seeing a widow who lives in Jupiter, and I hope that he will be happy.

When I reach the pew near the front of the church that has been reserved for me and my sisters, Beatriz nudges me.

"In the back," she whispers.

Confusion fills me, and I turn, and in the very last pew I see him, standing there, wearing a dark suit.

Diego.

His expression is solemn, his gaze trained on me.

Beatriz reaches out and takes my hand, and I know this was

somehow her doing, that she told him our mother had died and that she knew I would want him here even before I knew it myself.

We hold on to each other, Beatriz and I, and she lurches, nearly stumbling, and I'm so caught off guard that I reach out to steady her, and that's when I look down a few pews from where Diego stands to the sight of Nicholas Preston, alone, his gaze on Beatriz.

It takes everything I have to keep from glancing over my shoulder, sneaking peeks at the back of the church. Beside me, Beatriz is equally tense, and our fingers are intertwined as we derive strength from each other, as Elisa takes Beatriz's hand on the other side, Maria holding Elisa's free one.

The last major family event at this church was my wedding, Beatriz absent then, and it hits me now that despite all that has passed between us, we are together once more.

It is, by everyone's accounts, a beautiful funeral. The flowers I selected are elegant and timeless, the musical selections appropriate, the entire event one that my mother would have likely approved of.

When the service is over, my sisters and I linger, thanking those who came. Beatriz is the first to break away, heading toward Nicholas Preston like a moth to a flame.

Diego stands near the back of the church alone, and my gaze sweeps over the crowd. Most of the guests are already gone, but there are still enough people lingering to give me pause. And still—

"I'll be right back," I say to Maria, casting a worried look over at Beatriz where she stands talking to Nicholas Preston.

I walk toward the back of the church, something inside me too tired and emotionally wrung out to care what others think.

He doesn't say anything as I approach him, but his gaze never leaves me.

"I can't believe you're here. 'Thank you' hardly seems enough."

"I'm so sorry for your loss, Isabel. When my mother passed— the grief hits you unexpectedly at times. I just wanted to be here if you needed to talk to someone. If you needed a friend."

There's so much I want to say, but everyone's gaze is on us, so instead I settle on, "Thank you. There's a reception at my parents' home later. I need to help my sisters with the guests. But after that—we should talk. When it's just the two of us. When we have some privacy."

"I would like that very much."

After the funeral, the guests arrive at my parents' home in Palm Beach for a reception. My sisters and I take turns playing hostess, thanking people for coming, accepting condolences.

In so many ways, it seems like the gatherings my parents have had in the past, and I keep looking at the group, expecting to see my mother there, winding her way through the crowd, playing hostess, making sure our guests are enjoying themselves.

For a moment, I do think I see her, and I freeze in the middle of the crowd. Then I realize it was only Beatriz.

It is strange watching Mirta and Rosa together, my mother absent from their circle. Normally, she would be sitting beside them as they all filled one another in on the latest gossip and news. Even though they aren't sisters, there's something in their interactions with one another that reminds me so much of the bond I share with Elisa, Beatriz, and Maria.

"Join us," Mirta says, waving me over.

I sit beside her and Rosa, listening as they trade stories about my mother, memories from when they were younger together, and then the conversation drifts from their childhood to their memories of Cuba.

"How are things in Cuba now?" Mirta asks Rosa, and I realize this is the first time they have been in the same room together since Rosa and Felipe defected.

It is a routine that has now become familiar for so many of us in exile. When someone comes from Cuba, we all gather round and ask about friends and family that have stayed behind, about the country and all the changes that have happened in our absence. So many times, I've sat in my parents' living room in Palm Beach doing the same thing.

"It's bad," Rosa answers. "Fidel has a hold on Cuba, and I am afraid I will never see my home again."

"When Fidel dies, perhaps things will change," Mirta replies.

"Hopefully, that will happen sooner rather than later," Rosa counters.

And still, if Fidel dies, will I ever go back to Cuba? To visit, perhaps. But at this point, it is beginning to feel like I have one foot in the past, one foot in the present, as though I am straddling two countries and two lives. How many times do you have to start over?

We have tried our best to create our own version of Cuba that we can preserve and nurture in exile. We speak Spanish for the most part at home, eat Cuban dishes more frequently than not, our favorite songs playing on the record player, the familiar sounds harkening back to the days when we used to sneak out of our parents' house in Miramar and go to fast parties. There are so many other little traditions, things I don't even realize I'm doing that have helped keep Cuba alive for me. But more than anything, it is the memories that sustain me. I speak of Cuba with my sisters, with my family, like you might speak of a loved one you lost whose memory you are desperate to keep alive through the force of your own remembrances. Cuba is as much a lost part of our family as Alejandro was, and in my heart, they will forever be as I remember and loved them.

We speak for a little bit longer, the conversation turning back to my mother, and I realize that these moments, these conversations with those who knew and loved her best are another way of keeping her memory alive. And in their stories, I learn about a side of her I never got to know before, who she was simply as Alicia, independent of being my mother.

After a couple hours, my head begins to hurt, the events of the day taking a toll on me, and I excuse myself and go upstairs to rest.

I don't realize where I'm headed until I reach the top of the stairs and walk toward my mother's bedroom, the desire to be near her and the things she loved overwhelming me. I open the door and step inside to her inner sanctum, the room that she kept separate from my father, the lingering scent of her perfume in the air.

And then I see it—hanging on the wall near her bed where it would be one of the first things she saw before she fell asleep and one of the first things she saw when she woke up—the painting I did for Beatriz of our brother Alejandro.

I've gone the whole day without crying, trying to be brave for my sisters, trying to be strong for my father, but for some reason the scent of my mother's perfume, the sight of her bedroom exactly as she left it, the sight of that painting, unleashes the first sob, and another, and another, and I sit down on the edge of her bed and cry.

The door opens, and Beatriz walks inside. "I saw you come upstairs. Are you—" She breaks off when she sees the tears streaming down my face, and strides over to the bed and sits beside me, wrapping her arms around me.

"I can't believe she's gone," I say. "She was such a presence in our lives, and now, to think that she just won't be here anymore—"

"I know," Beatriz says. "I know."

My gaze drifts to the artwork on the wall, at the image of my brother staring back at me. "How did she end up with the painting I sent you in Barcelona?"

"I realized it belonged with her. I shipped it to her about a month ago. Alejandro will always be alive in my memories, in my heart. He will always be with me. But I thought about what it was like for her, how much she loved him, how much she lost in Cuba, to not even have had a picture of him. It didn't seem right. She sent me a thank-you note in Barcelona. She said it was a beautiful painting. She said you were talented."

It might not be much in the way of praise, but considering how infrequently our mother doled out such sentiments, it means everything.

Beatriz is silent for a beat and she says, "If you want to get out of here, Maria, Elisa, and I can take care of everyone. You should go to him."

"I can't."

"Of course you can." She rises from the bed and walks over to the door. "By the way," Beatriz says over her shoulder, "he's staying at the Breakers."

My heart pounds as I knock on Diego's hotel room door. I've nearly talked myself out of coming up here a dozen times, but for all my nerves, I think I knew I was headed here from the moment I saw him standing at the church.

I don't have much of a wait before he opens the door.

"Come in." Diego steps back as I walk in the room, closing the door behind me.

I don't speak, words eluding me.

Diego takes a step forward and another, stopping right in front of me.

"Can I?" he asks, and I nod, as he wraps his arms around me, holding me against him.

"I'm so sorry, Isabel."

We stay like that for a while, neither one of us speaking before he releases me, and Diego walks toward the bed and sits down on the edge, patting the space next to him for me. I follow suit, leaving a sliver of space between our bodies, my palm resting inches away from his hand braced next to him.

We talk about the funeral, about our mothers, we talk while Diego orders us room service and we sit and eat dinner, hours passing, and he asks me, "What will you do now? Will you stay in Palm Beach with your family or go back to New York?"

"New York, I think. I'll stay for a few days to help settle my mother's affairs, but I'm not sure there's a place for me here anymore. Beatriz is going back to Barcelona, and Maria is going to move in with Elisa in Coral Gables. They'll be fine without me, and I'll be close enough that I can visit if need be. I thought I'd take some art classes. There's a gallery in the city that has begun selling my artwork. I'm building a life for myself there. I need to know that I can take care of myself. That I can be on my own."

"That's wonderful about your art. I'm happy for you that you've found something you're passionate about, that you have such talent for, and that you're able to share your gift with other people. That's no small thing."

"And you? Will you go back to Barcelona soon?"

"Actually, I thought I might spend some time in New York," he says cautiously.

My heart pounds.

"I've been thinking about it for a while. I grew up in New York, and while I'll miss Barcelona, I'd be lying if I didn't tell you that I want to spend time with you. That I want a chance with you.

"What you said earlier, about wanting to be on your own, about needing to be independent—I understand and I don't want to rush you into anything. I know you've been through so much, already, but if you're interested, if you think you could be interested, I would very much like to be with you, to have a chance to spend more time with you. I would very much like to date you, Isabel Perez, whenever you're ready."

"I would like that, too," I reply softly.

He hesitates. "My job—"

"Isn't just manufacturing," I finish for him.

"No, it isn't."

"You pass information to the CIA."

"Yes, I do. It's dangerous and it's unpredictable, and there will be things I won't be able to tell you, things I won't tell you to keep you safe. Can you live with that?"

"I don't know. I can try, though."

I lie back on the bed, staring up at the ceiling.

I may not have an impulsive bone in my body, but tonight, I am daring. Tonight, I want to feel passion. As imperfect as the timing is, as reckless and foolish as it might be, I reach for the buttons at the front of my dress and begin undoing them, one by one.

Diego sits on the edge of the bed, his gaze on my face, and drifting lower, at the first sight of skin and then the swell of my breast, the lace of my bra.

"Isabel."

He moves quickly, covering me with his body, and for the first time, our lips meet even though it feels like we have been kissing each other for years, even as our bodies fit together as though they were meant to be together.

It is everything I never knew I wanted, some things I never imagined I would need, and all at once, all the emotion that I put in my paintings that for so long remained bottled up inside of me finally is free.

We lie together in bed, our naked bodies pressed together, limbs intertwined. He holds my hand, pressed to his heart, and we remain like that, not speaking, as though we both know there are no words, have been through enough loss that we are cautious, in awe, utterly wrecked.

Diego leans down and kisses me once more, and something turns over in my chest, hard and fast, and unpredictable, and I know without a doubt in my mind that I am falling in love, and I couldn't be happier.

epilogue

I stand in the courthouse in New York City, my dress the palest of pinks, the color of the inside of the shells we used to collect in Varadero when we were children.

Diego's eyes widen as he sees me, and I think that I will remember that look for the rest of my life.

There's no long aisle waiting for me, no pomp and circumstance. I wear a simple dress that I loved from the first moment I put it on, Beatriz, Elisa, and Maria there by my side as bridesmaids when Diego and I exchange vows, as he slides the gold wedding band that makes me his wife on my ring finger.

This time, there are no nerves, no worries that I am making a mistake, no voice in my head filling me with doubt. There's only love, and happiness, and laughter, and in this moment, despite all that has been lost, all the ways my life has led me down unexpected, winding paths, I am at peace, even if our life together is far from the one I envisioned for myself.

Diego travels often for work, and when he is gone I worry, checking the news constantly, unable to rest easily until I see him walking through our apartment door once more. Sometimes he comes back with scrapes and bruises, often I don't know where he is, and as much as I craved security, now I am learning that there can be peace even in the unpredictability of life, that I can carve out a space that is mine in an uncertain world.

When he is gone, I paint late into the evenings, sometimes finishing a piece as the sun is coming up. The more I paint, the more comfortable I become, and I am growing into a version of myself who is both the girl I was and the woman I am now.

After the wedding, we all have a private lunch at a Cuban restaurant in the city, Mirta and Anthony joining us. There are toasts and stories, and Beatriz is extremely smug about the role she has played in all of this, taking credit for bringing us together, praise I'm happy to give to her.

Following the dinner, Diego and I go to the Museum of Modern Art by ourselves, walking through the rooms, fingers laced.

We separate as a painting in the corner strikes my fancy, and I study it—the colors, the shapes, the emotions it evokes inside me. My artwork continues to find buyers, and each time I am notified of a new sale, I am taken aback by how much it moves me, the idea that people care about my paintings enough to want to hang them in their homes something I am not sure I will ever get used to. When you spend so much of your life feeling as though you are not meant to exercise your voice, it is an extraordinary thing to suddenly be rewarded and praised for having one, but more than anything I am moved by the fact that there are people out there connecting with my artwork, that what I have painted resonates with them on some level, that perhaps they may see parts of themselves and their lives in the images contained there.

I walk through the gallery, making my way toward the familiar painting that dominates the wall, the colors stark, unforgiving, daring the viewer to look away, the grotesque images representing the worst of what man is capable of illuminated before us, a moment in time when mankind's ability to wage war exceeded their humanity.

Diego stands in front of the painting, his back to me.

I walk up beside him, and he reaches out, his hand taking mine, lacing our fingers together, the metal of our wedding bands rubbing together in a sensation I have yet to be accustomed to, but I feel that spark in my chest when it happens, a little moment of joy at the reminder that I am his and he is mine.

His gaze is on an image of a mother in the painting, her baby cradled in her arms.

We stay like that, together, while people mill around us in the gallery.

What strikes me most about *Guernica*, the thing I didn't notice at the time when I first looked at it, is that without the title, without the background story of what happened that horrible day in April, you wouldn't know where it took place. It could be anywhere. It could have happened anywhere.

It is an audacious thing to create something for the world, to make a statement and share it with others with the hope that they will find meaning in it, that they will see themselves reflected in that which you have said, to believe that your voice can have some impact in this fractured world we live in. But without that hope, that audacity, what do we have?

Perhaps that's what men like Franco and Fidel fear the most, the power of speech, the power of art to galvanize the will of the people, the power of some positive creation to counterbalance the destruction they have wrought. To conquer, to destroy, you must subvert and eradicate the will of the people: their joy, their spirit, their hope.

And what is art, if not a manifestation of that hope?

For the first time in a long time, I have power, the ability to speak, to take the pain I have lived through and turn it into something that hopefully people can relate to, to offer them a piece of my memories with the hope that they, too, can see themselves in the canvas, can remember walking along the Malecón or the beauty of a Havana sunset.

Maybe there's a little magic in that, a power no dictator can take away.

When you love something with every fiber in your being, and you lose it, I don't know that you ever recover. You move on—physically—and you start a new life in a new country, and you make dreams and find new love, and yet there is always a part of you, a version of you, that is in the past, as though exile requires some transformation, a splintering to survive. I will always mourn Cuba as the love that I lost, the people I loved who were stolen away from us.

And today, more than ever, as I am a wife once more, I think of my mother.

I wish she were here with me today, wish she were able to see me and know that I have found a place for myself in this world. I wish she could know that the legacy she has passed down to her daughters will never be forgotten, that we carry on in her absence. That we will thrive.

As we walk out of the museum, on our way home, I look down at the ring on my finger and shake my head in wonder.

"I can't believe we're married." I smile. "Thank you for my wedding band, by the way. It's beautiful."

"It's a family heirloom," Diego answers.

I look down at the beautiful gold band, touched by the fact that I am wearing a piece of his family's history, something that links our pasts and present together.

"When my mother was leaving Spain, she was pregnant with me and she said she met a woman in Bilbao who helped her. My mother told me she saved her life—and mine. The ring was her wedding ring and she took it off her finger so that my mother would have something to sell if she needed money, but my mother never could part with it. She told me to give it to the woman I loved so I would never forget where I come from."

Tears fill my eyes as I stare down at the band, at the history contained there, at the legacy of courage I am honored to wear on my finger, the love and sacrifice I carry with me now, and I offer a prayer of thanks to the brave woman who saved my husband's life.

When I first wrote *Next Year in Havana*, I wasn't sure if I would write another novel about the Perez sisters. But then Beatriz came to me, standing on a balcony in Palm Beach, filled with passion and fury, her story bursting to be told, and I couldn't write the first scene of *When We Left Cuba* quickly enough. When I finished Beatriz's novel, I thought I'd left the Perez sisters as I traveled back in time to visit with Perez ancestors in *The Last Train to Key West* and *The Most Beautiful Girl in Cuba*. But I started getting messages and comments from readers, asking me if I planned on writing a story for Isabel and Maria, and the more I thought about it, the more I couldn't shake the sensation that there was another story that needed to be told.

While drafting *When We Left Cuba* and spending so much time in Beatriz's head, I often found myself at odds with Isabel. Of all the siblings, Isabel and Beatriz tend to clash the most, so naturally, at first, I struggled with the idea of writing from Isabel's perspective. But the more I thought of Isabel—who she is, the events that shaped her, and where her life was headed—I knew I wanted to tell her story. What I never could have predicted was that I would end up with a new favorite Perez sister as I fell in love with Isabel's loyalty and conviction as she embarked on this new chapter in her life.

Starting *Our Last Days in Barcelona* where we left the Perez family in *When We Left Cuba* felt like visiting old friends. When we last met Beatriz, she was jetting off to Spain to continue her intelligence work, and as I envisioned her there, I knew it was the perfect opportunity to both mend a rift between the sisters and to send Isabel on an unforgettable journey of her own. The setting particularly felt right given the research I had just done on the relationship between Spain and Cuba while writing my previous book *The Most Beautiful Girl in Cuba*. In reading about Cuba's fight for independence from Spain, I came across a mention of how Cubans later rallied their support for the Republican cause during the devastating Spanish Civil War, a conflict which had an enormous impact on Spain and the rest of the world.

As a Cuban-American writer with Spanish ancestry, I wanted to further explore this moment in history and this intersection between Cuba and Spain while traveling back in time and looking at the lives of two Perez women in the 1930s: Alicia Perez—Isabel's mother—and Rosa Aguilera—Marina Perez's granddaughter. Writing *Our Last Days in Barcelona* took me on a powerful journey as I learned more about this pivotal moment in history and the influence it had on both countries. These characters have left an indelible mark on my heart. Thank you for letting me share their story with you.

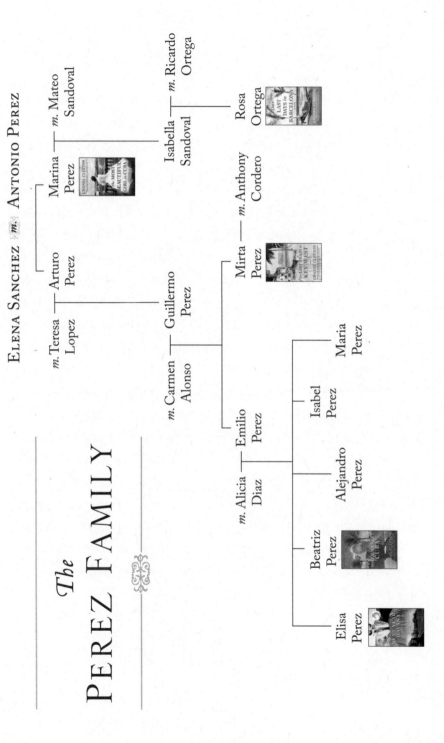

The
PEREZ FAMILY

ELENA SANCHEZ *m.* ANTONIO PEREZ

m. Teresa Lopez — Arturo Perez

Marina Perez — *m.* Mateo Sandoval

Guillermo Perez

Isabella Sandoval — *m.* Ricardo Ortega

Rosa Ortega

m. Carmen Alonso

Mirta Perez — *m.* Anthony Cordero

Emilio Perez — *m.* Alicia Diaz

Elisa Perez — Beatriz Perez — Alejandro Perez — Isabel Perez — Maria Perez

ACKNOWLEDGMENTS

This book wouldn't have been possible without the love readers have shown to the Perez family and the support you've given my books. Thank you *so* much for embracing these characters and thank you to everyone who asked when it was the other sisters' turns to have their story told. I am so grateful to all of you.

Thank you to my amazing agent Kevan Lyon for your wisdom, guidance, and encouragement. I am so fortunate to have the opportunity to work with my extraordinary editor Kate Seaver at Berkley. Thank you for all of your support, enthusiasm, and editorial magic. I adore working with you.

My fabulous publicists Erin Galloway, Tara O'Connor, Stephanie Felty, and marketing representative Fareeda Bullert share their immense talents with me and my books. Thank you for all that you do to share my work with readers and for your passion and creativity.

The team at Penguin Random House and Berkley has given me and my books such a wonderful home, and I am so grateful for all of the incredible work you do on my behalf. Thank you to Madeline McIntosh, Allison Dobson, Ivan Held, Christine Ball, Claire Zion, Jeanne-Marie Hudson, Craig Burke, Tawanna Sullivan, and Mary Geren. I am so grateful to the sales and subrights departments, as well as the art department and Sarah Oberrender for designing another gorgeous cover.

Thank you to Reese's Book Club for championing my books and welcoming me into your vibrant and passionate community. It's such an honor to be part of the wonderful readership you've built.

To my colleagues and friends and my family—thank you for your support and love. It means the world to me.